He nee[...]
the tru[...]

Before it was too late—if it wasn't already. Memories of holding her in his arms rose in his mind, letting him know that he was already having trouble seeing the situation objectively.

He left her fixing the coffee and headed for the den. He had a small tape recorder in his briefcase, and he wanted to make a note of what she'd told him so far. This had to be the breakthrough they were waiting for. Now that she'd started to get her memory back, it was just a matter of time before she remembered everything.

Then it would all be over. So why didn't he feel the glow of anticipation or the familiar excitement at the prospect of finally settling with Hanover? The answer formed in his mind as he remembered the way Yvonne had looked just before he kissed her. What if finding her memory meant losing Yvonne forever?

Dear Reader,

One of your favorite authors is on tap for this month: Nora Roberts. It's been a while since she last appeared in the line, but I think you'll find *Unfinished Business* well worth the wait. I'm a particular fan of stories that reunite past lovers, so I was really rooting for Vanessa Sexton and Brady Tucker, and I think you will be, too.

The rest of this month is pretty exciting, as well. Ann Williams is back with *Without Warning,* a complex tale of greed, revenge and—of course!—passion. Hero Michael Baldwin was reported dead years ago, but as Blair Mallory discovers, the reports of his death were greatly exaggerated! In *True to the Fire,* Suzanne Carey uses her lush island setting to full effect as she spins a tale about a woman trying to carry on her father's legacy and the handsome revolutionary who wins her heart. Finally, welcome Blythe Stephens to Silhouette Intimate Moments. In *Wake to Darkness* she grabs your attention right on page one and never lets go. I found myself completely involved with heroine Yvonne Worthington's search to regain her memory—and find love.

In coming months, keep your eyes out for more great reading from Silhouette Intimate Moments. We'll be bringing you books from favorite authors such as Marilyn Pappano, Paula Detmer Riggs, Joyce McGill and—very soon!—Linda Howard. You won't want to miss a single one of the books we have scheduled for you.

Yours,
Leslie Wainger
Senior Editor and Editorial Coordinator

BLYTHE STEPHENS

Wake to Darkness

SILHOUETTE·INTIMATE·MOMENTS®

Published by Silhouette Books New York

America's Publisher of Contemporary Romance

SILHOUETTE BOOKS
300 East 42nd St., New York, N.Y. 10017

WAKE TO DARKNESS

ISBN: 0-373-07434-4

First Silhouette Books printing June 1992

Books by Blythe Stephens

Silhouette Intimate Moments
Wake to Darkness #434

Silhouette Romance
Gift of Mischief #786

Silhouette Special Edition
Rainbow Days #554

BLYTHE STEPHENS

penned her first story when she was in third grade. Years later, after college and marriage, she became seriously involved with writing and published several short pieces. She soon discovered that novels were more fun, and with over fifty published books, she hasn't returned to the short-story form. Her books range from children's and young adults'—including a few Nancy Drews, written under the pen name Carolyn Keene—to Gothics, historicals, family sagas and contemporary romances. She loves the challenge of trying different genres.

Born in Idaho and raised in Montana, Blythe has followed the sun and currently resides in Mesa, Arizona. She shares a home with her mother (who is also her assistant editor and chief critic) and their cairn terriers. Blythe enjoys reading and traveling, and is constantly seeking new settings for her books. Her only regret is that she can't travel to the past to do on-the-spot research.

To my mother, Dorothy Wagner,
whose belief has ever given my heart wings.
Thank you, and all my love.

Chapter 1

Curtis Macklin slowed the Jeep at the top of the ridge and peered into the deep desert shadows that were only just now being erased by the first light of the Arizona dawn. The harsh land below showed no signs that anything unusual had happened here, so why didn't he have sense enough to turn back? Hadn't he had more than enough frustration for one night? His curiosity refused to go away.

It had been about 2:00 a.m. when he'd spotted the first car speeding away from the Hanover Ranch. Since he'd been sitting in his cliff-top lookout watching the ranch with binoculars from nightfall on, he'd been delighted by the diversion. It was the first since a small jet had landed on Hanover's airstrip just before midnight. Could it mean that the mysterious meeting was breaking up? But, if so, where the heck were they going? The dirt road the car followed led into the hills, not back to civilization.

While he was still trying to make sense of the first car's action, a second had come barreling down the ranch road, obviously in hot pursuit of the first. He'd been able to follow their progress with his glasses until they reached this area and disappeared below the ridge. That's when he'd heard something that sounded a whole lot like a gunshot. He'd been trying to decide if he should abandon his watch on the ranch to follow the cars and see what was going on, when both cars reappeared on their way back to the ranch.

Because of the trees that sheltered the front of the ranch, he hadn't been able to see much beyond the fact that several people got out of each car. After that nothing else had happened until the jet had left about 4:00 a.m. Unfortunately he hadn't been able to see who got aboard the jet, either, which made the whole night a study in frustration.

Curt sighed, hating himself for his insatiable need to find out what Hanover was up to. Telling himself that he wasn't a cop anymore didn't help. It would take more than being head of a successful investment business to distract him from his plan to make Hanover pay for what had happened to Genna.

Forcing away the painful thoughts of Genna, he concentrated on maneuvering his Jeep down the rough slope to the shadow area that separated the ridge from the dirt track where he figured the cars must have stopped. Not that he really expected to find anything, but there had been that gunshot... Not unusual in the desert, where a man could run afoul of a rattler at any given time, but whenever Hanover was involved, Curt always had a feeling the snakes might be the two-legged variety.

The land between the ridge and the road was depressingly clear in the brightening dawn. Curt smothered a yawn and twisted the wheel. Score another one for the wild goose. He dodged a rocky outcropping and nearly slid a tire over the lip of a deep cut in the ground that had been totally hidden by brush. A flash of something pale within the shadows ahead caught his eye. He gunned the tough old Jeep along the edge of the tiny ravine, curiosity banishing his weariness.

The Jeep bucked when he hit the brakes, dying even before he switched off the ignition. Curt stayed where he was for a moment, watching the march of sunlight as it illuminated more of the scene. Memories of several grisly, desert discoveries during his six years as a Phoenix cop made him sure he didn't want to see what the ravine might be hiding. He'd loved the challenge of police work, but there were parts of the job that he didn't miss at all.

Groaning slightly, he climbed out of the Jeep. If he really had heard a shooting, he'd better find out what had happened before he radioed the authorities. He shrugged the tension from his shoulders and back before he scrambled through the brush and down into the ravine, wishing that he'd come out to investigate sooner. Not that he'd have had a chance in hell of spotting anyone in the dark. It was mostly luck that he'd even found the ravine.

"Damn!" Bile burned in the back of his throat as he got a good look at the silky gold fabric partially covering the long, slim nylon-clad legs. Thick, curly black hair spilled over the pale skin bared by the low-cut back of the jumpsuit. The last person he'd expected to find lying out here was some damned girl. Feeling sicker by the minute, he touched her shoulder gently, knowing that he'd have to turn her over, but dreading it. He didn't need any more dead faces haunting his dreams.

"No, don't! David!" The words came out soft, barely more than a moan, but they cut through him like a scream. She was alive!

As he eased her over on her back, her blue eyes opened wide. She stared past him, seemingly transfixed with horror by something he couldn't see, then a terrible shudder shook her whole body. Her eyes closed again without ever focusing in his direction.

"Hey, come on, it's okay. I'm not going to hurt you." Curt shook her gently, hoping to get her to open her eyes again, but there was no response. Unconscious? He checked her pulse, which was steady and strong. Her breathing seemed a little shallow, but not labored in any way. Her skin felt warm and neither too moist nor too dry. Obviously a couple of hours in the night-cool desert hadn't hurt her.

He sat back on his heels, staring at her in the improving light of the rising sun. The gold lamé jumpsuit, which was zipped up to a deceptively high neck in the front, was snagged and dirty, probably from the brush and her fall into the ravine; but there didn't seem to be any blood on the front, either. He ran a gentle hand down one arm, then the other, then carefully moved her elegant legs. Everything seemed intact, though both her slim wrists and her arms were scraped and bruised as though she might have been held roughly or even tied up.

Frowning, Curt turned his attention to her torso, probing at her rib cage, watching for a pain reflex, since she didn't seem too deeply unconscious. As he moved his hand up her left side, she winced away from his fingers, whimpering. Curt hesitated a moment, then reached for the ornately carved gold zipper pull at the base of her pale throat. He eased it down slowly, doing his best to ignore her swelling breast as he pulled the silky cloth out of the way so he could examine her side.

"Bastards!" When he'd still been a cop, he'd seen plenty of bruises like the ones that marked her pale skin, but that didn't make them any easier to look at. She'd been battered, no question about it. Adding a few choice comments about her attacker's family tree, he closed the zipper again.

That's when he noticed the mark on her jaw and the dried blood in the corners of her mouth. Now what? He gently parted her pale lips. The soft flesh inside her lower lip bore teeth marks, probably the result of someone slapping her around. She'd definitely been roughed up, but none of the injuries he'd seen so far explained why she was unconscious. If she hadn't been shot, what the heck had happened to her?

Curt sat back again, frowning at her, then got stiffly to his feet and climbed out of the ravine to check the ground nearer to the road. He found plenty of fresh tire tracks there, but none close to the area where the woman was lying. If someone had taken a shot at her, maybe she'd run and...and what? Dived into the ravine headfirst? That made as much sense as anything he could think of—especially since she would have been nearly impossible to find in the dark.

"So what the hell were you doing out here with that crew, little lady?" he asked, sliding down beside her again. She whimpered, rolling her head from side to side; then he saw it. The hair on the side of her head that had been hidden from him before was damp and matted. He touched the area lightly and she winced away from his fingers, but not before he'd felt the deep groove and the stickiness of blood.

A quick check of the ground near her showed no sign of a sharp rock that she could have fallen on and the only traces of blood were beneath her head. Curt sighed. So the shot he'd heard had hit its target, but what did that mean? He closed his eyes, trying to imagine what might have happened.

Had she been in the first car or the second? And why bring her out here? To keep her from being seen by someone at the mysterious meeting or just for disposal? Either way, it seemed odd that they hadn't come back to make sure she was dead. Still, injured people didn't last long in the Arizona desert sun and this area was as desolate as any around.

Curt squinted at the rising sun, feeling the heat already. He studied the woman again, wondering if she'd wake when he moved her. The trip to the cabin wouldn't be a problem, since it was early, but if he had to take her into Phoenix for medical treatment, they'd be easily spotted by anyone leaving the ranch for town.

"Well, little lady, I guess you're going to be my guest for the day." He leaned closer to study her smudged face. She wasn't as young as he'd first thought, he realized as he traced what looked like a tear track down her tanned cheek. Closer to thirty than twenty, he'd guess. A long way from innocence.

But she looked innocent, sleeping so deeply, her thick black eyelashes like fans against her cheeks. Anger ate at him. For a moment, all he wanted to do was smash the creeps that had abused her, then bitter laughter washed his fury away. Before he got up on his white charger, he'd better find out something about the fair lady. Evil was quite comfortable wearing the face of innocence—he'd learned that the hard way, not once but several times in his thirty-eight years.

Shaking his head at his own peculiar thoughts, he carried her to the Jeep. She moaned in protest as he settled her in the narrow space behind the seat. He carefully padded her head with his jacket, then wrapped her in the battered blanket he always carried. She'd need its protection against the jouncing that would come as he drove cross-country to the cabin.

She hurt! The pain was swelling through her body. She was being battered against something hard; it cut into her hip and when her head moved... She tried to force her eyelids up to see where she was. Light lanced into her brain like a sword.

She reached out for the darkness, wanting to wrap herself in it. Darkness would protect her, hide her. But she was going to die. She'd die if they didn't stop beating her, but how could she make them stop? She tried to turn her head away from the pain, but it exploded again, banishing everything for a while.

The darkness began to recede again. She felt something cool touching her lips. Suddenly water spilled into her mouth and she swallowed eagerly. The water tasted slightly of blood, but her dry throat didn't mind.

"That's a good girl," a male voice said. "Have another sip. Can't let you get dehydrated. You're going to have to wake up enough to take liquids."

More water spilled into her mouth. She kept swallowing desperately, afraid that she'd choke if she stopped to protest. Just swallowing took all her concentration, so she didn't even try to open her eyes. Nothing mattered but the cool liquid that eased the grittiness in her throat.

"Well, I think that's enough for this time. I'm going to wash out that wound now, so you don't get infection from it." The voice had a rough, almost unused quality to it. His touch, though gentle, brought waves of pain, so that she whimpered in protest, but he didn't stop. Unable to fight him, she escaped back into blackness.

Curt sprawled wearily in his battered lounge chair and glared at the woman sleeping peacefully on his bed. What the hell was he going to do now? He roundly cursed the Jeep, which had died about a quarter of a mile from the cabin. At the time he'd been too anxious to get her away from the relentless heat to even look at the engine, but he had a strong hunch that whatever had gone wrong was going to take more than a few minutes of tinkering to fix.

So where did that leave the woman? He looked across the cabin to his one link with the outside world—the short-wave radio on the cupboard. He could call the authorities and have a medivac chopper out here in no time, but then what? She had what was obviously a gunshot wound on the side of her head and that would mean a police investigation. He could see the headlines now—*Mystery Woman Found Shot In Desert*.

Nothing like a hot news story to let whoever shot her know that she'd survived. He sighed. At the moment, she was a lot safer if they believed her dead. Besides, her head injury didn't seem that serious. It had been a while since his medic training days, but he remembered that being easily roused was a good sign.

Also, once the local media started digging into the story, it wouldn't take long for his name to surface. Thanks to the success of BCM Investments, the firm he'd inherited from his uncle two years ago, they sure wouldn't ignore him. And how would he explain finding her? The answer was painfully obvious—as was the logical result of making his presence in this area of the desert public knowledge.

Once the media discovered that he owned a hidden cabin on land adjacent to the Hanover Ranch, all hell would break loose. Every accusation he'd made against Hanover after Genna's suicide would be reprinted in great detail and the speculation would start all over again. He'd never have another chance to watch the man he believed was to blame for the complicated drug frame-up that had driven Genna to kill herself.

He closed his eyes, not wanting to think about Genna ending her life in a carbon-monoxide-filled garage. His stomach rumbled, but he was too tired to get up and fix himself something to eat. Curt slipped into restless sleep, twitching as his overstrained muscles sought relief.

Outside, the late May temperature climbed steadily toward a hundred, but inside, the generator fed electricity into the air conditioner, keeping the cabin cool. To anyone curious enough to look, the outside of Curt's hideaway might appear run-down and neglected, but he'd made sure that the inside was well insulated and completely modern.

Curt woke suddenly, tense, sure that something was different in the cabin. He held his breath, listening for a foreign sound, firmly controlling his urge to reach under the chair for his gun. A soft whimpering came from the bed where the woman was thrashing around, obviously lost in some kind of nightmare.

Feeling older and more battered than the Sphinx, Curt groaned his way out of his chair. Who the devil was she? he wondered as he glared down at her. And was she in pain or did her agitation come from terror? As she rolled over, he noticed the slit pocket in the sideseam of her jumpsuit.

Should he search her? He hadn't even thought about it before, probably because he'd been too busy making sure she got some water, but now... Uncomfortable with the invasion, he eased a hand over the curve of her hip into the warmth of the pocket, seeking something that would give him a lead to her identity. He pulled out a piece of fabric.

"Damn." He glared at the neatly folded, lace-edged handkerchief. Obviously it was too much to hope that she'd stuck her driver's license in her pocket. He started to put it back, then noticed that a name had been embroidered in one corner.

"Yvonne." A pretty name for a pretty lady, but not exactly the kind of information he'd been seeking. He slipped it back into the pocket, then eased her over, hoping to have better luck on the other side. Somehow, he wasn't surprised to find that there was no second pocket.

"Travel pretty light, don't you, Yvonne?" He studied her, hoping that the sound of her name would rouse her, but she slept on. Feeling guilty, he checked her pulse, then got some fruit juice from the refrigerator. As before, she swallowed obediently when he held her against his chest and slipped the edge of the glass between her lips, but she didn't open her eyes or respond to him in any other way.

Curt fixed himself a couple of sandwiches, hoping that food would ease the knots of frustration forming in his belly. The silence was beginning to bother him, so he switched on his transister radio to check the news. A local commentator spoke of robberies, a small drug bust and a couple of murders, but there was no mention of a woman reported missing. Too weary to think, Curt dozed off in his chair.

She woke suddenly, every sense alert. For the first time she was fully aware of the roughness of the fabric beneath her bare back, the softness of the pillows behind her head. She listened intently to the sighing of the air conditioner and the snore of... A chill of fear stiffened her. Someone was here! Shaken, she opened her eyes.

Where the heck was she? Nothing looked familiar. Not even the sounds seemed right. Where was the person snoring and what was she doing lying here on a bed in a room she'd never seen and couldn't remember entering? She turned her head slowly in the direction of the sounds.

He was stretched out in a lounge chair across the room, his face half turned away from her. She squinted, confused by the dimness of the room. She could make out little about him beyond the fact that he appeared to be a big man and he was definitely snoring enthusiastically. The fact that he was sleeping didn't seem particularly reassuring.

Her panic grew; she had to get away from this place, from the stranger. Maybe if she moved very carefully... The bed creaked, the sound ominously loud in the silence. The snores died instantly and suddenly, the man was looking her way.

"Well, hello there, Yvonne. How are you feeling?" He straightened up in the lounge chair, looking even bigger.

Terrible memories swamped her, freezing her to the spot. Someone was twisting her arms behind her while a fist crashed into her side. Voices were shouting questions, but the words made no sense. What did they want? Terror kept her gaze locked on the man.

He was smiling, but she didn't believe it was real. What should she do? Maybe if she didn't move, he wouldn't hurt her again. She longed to close her eyes and seek the safety of unconsciousness. The darkness had saved her before, but now her eyes were open and her head ached with the strain of trying to make sense of what she saw.

He was getting up! She tried to melt back into the pillow as tides of terror washed over her. He'd come over and then he'd... The horrible memories faded from her mind as suddenly as they'd come, but the icy fear shivered through her with such force she knew she could never pretend to be unconscious.

All at once, she realized that he was moving slowly, almost as though he didn't want to frighten her, but that made no sense. Why should he care about her feelings? Who was he? Where were they? What did he mean to do to her now?

"Thirsty?" he asked, his tone casual, as though she were a guest and not his prisoner. For a moment she wondered if she could be trapped in some crazy nightmare.

Curt watched the shivers tracing over the woman, felt her eyes following him as he moved carefully past the bed to the kitchen area of the cabin. She looked frightened out of her mind. But why? Could she think he was the one who'd hurt her? Didn't she know who'd shot her? As he poured another glass of juice for her, he could think of at least a dozen questions he needed to ask.

She cowered back when he started toward her, so he stopped well away from the bed. "Can you manage the glass yourself, Yvonne?'' he asked, trying hard to sound as though this was an ordinary conversation.

She hesitated, fearful, yet so thirsty she couldn't resist the promise of the glass. When she reached out to take it, pain tore in her side, taking her breath away, but she clung to consciousness. The sweat-beaded glass was amazingly heavy; it took both her hands to hold it. The sweet juice tasted like ambrosia.

Drinking slowly, savoring each swallow, she kept her gaze on the man. Was he her jailor? But why keep her captive? Who was he? Questions filled her mind, but the act of drinking sapped her strength. By the time she'd finished her juice, she was so tired, she couldn't even move away when he came to take the glass from her loosening fingers. She closed her eyes, willingly surrendering to sleep.

Curt watched her for a moment, trying to judge whether she was really asleep or feigning. Her total relaxation irritated him. Though he'd slept only a few hours, he was too edgy to settle down again. He glared out the window at the sunburned desert. What he needed to do was check the Jeep, but by now the baking sun would have made the hood and the engine beneath it too hot to touch. They were trapped here at least until evening.

The woman's presence made the cabin feel smaller, confining, and he quickly discovered that it was impossible to pace quietly or to concentrate on the spy novel he'd brought out here with him. By the time he activated the shortwave radio for his three o'clock transmission, Curt was ready to explode with frustration. Luckily Jackson was waiting for his call.

Curt reported the arrival and departure of the small jet in their prearranged bird-watching code, then asked, ''Any unusual activity kicking up in Phoenix?''

''Haven't heard a thing.'' Jackson sounded bored. ''Do you think maybe you could be wasting your time out there?''

Curt swallowed a sharp retort, reminding himself that he couldn't expect anyone, least of all his gifted, but single-minded partner in BCM Investments, to share his preoccupation with Hanover's guilt—not without proof. "Matter of fact, it's lucky I took a couple of days off since a little bird fell out of a nest I've been watching. Found it early this morning."

"What?" Jackson Palmer's tone reflected sharp interest. "Is the...uh...bird okay?"

"Slight damage. I've been taking care of her since my Jeep died out in the open about a quarter of a mile from home base."

Silence followed that cryptic statement, but Curt didn't add anything. He trusted Jackson to sort it out without asking the kind of questions that would give too much away, should anyone be monitoring their radio transmissions. They'd learned to read each other loud and clear during their dark days in the muddy hell of Vietnam, so he figured Jackson would make the necessary assumptions.

"You need transport?"

Curt heaved a sigh of relief, leaning back in his chair for the first time. Even though Jackson thought that his playing cop in his spare time was crazy, it meant a lot to Curt to know he had someone he could count on for backup should he need it. "I may. I'll check the Jeep as soon as it cools off. Meanwhile, you might touch base with Pete and see if anything is stirring about our friend."

"You sure you don't want me to come pick you up now?"

Curt studied the sleeping woman, weighing his options. The offer was tempting, but he had a feeling that he'd learn more if Yvonne woke up here with no one to depend on but him. If he took her into Phoenix she'd have far too many options. "I think everything is okay here for now."

"Damn it, Curt, I wish—" Jackson broke off without finishing his all-too-familiar request that Curt give up his investigation of Hanover and concentrate his energies on his expanding financial empire. His sigh was audible. "I'll radio if I pick up anything hot, otherwise, you can let me know if you need a ride." That said, Jackson ended the transmission.

Feeling the full weight of his decision, Curt remained at the counter for several minutes. Could Jackson be right? Was it time to give up trying to tie Keenan Hanover to Genna's death? The police had tried and failed, so why should he think that he could? Maybe Genna had been wrong to suspect the wealthy financier and local power broker of being involved with the laundering of drug money.

He sighed. It didn't really matter now, since he'd found Yvonne. What had happened to her definitely was tied to Hanover. He couldn't just walk away. And maybe once he found out exactly what had happened to Yvonne, he'd finally be able to find a way to put to rest his guilty feeling that he'd let Genna down just when she needed him the most.

Not wanting to think about the past, Curt went over to check on Yvonne. It was time to concentrate on her. By bringing her here, he'd made her his responsibility and he had to take care of her until he learned exactly where she fit into last night's gathering at the ranch.

He watched her closely. Had she been listening to his transmission? Her relaxed muscles and slow, deep breathing seemed to indicate that she hadn't. But was she sleeping or unconscious? Not knowing for sure bothered him. There was always a possibility she was in worse shape than he thought. Keeping her out here could put her in more danger. . . .

He trailed a finger along the velvety skin of her jaw, tracing the edge of the darkening bruise and remembering the others on her side. She looked so fragile and innocent lying here, completely vulnerable, yet she'd come from the Hanover Ranch. And someone had tried to kill her. He pulled his hand away, wishing that he could forget the sweet curves he'd uncovered when he examined her.

The cabin was closing in on him again. Mumbling curses, he got his gun from beneath the chair and tucked it into his pocket, then opened the chest under the window and got out a camouflage tarp. It was time to make a reconnaissance of the area around the cabin and cover the Jeep. He

badly needed the distraction of physical activity. Having a
woman around brought back feelings he was far from ready
to deal with.

She opened her eyes the moment she heard the door
close. He was gone! She sat up, fighting dizziness and nausea as stabbing pains radiated from the side of her head.
The need to escape forced her to ignore the pain. This was
her chance to flee, to run to...to where?

Confusion froze her to the bed. Memories of the man's
gentle touch, the concern she'd sensed as he forced water
and juice down her throat warred with her violent need to
escape. Slowly, carefully, she tried to stand. Every muscle
and nerve in her body screamed in protest.

What had happened to her? Had he done this? Or had
she been in some terrible accident? She tried to concentrate, to remember, but the pain swelled, throbbing so
fiercely it set sparks of light to exploding behind her eyes.
Swaying, she clung to the headboard of the bed, trying to
determine where she was, but the room continued to spin
and tilt sickeningly around her.

Trying to ease the dizziness, she focused on the window,
seeking a clue to her whereabouts. Since the curtains were
open, she had no trouble seeing what lay outside, but it only
intensified her terror. She was in the desert! Beyond the
shadows that shrouded the cabin, she could see nothing but
cactus-punctuated emptiness.

She turned quickly, hoping to find a more rewarding
scene beyond the window on the kitchen side of the large
room, but the sudden movement was too much for her
abused body. A shaft of pain ripped up from her side, cutting off her breath and setting the room to spinning so fast
that she was spun off, crashing into the welcoming darkness without a whimper of protest.

Curt was sweating heavily by the time he reached the
shelter of the brush and palo verde trees that shaded and
concealed the cabin. His reconnaissance hadn't turned up
anything of interest, which pleased him. Even though he'd

found Yvonne a fair distance from the cabin, he couldn't help worrying that someone might have come back looking for her.

Not that anyone driving along the road was likely to notice his cabin, since it was nestled in the rocks beneath an overhanging cliff, but he'd been forced to leave the disabled Jeep out in the open. He cursed himself for not taking the camouflage tarp out sooner.

It was enough to make him wonder if Jackson could be right—maybe he was getting too old and careless to keep this up. It would be a year in July—a year since Genna's death—and he was still no closer to tying the whole sorry mess to Hanover.

Could he be doing all this just to prove that someone else was to blame for her suicide? Was he really looking for a scapegoat to take on the guilt he still felt? The voice deep inside him had been asking those questions more often lately, but that might just be frustration.

His six years on the Phoenix police force had taught him a lot about the various stages of an investigation. Turning over rocks looking for clues was always a frustrating and thankless task, but every once in a while, something interesting turned up. Like this morning.

Curt felt his depression lifting as he neared the cabin door. Every case had its turning points and he had a good feeling about his discovery of Yvonne. She'd come from Hanover's secret meeting and someone had wanted her dead—that had to mean something. All he had to do was find out what she knew.

Chapter 2

The cabin was as cool and dim as a cave after the blazing brightness of the sun-drenched desert. Curt downed two tall glasses of cold water before he even glanced toward the bed to check on Yvonne. His glass clattered into the sink, as shock numbed him. She was gone!

The soft whimpering broke through his momentary paralysis, drawing him around the bed to where he found her crumpled on the rag rug. Worried, Curt dropped to his knees beside her. "Damn it, lady, what have you done to yourself?" he asked, torn between worry and anger.

His words went unanswered as she continued thrashing around as though fighting off some nightmare demon. Not sure what to do, he reached out to touch her cheek, instinct telling him she would be calmer if he let her know she wasn't alone. To his surprise, she stilled at once. Now all he needed to do was lift her back up on the bed so he could check her over, make sure she hadn't hurt herself. He slipped an arm under her shoulders.

She sat up immediately, as though afraid to accept his support, then her fingers snagged in his shirt front. Curt froze, making no move to pull away from her even though her grip was so fierce he could feel the scraping of her nails against his chest. Still operating out of instinct, he gathered her gently in his arms, cradling her.

For a moment he could feel the stiff tension of her body, then it seemed to ease and she relaxed against him, her fingers loosening, but not releasing their hold on his shirt. Instead of lifting her, he continued to just hold her, suddenly aware of her heart beating strong against his chest. He drew in a deep breath and caught the seductive scent of jasmine from her hair. A deep longing stirred within him and it took all his self-control not to tighten his embrace.

Yvonne sighed and rubbed her cheek against his shoulder like a sleepy child. Curt grinned, pleased that his embrace had soothed her fears and comforted her. Still holding her slender body close, he got to his feet. He eased Yvonne down on the bed, then stepped back, sudden awareness chilling him.

What the hell was this? Since when did he react like a hormone-ridden teenager to just holding a stranger in his arms? If he was that susceptible, he'd damned well better start listening to Jackson's advice about letting go of the past. Maybe it was time he thought about finding a woman to fill the void Genna's suicide had left in his life.

He turned his attention back to Yvonne, his emotions once more under control. To his surprise, her eyes were open. "Are you all right?" he asked, pleased to find that his voice sounded perfectly normal.

He'd been holding her. She remembered the warm strength of his arms, the same sense of security that had lured her back from the brink of terror. She'd cried out and he'd been there to comfort her, to drive away the demons that had somehow found her even in the depths of unconsciousness. She wanted to thank him, yet he was still a stranger and that frightened her.

"Did you hurt yourself when you fell out of bed?"

The words meant little to her as she studied him. The face beneath the thick growth of golden brown hair wasn't handsome, his features were too rough-cut and his expression too hard; but his dark eyes met hers with such compassion, she found herself responding. Her anxiety faded and she found it easier to breathe. Somehow she couldn't believe that he meant to hurt her.

"What happened?" Curt felt he had to keep pressing her for answers, he needed to keep her awake and alert. Though he longed to touch her again, the fear in her wide blue eyes kept him away. When she didn't answer, he tried another tack. "Are you getting hungry?"

Her body answered for her, her stomach rumbling its need. Yvonne nodded timidly, afraid to move after what had happened earlier. The throbbing in her head increased slightly from the movement, but subsided when she lay still.

"Who...who are you?" Her voice sounded strange, too soft, almost childlike. But she wasn't a child, she was... She couldn't seem to remember her age, which seemed odd.

Curt watched the emotions flickering over her delicate features. Fear was still dominant, but confusion seemed to be blunting her fright. It was easy to smile at her. "I'm Curt, Yvonne. We're in my cabin." He hesitated, wanting her to speak again; but she just continued to watch him, reminding him of a doe trapped in the lights of an oncoming car.

Maybe she needed help to begin talking, someone to give her an idea of what had happened, bring it back to her. He decided to give it a try. "I know you're frightened and confused. You were unconscious when I brought you here, so I'm sure you have a lot of questions. Do you remember how you got hurt?"

Something flickered in the depths of her dark blue eyes, but she only shuddered, then closed them. He waited, watching the slow rise and fall of her breasts beneath the stained gold cloth. Was she really asleep or just faking unconsciousness to avoid his questions?

Swallowing a curse, he headed for the kitchen. Since she'd admitted to being hungry, the smell of frying bacon should rouse her and eating would keep her awake long enough for him to ask a few questions. He couldn't wait forever to find out what had happened last night.

She heard his soft footsteps as he moved away from the bed. Curt. He'd said his name was Curt and he'd called her Yvonne. Was that her name? She kept her eyes tightly closed, waiting for the answer, but it didn't come. What had happened to her? The pain in the side of her head swelled viciously until it seemed to fill her skull. She clenched her teeth to keep from screaming.

Suddenly sounds from the kitchen part of the cabin broke through her wall of pain, distracting her. She recognized the pungent scent of brewing coffee, then the mouth-watering smell of bacon frying. To her surprise and relief, the pain in her head subsided. She opened her eyes cautiously. The room stayed still and the pain remained bearable.

Slowly, carefully, she inched up, supporting herself against the pillows. She might not be able to stand yet, but she could sit up. She needed to face the man on a more equal level. She'd had enough of cowering like a terrified child. She wanted answers and instinct told her that she'd have a better chance of getting them if she showed her determination when she asked Curt what had happened to her.

Curt kept an eye on his guest while he scrambled eggs and rescued the toast from a future as charcoal. So she had been pretending unconsciousness to avoid answering his questions. He couldn't really blame her; she had no reason to trust him, since she'd been unconscious when he found her. Whoever had left those bruises on her ribs and jaw, not to mention fired the bullet that had nearly killed her, had laid a heavy burden of fear on her slender shoulders. He had a feeling it was going to take more than a few kind words to win her trust.

Which could be a real problem since he didn't have much time. But what kind of approach would work? He could pretend he was still a policeman, but that would be productive only if she was an innocent victim and not a player in whatever had been going down at the Hanover Ranch. He sighed, realizing that he was hoping that she was innocent; he didn't want her to have any part in Hanover's dealings.

By the time he carried the small table over to her bedside, he'd discarded all his schemes for winning her trust and decided to play it straight with her. No big lies, just selective truth. She didn't need to know why he was out here or why he cared what was going on at Hanover's ranch—at least not until she'd told him everything she knew.

"Do you need any help?" he asked as he moved a chair up to the other side of the table, then went to get their plates of food.

She shook her head, then winced as the movement jarred her aching brain. Though she'd welcomed his gentle embrace when she was lost in the terror of her nightmare, she didn't want him to touch her now. She hadn't known then that he was a stranger. "I can manage," she assured him as she carefully slid her legs over the side of the bed and reached for her fork.

Curt concealed a grin as he poured two mugs of coffee and brought them to the table. There was sure nothing wrong with her appetite as she attacked the bacon and eggs. Not that he didn't understand: he was starved, too, and he'd eaten while she slept.

Out of consideration for her physical need for nourishment, he concentrated on his own meal; the questions could wait. Even so, he found it impossible to keep from watching her. It had been a long time since he'd shared a meal with such an attractive woman.

Once again his own thoughts sobered him. Anyone associated with Hanover had to be considered suspect and suspects weren't attractive, they were simply people to be investigated. He'd damn well better keep that in mind and get on with unraveling what had happened last night. He wasn't here to play house.

"Feeling better now?" He put down his fork and picked up his coffee with a show of casualness.

She nodded, meeting his gaze for a moment before giving all her concentration to lifting her own mug. Her hand

was shaking and the coffee sloshed back and forth until she
steadied it with her other hand.

"Could you tell me what happened to you?" He did his
best to keep his tone lazy, as though her answer meant little to him.

"Happened?" The question brought confusion as well
as pain. She frowned at him. "What do you mean? How
did I get here?"

Impatience surged through Curt, but he controlled it.
This wasn't the response he'd expected. She'd seemed perfectly calm while she was eating, but now he could sense the
tension building inside her. Still, he couldn't take back his
question, so he tried again. "I told you that I brought you
here. What I want to know is how you were injured."

Unable to answer him, she took another sip of her coffee, but her throat closed, making swallowing difficult. Her
hands began to shake, so she had to set the mug down before she dropped it or spilled the hot liquid. Questions
flooded into her mind, questions that hadn't occurred to
her before.

Why was he staring at her? Was she badly hurt? What
had happened to her? Her head ached and her side ... The
food that had tasted so good before, now seemed to twist
inside her and burned nauseatingly in her throat.

Gritting her teeth in spite of the soreness of her jaw, she
fought for control of her emotions. She clasped her hands
together tightly, hoping to still their terrible shaking, but it
was impossible. Her strong will was overwhelmed by the
riptide of terror that swept over her, setting her whole body
to shivering and shuddering out of her control.

"Yvonne?" Curt leaped to his feet, sending his chair
crashing over behind him. Her golden skin was now deathly
pale and nearly translucent, while her eyes seemed glazed
as she looked wildly around the room, focusing on nothing. Wanting to soothe her as he had before, he tried to
capture her shaking hands, but she jerked away from him.

"What is it?" He fought down his protective instincts,
moving back a step to give her space. She looked half-mad

with panic and he didn't want to risk her injuring herself trying to escape his touch.

And what if it was more than panic? Could her head injury be more serious than he'd thought? What if her reaction to him was caused by pressure on her brain, instead of fear left over from whatever had happened to her before he found her? The idea sickened him. He'd kept her here to protect her, not put her in more danger.

Yvonne fought to control her panting, wanting desperately to stop the terrible emotions that seemed to be tearing her apart. She'd felt safe a moment ago, so where had this awful fear come from? What was happening to her? Was she losing her mind?

The blackness seemed to beckon almost irresistibly, but this time Yvonne drew back from the abyss. She closed her eyes, willing herself to fight instead of giving in. Suddenly a flood of tears burned behind her eyelids, then spilled over to stream down her cheeks. Strangely enough, her tears seemed to wash away the worst of her panic.

After a moment, she was able to pull in one deep, steadying breath, then another. The blinding panic receded and she immediately became aware of the man standing beside the bed. As she met his gaze, she realized that he looked frightened. Somehow that fact made her feel less alone.

"Are you all right?" As Curt handed her a box of tissues, he noticed that his own hand was shaking, yet what he felt most was relief. For a moment there he'd really been afraid for her, but now the wildness was fading from her eyes.

"I don't know." Pride forced her to keep her voice level. "I don't know what happened to me. I don't know where I am or who you are or... or anything. Please, if you could just tell me what happened to me."

Curt studied her, intrigued by the mixture of courage and quiet strength he could read in her face. The panic was gone, vanished nearly as quickly as it had come, a fact that disturbed him. Had the tears really washed it away? Or had the whole thing been a skillful performance meant to win his sympathy and trust?

The instincts he'd honed so carefully during his years as a cop told him that Yvonne's panic had been genuine, but it had been four years since he'd carried a badge. Could his instinct about people be as rusty as some of his other police skills? He hated the doubts that continued to haunt him.

He forced his speculation aside, aware that he couldn't just ignore her question or the plea in her eyes. But what should he tell her? If her emotions were as fragile as they'd seemed a few minutes ago, could she handle his theory about what had happened to her or would she fall apart completely? Perhaps if he stuck strictly to the truth...

Curt took a deep breath and plunged in. "I don't know exactly what happened to you. I found you unconscious in the desert at about dawn today. You have some bruises and an injury to the side of your head." He righted his chair as he explained, then sat down, hoping to reassure her with a semblance of normal behavior.

Yvonne watched his eyes as he spoke. His words had the ring of truth, yet she sensed that he was holding something back. She tried to force her aching brain to produce images that would clarify his words, but that only made the pain worse. The throbbing threatened to overwhelm her and she felt the panic rising again. To fight it, she asked, "Do you know me?"

Surprised by the question, Curt felt a stirring of admiration. He'd seen the doubts and fears rising in her eyes and sensed the battle she was waging against her own terror. Suspect or victim, she was doing a terrific job of controlling herself. He wished he could help her, but he didn't know how.

Choosing to play it casual, he extended his hand to her. "Actually we've never met, so let me introduce myself. My name is Curtis Macklin and I'd like to welcome you to my cabin."

His gesture was so natural, Yvonne took his hand without even thinking about it. There was something reassuring about the strong, hard feel of his palm against hers, his warm fingers closing over her cold ones in a casual handshake. "It's a pleasure to meet you, Mr. Macklin. I'm...uh..." Her throat closed, making breathing difficult as the tide of panic rose inside her again. She forced more words out. "My name is..." Nothing came. The injured side of her head began to pound as though her effort to think had probed into a festering sore.

"Yvonne?" Curt winced as her fingers tightened around his, her fingernails digging into his flesh even as her eyes darkened with terror. "What is it?"

"I don't know my own name." The words came out like a harsh sob. "How do you know I'm Yvonne?"

Amnesia? With a head injury, it was possible. He knew that from the wounded he'd seen in Vietnam and the victims he'd cared for as a cop—first in his hometown in Nebraska, then later in Phoenix.

Curt sought through his mind for an explanation that might ease her suffering, but again, he had nothing to offer but the truth. "I don't know, at least, not for sure. I just found the name Yvonne embroidered on a handkerchief in your pocket. I had to call you something, so..."

Yvonne closed her eyes, wanting to deny his words, and was startled to realize that she could picture the handkerchief in her mind. For a moment she felt the warmth of the love that had gone into the embroidery, then the faint memory vanished, leaving only dark emptiness. She fought back the fear, clinging to his hand as though it were a lifeline.

"The handkerchief is mine." She stated it firmly, as much to reassure herself as to enlighten him.

"Then your name is Yvonne." He could feel the tremors that shook her and he ached to take her in his arms. If he could hold her the way he had when he'd found her on the floor...

"When you found me, did you find anything else?" She forced herself to focus on the ordinary, afraid to even think about the abyss that seemed to have swallowed her memories.

"I'm afraid not. There was no sign of a purse or bill-fold." Sympathy filled him as he watched the hope fading from her face. He could no longer doubt her honesty; every thought and emotion was clearly reflected in her eyes. But if she really didn't know who she was, where did that leave him?

"You don't know anything about me?" She knew the answer even before she asked and with the knowledge came weariness. She released his hand, not even noticing the marks her nails had left in his flesh.

"I know that you took a severe blow to the side of your head. I expect that's why you're having difficulty remembering right now. What you need is rest. Once you're feeling better, I'm sure..." He let it trail off, relieved to see that she seemed reassured as she slumped back against the pillows, her eyes already closing. This was obviously not the time to tell her what had caused her head injury.

Moving cautiously, he lifted the table out of the way, then eased her legs back up on the bed. She sighed and moaned as he covered her with the quilt, but she didn't pull away when he smoothed her tangled hair from her forehead. Curt watched her sleep for several minutes, not really thinking, just enjoying the sensation of having her here, safe from whatever fate had awaited her in the desert.

Now what kind of idea was that? Curt turned away, shaking his head. He was definitely too old and wise to ro-manticize what had happened. Desert fever must be rot-ting his brain. He cleared the table, then checked the view from the window. The sun was now low enough for the day to be cooling down and he had at least an hour of daylight left, so he'd better use it.

Since Yvonne appeared to be sleeping deeply, he decided to see if he could fix the Jeep. If he could get it running, maybe he'd take her out of here tonight. A cheering thought—until he realized that he hadn't a clue as to what to do with her once he got her into Phoenix.

She was sitting at her desk, papers spread out before her, the distant sounds of telephones ringing hardly disturbing her. She was trying to figure out which... A sound penetrated the dream, shattering the familiar images and waking her instantly.

Yvonne opened her eyes cautiously, hoping to find herself in the office she'd been dreaming about, but even in the fading light, she recognized the cabin. Curt's cabin, she reminded herself firmly. With everything else in her memory so hazy, she needed to keep each fact she knew sharp in her mind.

Since her head felt better, she sat up. The room seemed steady enough and she knew instinctively that she was alone. Curious, she tried to stand. Movement brought a few twinges of pain, but they quickly subsided into a bearable ache. Obviously eating had helped a lot.

She eased away from the bed, discovering that she felt as stiff as she had the first time she'd fallen off a horse. The tiny flicker of memory made her smile, then she gasped as she realized what it meant. Her memory was coming back! She was Yvonne... Instead of remembering her last name, she gasped as the blinding pain hit. She grabbed the back of the straight chair to keep from falling.

Take deep breaths, she told herself. Focus on something. She did her best to concentrate on the dishes Curt had left in the sink, the pattern of shadows cast by the bushes outside the window. Much to her relief, it worked; the pain eased almost immediately.

Yvonne moved her head slowly from side to side, testing her limits. Motion didn't seem to make it hurt worse; but the moment she tried to think about the past, the throbbing nearly forced her to her knees. She swallowed hard, sure that such strange behavior must mean something, but afraid of the pain that might come from even speculating about it.

She didn't have to remember anything just now, she decided. What she needed to do was find the bathroom. She reluctantly released the chair back and headed across the room, grateful that it was no larger. Her legs were wobbly by the time she reached the closet-sized bath that opened off the main room.

Yvonne switched on the light as she stepped through the door, then stopped, appalled as she caught a glimpse of her reflection in the mirror over the sink. She looked terrible! Her face was scratched and bruised and her hair... She lifted a hand to smooth it down and gasped as she found the gauze-covered welt hidden beneath the tangles.

He'd been right about her head wound. She probed her injury delicately, exploring the possibilities of pain. It hurt, but not a whole lot more than her ribs or her jaw. So why couldn't she remember anything? Just getting a bump on the head shouldn't be enough to...

The rising wave of pain forced her to drop that train of thought. Instead, she studied herself in the mirror, relieved that her face was familiar. Somehow, she'd been afraid of finding a stranger staring back.

She looked longingly at the small shower, then rejected the idea. No way was she going to take off all her clothes while she was here at the mercy of a stranger. Still, it was pure luxury to wash her arms and shoulders as well as her hands and face. Unfortunately the effort of bathing all her scrapes and scratches left her so exhausted, she could barely stand.

"Time to rest again, Yvonne," she told herself as she slowly made her way back to the bed. Though she was pleased with her explorations, she needed the sound of her own voice to dispel the unreality of being here. She was asleep the moment her head touched the pillow.

Curt frowned as he rounded the small ridge that had hidden the Jeep from him. Someone had removed the camouflage tarp and the hood was up. The muscles in his belly tightened and he was glad that he'd brought his gun with him. If one of Hanover's men had found the Jeep's registration...

A familiar shape appeared on the far side of the Jeep. "'Bout time you got out here," Jackson observed, his even white teeth making a nice contrast with his black skin as he grinned at Curt. "I was beginning to think I'd have to hot-wire this bucket of bolts to find out if it would run."

"What the hell are you doing here? Why didn't you come to the cabin?" Curt was digging the ignition key out of his Levi's as he moved forward. As he neared the Jeep, he caught a glimpse of Jackson's big van, which was parked in a clump of brush a short distance beyond the exposed Jeep.

"I'm fixing your Jeep, of course. I figured you'd be coming to work on it soon as you woke up." Jackson positioned himself over the engine as Curt climbed behind the wheel. "Why you insist on keeping this old…" He sighed. "You want to try it and see if I'm having any luck at breathing life into it?"

The next half hour was devoted to the fine art of finding out which connection had shaken loose during his drive back to the cabin with Yvonne. As always, they worked well together, so it was no surprise when the engine finally roared to life.

Curt nursed it tenderly as he frowned at his friend. "I appreciate the help, but I didn't expect you out here tonight. Has something happened?"

Jackson sighed, his look of satisfaction fading. "I'm not sure, that's why I came. I think we need to talk."

Curt nodded. "Let's get the vehicles under cover, then you can tell me what's going on."

Uneasiness twisted inside Curt as he drove to the rocky area of the cliff, easing the Jeep around the wild brush and into the deep shadows beneath the palo verde trees. Thanks to the runoff from the spring that supplied water to the cabin, there was plenty of vegetation near the cliff. He turned the engine off, as Jackson pulled in beside him.

"You want to go topside to talk?" Jackson asked.

Curt nodded, aware that having Yvonne in the cabin made talking there impossible. He peered through the window to make sure she was still on the bed, then led the way up the steep slope to the rocky outcropping high above the cabin that was his lookout. "So what's up?" he asked, sinking onto the rocks. He patted his shirt pocket, seeking a cigarette, then muttered a curse. He'd quit over a year ago, but tonight his jumping nerves brought back the old craving.

Jackson's mocking grin told Curt that his friend was well aware of his discomfort. An admitted health nut, Jackson had burned Curt's last carton himself, so Curt knew better than to expect any sympathy from him. To distract himself, he turned his thoughts to the request he'd made when he radioed Jackson. Maybe Pete had come up with something new on last night's mysterious meeting. "So, what's up? Did Pete have something for you?"

Jackson's grin was replaced by a scowl that had been known to freeze a grown man in his tracks. At six foot one, his partner was an inch shorter than Curt and carried about twenty more pounds on his heavily muscled body. Jackson looked like a fullback, which was why people so frequently failed to notice that he was a financial wizard—a mistake that had proved profitable in the two years since Curt had offered Jackson a partnership in BCM Investments, the firm he had inherited from his uncle Bennett Macklin.

"Turns out I didn't even have to call Pete. Since he knew you were doing your surveillance thing out here, he came by the office on his own. Wanted to know if you'd seen anything special last night. Seems one of his snitches told him that something big was supposed to be going down at that meeting. He was real interested to hear about the jet and the fact that you'd found someone out here."

Curt frowned, suddenly wishing that Jackson hadn't mentioned Yvonne to Pete. He trusted Pete completely. Hell, they'd been friends and partners for most of the six years Curt had been on the Phoenix police force. It was just that Genna had told him once that she suspected Hanover had friends high up in the department and if Pete trusted the wrong person . . .

"You didn't want me to mention that you'd found someone?" Jackson looked confused, reminding Curt that he hadn't exactly been able to explain things on the radio.

"I found a woman." Curt gave Jackson a quick rundown on everything that had happened from the time he'd

seen the cars leaving the ranch until he'd left Yvonne to
come work on the Jeep, stressing her seeming amnesia and
his failure to learn anything about her—including her last
name.

Jackson listened without comment, but his frown didn't
go away. "Damn." He shook his head. "I was hoping your
'little bird' wouldn't fit in with what Pete told me."

"What do you mean?" Curt's belly knotted.

"That's why I'm here. Pete called me at home to tell me
that someone spent the afternoon making discreet inquiries about an injured woman. Seems they called pretty near
every hospital and clinic in the Phoenix metropolitan area.
I thought you should know."

"They must have come back looking for her this morning after I found her." Curt swore wearily. "I was hoping
they'd assume she was dead. This could mean trouble."

Jackson nodded. "We can load her into the van and take
her to town now, if you think she'd be safer there."

Curt considered, then shook his head. "I think she's
better off here where I can keep her hidden. Since they
didn't find her in any clinic or hospital, maybe they'll just
figure she wandered into the desert and died. I hate to leave
now she's starting to trust me. Once we're in town, I won't
be able to keep her away from everyone. She could end up
in a lot of danger."

Jackson frowned. "I don't want to leave you out here
with such unreliable transport. Besides, the Jeep's too easy
to spot. I'll leave the van and drive the blasted thing to
town. But don't wait too long, Curt, this place is too close
to Hanover's ranch. The minute she's ready for transport,
bring her in. If you need to keep her hidden, we'll figure
something."

Curt nodded. Jackson's assessment of the situation
matched his own. "I'll get out as soon as I can. Meantime,
I don't think we'd better risk using the radio again. I'll call
you when I get to town, okay?"

"Sounds good to me." Jackson stood up. "Well, I'd
better be on my way. Anything I should know about that
miserable hunk of junk you drive?"

"It shimmies when you get it over a hundred."

Jackson chuckled. "That Jeep couldn't make fifty headed downhill."

Curt joined in his laughter, well aware that Jackson had no patience with his fondness for the old Jeep. "Treat it gently, man, it's damn near as old as we are."

"Nothing is that old." Jackson's tone was sober as he started down the trail, then he stopped and looked back. "You watch yourself out here, buddy. No stray is worth dying for and even if she can help you hang something on Hanover, it won't bring Genna back. Life goes on."

Curt couldn't argue with Jackson's logic, but at the same time, he knew that he wasn't going to give up, not yet. Maybe once he'd cleared Genna's name, he'd be able to let go of the guilt and walk away from what they'd come so close to sharing; but until then... He watched Jackson drive away, then turned toward the cabin. It was time to check on Yvonne.

Chapter 3

Curt frowned as he turned to the cabin, which was nearly invisible now that the sun had set, bringing instant night to the desert. He'd left Yvonne alone for far too long, he realized. What if she'd awakened in the dark? Would she be afraid? He quickened his steps, trying not to remember the way she'd felt in his arms, telling himself that he only wanted to protect his potential source of information from another panic attack.

Cursing an attraction he couldn't deny, he entered the dark cabin and reached for the light switch, then checked himself. After what Jackson had told him, there was no reason to take chances. He moved to the desk and picked up the small flashlight he kept there.

"It's just me, Yvonne," he called, realizing that he might frighten her by his actions. "Are you all right?"

There was no answer, but when he trained the light on the bed, he could see that she was pretty much where he'd left her. Reassured, he made a quick check of the cabin, easily spotting the blood-smudged towel in the bathroom. Curt grinned, pleased at the proof of her recovery. No wonder she was sleeping so soundly now, she'd probably worn herself out exploring.

Since the dark cabin offered little in the way of diversion, Curt retired to his lounge chair, hoping to catch up on the sleep he'd missed last night. It didn't take him long to discover that it made a lousy bed. The whimpering cries started just as he'd decided that he'd do better sleeping on the damned floor.

"No. Please, I can't...I don't know...I didn't...David? David, no...I..."

He was at the bedside in three strides, then he hesitated, remembering the way she'd pulled away from him after dinner. "It's all right, Yvonne," he whispered, touching her cheek very lightly. It was wet with tears. He stroked it more firmly. "You're safe. I won't let them hurt you again."

She caught his hand with surprising strength, clinging to him. Curt eased down on the edge of the bed, sensing her need. For a moment she stiffened, then he felt the tension ebbing from her trembling body. He lifted her gently, sliding an arm beneath her, settling himself on the bed beside her. She pressed her head against his chest as he gently stroked the soft skin of her bare back.

Her trembling ceased. Her sigh stirred the thick mat of hair on his chest as he allowed himself to relax, adjusting their positions until he, too, felt comfortable. He should get up now that she was quiet, he told himself sternly, but he didn't move. Instead, he closed his eyes and drifted off to sleep.

The familiar dream stalked him. He and Genna were in a mountain meadow, laughing and making love under the stars, planning and dreaming about their future. They'd worked through their doubts and Genna had finally accepted his proposal; she just wanted to wait to get married until after she finished the case she was investigating.

Curt twisted, tightening his hold on Genna as the scene in his dream shifted inexorably from the glorious meadow to a dark, fume-filled garage. He had to hold on to her. She couldn't die! He wouldn't let the paramedics take her away. He had to make her live again, so that they could...

Reality broke through the dream-turned-nightmare as the woman in his arms whimpered in protest. Curt opened his eyes, paralyzed until his mind made the shift from past to present. He was in the cabin and the woman in his arms was Yvonne, not Genna. She whimpered again, pulling away from him and this time Curt gladly let her go, nearly falling in his hurry to get off the bed and away from her.

Still in a cold sweat, he moved through the darkness to the sink and downed a glass of cold water. It wasn't enough to calm the hammering of his heart or to ease the twisting in his guts. He felt the old hunger for a cigarette. He needed to get out of here, away from the memories activated by sleeping with Yvonne in his arms. He used the flashlight to check her, then grabbed his gun and binoculars and left the cabin.

Force of habit led him to the highest point of the cliff. It wouldn't hurt to check the whole area, he decided, though he didn't expect anything to be happening at the Hanover Ranch. Old Keenan would be long gone now that his mysterious gathering was history—history except the woman who'd been left behind.

Thinking of Yvonne, he turned his attention from the ranch to the direction of the area where he'd found her. At first, the distant stretches of cactus-marked desert landscape soothed him, then he became aware of shadows moving across the pale ground. Horseback riders! It took him only a moment to spot four of them, all riding in the orderly pattern of a search. His belly knotted. He knew exactly for whom they were looking.

Yvonne shivered, moving restlessly, seeking the warm embrace that had comforted her earlier. The cold emptiness of the bed forced the final cobwebs of sleep away. She struggled to sit up, listening intently, since she could see very little in the faint light that came from the two windows. The empty silence told her she was alone again.

Still cold, she pulled the quilt over her bare back. Had the comforting embrace been real or a dream? Had Curt really held her in his arms, stroking her back so gently that she'd forgotten her fear? She bent her head to the pillow, drawing in a long breath. His scent was there, the unmistakable male musk that had filled her senses when she buried her face against his hard-muscled chest. She shivered again, but this time it had nothing to do with the cold desert night.

What was happening to her? Why had she willingly accepted comfort from the stranger who'd brought her here? She wasn't the sort of woman to... Or was she? The chill of doubt slipped down her spine. If she couldn't remember her own name, how did she know what kind of person she was? Just thinking about it brought back her headache.

So where had Curt gone? What did he do out in the desert? Was he going for help? Maybe he'd bring a doctor or someone who could help her find the missing pieces of her life. She found little consolation in that idea, but the ache in her head kept her from wondering why she wasn't more eager to remember. She found it easier to think of Curt.

She knew so little about him, besides the fact that he was a very attractive man in his tough, silent way. And that he could be wonderfully gentle. She remembered his touch even from the times when she'd been too out of it to respond. He'd taken good care of her today; she just wished that she knew why.

Questions continued to haunt her. How had she been hurt? And what was she doing in the desert? Had she... The pain intruded, forcing her to stop thinking about herself. Fighting it, she focused her thoughts on Curt once again.

How had he come to find her and what was a man like him doing living in an isolated cabin in the middle of nowhere? Or was he living here? The pain subsided as she considered the few possessions she'd noticed during her brief exploration of the room. The cabin was adequately furnished, but it didn't really look lived-in. It was more like the weekend place her aunt and uncle had in the mountains outside Denver.

She smiled, remembering her long-ago visits to their cabin. She'd been nine or ten when they sold the place, but she'd never forgotten... The memory faded even as she realized what it was—a clue to her past. Desperate for more, she tried to focus on her aunt and uncle, but the images refused to come and the throbbing in her head warned her to stop.

Frustrated, she sank back against the pillows. She closed her eyes, seeking escape in sleep, but she was too thirsty to relax. Maybe if she got a drink... A sound from the direction of the door brought her back to a sitting position. Fear and hope paralyzed her as a small beam of light moved toward her, trapping her in its brightness.

"You're awake." Curt sounded relieved. "Are you all right?"

"Curt." It was the only word she could force past the lump that filled her dry throat.

He recognized the relief in her face, the shadows of fear in her eyes and something inside him softened. She trusted him. She'd been afraid until he'd come back to her. He wanted to take her in his arms and hold her the way he had earlier, but what he'd seen from the top of the cliff made that impossible.

"We're going to have to leave now," he told her, doing his best not to let his worry show.

"Leave?" Though she'd wanted to get away from here before, the idea of change was intimidating.

Curt hesitated, not sure how much he should tell her. How much she could handle. Still, he couldn't keep her in the dark any longer, he realized. Once they were in Phoenix, she'd find it all too easy to walk away from him and she'd be totally vulnerable if she didn't know that someone wanted her dead. "There are some people looking for you, Yvonne. At the moment, they're searching the area where I found you, but they're bound to come this way soon."

"People who know me?" She should have been excited at the prospect, but she felt only a chill of fear. Was it because she could hear the concern in Curt's voice or was it something else, something she sensed might be hidden behind the pain that masked her past.

"I don't know about that." Curt chose his words with care, sensing that she was uneasy, but not sure why. "I'm afraid they might be the ones who hurt you. I want to get you safely away from here until we can find out. Will you come with me?"

"Hurt me?" Shivers moved through her as the ache in her ribs suddenly intensified. For just a heartbeat, she remembered being struck, then the stabbing in her head banished the glimpse into her past.

Though he could see her eyes narrowing as though she were in pain, he had to go on. Time might be running out for her. "The bruises on your jaw and your side came from a beating, the wound on the side of your head was made by a bullet. I don't know why it happened or who did it, but I do know that someone is looking for you now."

The idea was so foreign that for a moment she felt only confusion. "A bullet? By why would anyone—" Yvonne stopped, the room fading as an image began to form in her mind. She could see the gun clearly in the moonlight, but it wasn't the gun that drew her gaze, it was the man holding it that... The pain swelled within her head, blotting out the scene, then exploded so violently that she was plunged into oblivion once again.

Curt caught her as she slumped forward. Swearing, he lifted her back onto the quilt, then wrapped it around her. She didn't show any sign of rousing, not even when he called her name and shook her. Furious at himself for telling her more than she was ready to deal with, he moved around the cabin, doing his best to remove all traces of occupancy.

Since he traveled light, it took only a few minutes to gather his clothes and other belongings, clean out the refrigerator and stow everything, including his revolver, in Jackson's van. Yvonne didn't even wake up when he carried her out. Curt wasn't sure whether he should be relieved or worried as he settled her on the front seat.

"Well, little lady, this is it," he whispered, tucking his revolver into his back waistband where he could reach it in a hurry—just in case. His denim jacket covered it perfectly. Taking a deep breath, he started the van and eased out of the shadows.

If he'd had the old Jeep, he could have headed across the desert, but there was no way he could do that in the van. Which was why he kept the Jeep and left his BMW home in the garage. New vehicles just weren't built to take abuse the way the old ones did. Sighing, he headed for the road. Maybe if he didn't use the headlights on the backroads, no one would notice him. And if, on his way out, he met someone coming to join the search party? He didn't even want to think about that.

The drive seemed to take forever, but Yvonne slept serenely through it all, her head pillowed against his thigh, her soft curls a constant invitation to his fingers. The knot in his belly didn't loosen until he reached the Apache Trail and headed toward Mesa, a Phoenix suburb. Even though it was well past midnight, there was still enough traffic for him to blend in. At least, he hoped he looked like just another weary camper heading back to town after a few days in the high country.

Back to what? Curt slowed his pace as he realized that he didn't have a contingency plan in mind. His condo in Scottsdale seemed a safe enough haven, but how would he explain Yvonne to his curious neighbors? He'd lived there nearly five years now, which meant that most of them knew more than he liked about his life-style. Had his relationship with her been a romantic one, he wouldn't have worried, but he couldn't subject an amnesiac to their curiosity.

Besides, she wouldn't be safe there. If the searchers happened to find his cabin, they'd be sure to check for ownership. Once Hanover learned that Curt owned a place so close to his ranch, Curt had no doubt that the financier would start looking for his missing guest in Curt's custody.

Thinking of Yvonne and Hanover together chilled him. Somehow, when he was comforting and caring for her, he found it easy to forget that she had come from Hanover Ranch, had been a guest at whatever secret gathering Hanover had been hosting. Could Yvonne have legitimate business ties to Hanover? He wanted to believe she did, but the bullet crease along her skull was hard to overlook. Legitimate business partners rarely ended up shot and left for dead.

So what choices did he have? Turn her over to Pete and let the cops protect her? They'd try, he was sure. They'd do their best to cure her amnesia so they could find out who'd shot her, but they wouldn't realize the danger she was in. Outside of Pete and a couple of others, most of the guys thought his suspicions about Hanover were crazy.

He sighed, remembering how painful that realization had been. Of course, at the time, he'd been trying to prove that the allegations of drug trafficking against Genna were lies. He'd been sure his old friends on the force would sympathize and help since Genna was a cop, one of their own. But he'd been wrong. Well, he wouldn't make that mistake again; no way would he abandon Yvonne to their care, not after what had happened to Genna.

Okay, so what did that leave? He peered ahead, aware that he was nearing Mesa. A motel? There were plenty of them along the road and most had vacancy signs, since the heat had driven the winter visitors away. He looked down at Yvonne, letting go of the wheel with one hand so he could smooth back her hair.

Why not? He was too tired to formulate a plan now and they'd be safely anonymous out here. No one would be looking for Jackson's van. He shook her shoulder. "Time to wake up."

Yvonne opened her eyes, suddenly aware of unfamiliar sensations. Where was she? What was happening? She looked up and felt a momentary flash of relief as she recognized Curt. She was safe with Curt.

Memories flooded back as she realized she was in a car or van. She remembered the dark cabin and the terrible things that Curt had told her. She'd been shot and the people who'd done it were looking for her. Her head throbbed the moment she tried to remember more, so she struggled to sit up instead of pursuing that line of thought.

"How are you feeling?" Curt was relieved to see that she didn't look too upset at finding herself in the van instead of the cabin.

"Confused." Yvonne peered out the window. They seemed to be in a town, yet there was nothing familiar about the scene. "Where are you taking me?"

"Do you remember what happened at the cabin before you passed out on me?" he asked instead of answering her question.

She nodded. "You said someone shot me and I tried to remember, but the pain—" She stopped, fighting panic as the agony in the side of her head increased. It eased when she focused on the present and asked, "Where are we?"

"Mesa, Arizona. It's just east of Phoenix. I was thinking of stopping at a motel here. We could get some sleep, then tomorrow we'll decide what to do next. Is that all right with you?" Curt slowed even more, relieved that she still seemed willing to trust him.

"Will we be safe?"

"Safer than we were in the cabin. I think we got away without being spotted." Curt stopped at a red light. There was a large motel complex ahead. "What about staying here?"

Yvonne nodded, feeling strangely content to allow Curt to make the decisions. Deep inside, behind the veil the pain drew over her mind, she sensed that this wasn't her normal behavior, but she was too tired to care. Besides, she reasoned, at a motel she'd have other people around and a telephone.

She found that thought exciting for only a moment, then she realized that she had no idea who to call. The police seemed the most logical, but what could she tell them? She had no idea why she'd been shot. What if she'd done something bad? What if the police were looking for her? She stole a glance at Curt, her fear ebbing when he met her gaze with a grin. The nagging pain in her head eased as she decided to trust him, at least for now.

"Will you be all right alone out here?" Curt parked right outside the motel office. "You won't try to get out of the van?"

Yvonne shook her head. "Where would I go?"

The desolation in her voice and expression made him sure he could believe her, so he left her in the van while he went in to make arrangements for a room. As he kept an eye on her through the window, his concern returned. He didn't want her freaking out with panic, but her lack of curiosity seemed unnatural. He couldn't help wondering why she so readily accepted everything he'd told her. If he'd found out he had a bullet wound, he'd have had plenty of questions.

Was all this coming from her injury or was there something more behind it? Damn, he needed some professional advice on the handling of amnesia victims. If she was an amnesia victim. The attraction he felt toward her made him afraid to trust his instincts where she was concerned. He was glad when they were finally safe in the motel room.

Yvonne settled on one of the beds as Curt moved restlessly around the room, stopping only to poke at the boxes he'd carried in. He seemed almost angry, yet she could think of no reason why he should be. She frowned, her curiosity about him reviving.

"Is something wrong?" She tried to break the growing tension with conversation.

"Wrong?" Curt glanced at her, surprised by the question. She looked different, he noticed, more alert, aware— less like a victim. "Of course not, why would you think that?" He shook his head, suddenly aware of the way he'd been acting. "I'm sorry, I was just worrying about keeping you safe. It would be easier for me to protect you if I knew why someone shot at you."

Yvonne ignored the throb of warning that followed his words. Stay calm and focus on the present, she told herself. "I have no idea why anyone would want to hurt me, but every time I try to remember anything that happened before I woke up in your cabin, my head seems to explode and I black out. That's what happened when you told me about the—" Her voice broke as the pain worsened.

"Don't think about it now." Curt's guilt flared as he saw the etching of pain lines in her face. He hated himself for adding to her suffering. "Are you hungry? I brought what food I had at the cabin, so we've got juice and sandwich stuff, anyway."

The change of subject worked like magic, the pain ebbed the moment her thoughts were diverted. "I suppose I could eat something," she admitted. "And juice sounds wonderful."

He could get to like this new Yvonne, Curt realized as they worked together fixing the sandwiches, then settled at the heavy corner table to eat them. He watched her as he devoured a sandwich. Viewed objectively, she was a bright, pretty woman; under different circumstances...

He forced that thought away, reminding himself that she must be involved with Hanover, there was no other explanation for her being at a private meeting out at his ranch. The amount of time he'd spent watching Hanover made him sure the man handled his legitimate business deals at his downtown office building; the ranch was used only for very private liaisons.

"So what do you do, Curt? Are you some kind of geologist?" Yvonne relaxed in the chair, feeling better. In spite of everything, she really enjoyed being here with Curt, and she obviously owed him a great debt for his rescue. Not that she dared even think about that.

"What?" He frowned, caught by surprise.

"Well, I thought since you were staying out in the middle of nowhere..." Yvonne let it trail off, obviously sensing his change of mood. "I didn't mean to pry."

Curt recovered, offering his standard explanation for owning the cabin. "You're not prying. And, no, I'm not a geologist—I'm an investment broker. The cabin is my getaway place. I like the peace and quiet of the desert." Not to mention his view of Hanover's hideaway.

An investment broker? Yvonne studied his rugged face and well-muscled body. He'd look terrific in a three-piece suit and she had no trouble picturing him taking control in a boardroom, but there was something very physical about the man that made her suspect there was more to his story. She decided to see what else she could find out. "Do you live near here?"

He could read the curiosity in her face and decided he might as well tell her what he could; since he wanted trust, he had to give it. Besides, it might make it easier for her to confide in him, if she knew more about him. "In Scottsdale, another Phoenix suburb. My company, BCM Investments is located in Phoenix. Have you heard of it?"

Yvonne considered the question cautiously, but the pain in her head remained bearable. "I don't know," she admitted after a moment, distracted by another thought. If they were near his home, why had he chosen to stop at a motel instead of taking her there? Was there someone at his house that he didn't want to see her—like a wife perhaps? For some reason she found that idea disturbing. "If you live near Phoenix, why did we stop here?"

Curt hesitated. Her feelings were easy to read—curiosity, a hint of suspicion, then a lack of expression that surprised him. For a moment he wondered what was bugging her, then he realized how confusing his words must seem. "I'm afraid to take you to my town house. If the men searching for you find the cabin, they won't have any trouble tracing the ownership."

"Oh, I hadn't thought..." Yvonne shivered. She didn't want to think about the men Curt had seen, but this time she couldn't seem to banish the fear.

As he watched, the blood seemed to drain from her face and he knew immediately that she was in pain again. Wishing there was a way to spare her, he caught her hand. "I'll think of something tomorrow, don't worry about it now. I'm not going to let them find you, I promise."

"I don't even know why they're looking for me! What could I have done to make someone want to kill me?" She stumbled to her feet, despair flooding her eyes with tears.

Curt rose, reaching out to her without thinking. He pulled her close, wanting to tell her that it would be all right, that she'd be safe. Yet deep down, he wasn't sure he had the right. There was too much he still didn't know.

Yvonne tried to force herself to pull away, but somehow, she continued leaning against his warm, strong body instead. Maybe it was all right for just a minute or two. His arms felt so good, so safe. She rested her cheek against his chest, closing her eyes so she could draw strength from the steady rhythm of his heartbeat.

This was insane! Curt willed himself not to notice the scent of her hair or the way her warm curves fit against him, but he couldn't ignore the immediate response of his body. Holding her felt so good. He'd definitely been alone too long, but this was no time to give in to his hormones. Luckily Yvonne seemed to feel the same way, for she stiffened in his embrace.

"Thank you, I'm all right now, just tired." She moved away from him, turning her back so he wouldn't be able to read the longing in her face. Memory or no memory, she knew it would be a mistake to give in to the need she felt.

"It's been a rough day for you," Curt conceded. "Maybe by tomorrow..."

"I'm sure everything will be better tomorrow." Yvonne slipped into the bathroom and locked the door behind her. As she stared at herself in the mirror, she wished mightily that she believed her own words.

Curt stared at the door. So now what? How did he keep her here? How could he stop her from calling the cops or running the moment he went to sleep? Trust? Handcuffs would be better, but since he'd handed them in along with his shield... He sighed, realizing that, in his eagerness to make sure Yvonne was safe, he'd forgotten to protect himself.

Feeling weary beyond words, he got up and moved the heavy table over in front of the door, then took the phone apart. She could, of course, break the window or raise enough of a ruckus to attract someone, but he had a hunch she wouldn't. Her fear and confusion seemed genuine, but he couldn't take any chances, not yet.

Yvonne stopped in the bathroom doorway, shocked at the changes that Curt had made in the room. Was he really expecting someone to try to break in? Or was she afraid that she'd run? Logic told her it was the latter. Sighing, she faced him. "I have nowhere to go, Curt. I don't know my own name, so how could I remember anyone else's? I have to trust you, I wish you could trust me."

"I want to." He was too tired to hide his feelings. "But I need to feel safe, too. So let's get some sleep, we'll sort everything out tomorrow."

Though he'd expected to sleep lightly and wake early, Curt knew the moment he opened his eyes that he'd failed. Sunlight streamed through the window and the other bed was empty. Fear brought him to his feet. "Yvonne?"

"Good morning." She was sitting in the corner, smiling at him. "Or should I say good afternoon?"

His relief turned to anger at her slightly amused tone. "Why didn't you wake me?"

"I thought you needed the sleep." Her smile faded. "Would you like some juice or a peanut butter sandwich? I had one for breakfast and it wasn't too bad."

Curt rubbed his stubbly chin, embarrassed by his display of bad temper. It wasn't her fault he'd overslept. He began to reassemble the phone. "I've got to call Jackson. Let him know where we are."

"Jackson?"

"My partner at BCM Investments. He's the reason I can occasionally play hooky from the office." He forced a grin, wondering how he could hope to talk to Jackson with her sitting there listening. Not that he had a choice. He'd done some thinking after they turned out the lights last night and he'd come up with a plan, but he needed Jackson's help to make it work.

Since it was near noon, Curt decided to try the office first. Jackson answered on the second ring. "Hi, man," Curt began.

"Curt? My God, where have you been? What happened?" His usually unflappable partner sounded frantic.

"I...a...saw a search party in the area where I found Yvonne, so we split after midnight last night. We're in a motel outside of Mesa. What's up?"

"I got a call half an hour ago from some rural fireman. He wanted to tell you that your cabin burned down last night. He said that they didn't think anyone was in the place, but they couldn't make a real search until it cooled down."

Curt swore expressively for several minutes before he remembered that he had an audience. Controlling his temper with a firm hand, he settled down on the bed and outlined his plan for Jackson. As he expected, Jackson wasn't thrilled with it, but he had to agree that, under the circumstances, Curt really didn't have a choice.

It wasn't until he hung up the receiver that Curt turned to Yvonne. She was staring at him in stunned disbelief. "You want him to rent a house for us?"

Chapter 4

Curt took a deep breath, wishing fervently for a cup of coffee and about an hour to get everything straight in his head. If he could. Yvonne's confused and angry gaze made it clear he didn't even have a minute. Not sure what she might do if he didn't explain, he gave her a quick résumé of what Jackson had told him.

"They burned your cabin?" Disbelief replaced the anger as the color drained from her face. "But why would they do that?"

"Who knows? As a warning, maybe. Or just bad temper." Curt sighed, missing the place already. "Whatever the reason, you can bet they'll find out that I owned the place, so there's no way I can keep you safe in any property that has my name on it."

"Oh." Yvonne swallowed hard, aching with emptiness. Her memories of the cabin were all she had and now it was gone. "They did that because of me?" It made no sense and the swirling confusion intensified her headache. "But why? What have I done that would make them do something so vindictive? Who are they Curt? You know something, don't you? Something you haven't told me. That's why you were so anxious to get me out of there last night."

Curt's gaze moved from her face to the food on the table. He got up and poured himself some juice, his face turned away from her. "I know someone tried to kill you, but I have no idea why. I was hoping you'd be able to tell me. Have you remembered anything at all?"

He turned to her again, his dark eyes probing at her like inquisitive fingers. It took all her strength to meet his gaze, but she felt better for doing it. She'd had plenty of time to think while she was watching him sleep and none of her thoughts had been pleasant. "Nothing," she admitted with a sigh. "I still don't know my name or anything about myself."

He studied her for a moment longer, sensing a change in her, yet not sure what it was. She endured his gaze without flinching, though he could see pain in her face. There was no way he could doubt her honesty.

"Well, don't worry about it. I'm sure your memory will start to come back soon. Meantime, we'll just keep you safely out of sight. You do still trust me, don't you?"

Did she? That was the question that had tormented her the most since she awoke. She wanted to trust him, to believe in the warm concern he'd shown her yesterday and last night—but could she? Should she? The answer was obvious—she had no choice. Someone had hurt her, Curt had saved her; until her memory came back, she had no other basis for making a judgment. "I think I have to."

Curt nodded. Not exactly a ringing endorsement, but he couldn't blame her. Actually he was rather glad she was showing signs of a healthy suspicion. In her position, trusting the wrong person could be fatal. What did worry him was the fact that Yvonne herself was fast becoming more important to him than the information she might be able to give him.

"Have you located her yet, Hanover?" The tone of the man calling was cold, demanding.

"I'm still checking." Keenan Hanover shifted in his well-padded executive chair. He didn't enjoy being interrogated like a hireling by someone he'd never met.

"How the hell could you have been so careless?" The man's tone reminded Hanover of his late father, an unpleasant memory.

"Why was G.P. two hours early?" Hanover fought back the only way he could, by attacking. "There would have been no problem if everything had gone as scheduled."

"Would you like me to relay that message to G.P.?" The voice dripped sarcasm.

Hanover ground his teeth. "It's not my fault your man didn't do the job right when he had the chance. If he hadn't taken it upon himself to..."

"At least my people have a pretty good idea how she managed to disappear so quickly."

"What do you mean?" Hanover sat forward, his antagonism momentarily forgotten. "What did you find?"

"Jeep tracks in the area led to a concealed cabin belonging to one Curtis Macklin. A cabin within spying distance of your ranch." The last came with a note of warning.

"What?" He knew his tone betrayed his shock, but he couldn't help himself. What the hell was Macklin up to now? "Where exactly is this cabin?"

"You can find the ashes at the base of that cliff to the northwest of your place."

"Ashes?" Relief brought a smile. Too bad the persistent bastard hadn't been inside.

"The boys were a little disappointed at not finding your missing guest. They're looking for Macklin now."

Hanover smiled, pleased at the opportunity this could afford him. "Well, if Macklin gets between them and the woman, tell them to go through him. He won't be missed."

The man's evil chuckle chilled away his momentary pleasure. "They have their orders, don't worry. But you'd better keep on checking. Remember, if she talks, you're the one who'll pay." The man broke the connection without giving Hanover a chance to reply.

* * *

Curt braced himself as he opened the bathroom door. He'd rushed dressing after his shower, but in his gut he knew that Yvonne could be gone. It was a calculated risk, but he needed to find out whether or not he could trust her before he moved into a house with her.

Yvonne looked up from reading the newspaper, which they'd found outside their door earlier, her gaze envious. "I wish I had some clean clothes."

Relief at seeing her right where he'd left her, hit him surprisingly hard. "You're welcome to anything of mine, but I have a hunch the fit might be a problem." He grinned, intrigued with the idea of her slender form enveloped in one of his shirts.

Her slow chuckle pleased him. "I'm almost tempted, I feel so grungy in this. If I could just remember where I live..." Her smile faded and her eyes were shadowed with pain.

"How about I arrange for you to have some new clothes—to tide you over until you get your memory back?" Curt made the offer without thinking, just wanting to bring the brightness back into her face.

"How? I thought you said we should stay here until you hear from your friend?"

Even with her memory gone, there was obviously nothing wrong with her mind, he decided, pleased to note the excitement in her gaze. "If you tell me your sizes and what you want, I'll call Sybil and ask her to pick up some stuff. She won't mind."

Sybil. Not exactly a maiden aunt sort of name. Yvonne was shocked by the way his mention of another woman's name made her feel. It was crazy. Why should she be jealous? She didn't know Curt, not really, and even if she had, what possible difference could...

"Yvonne, is something wrong?" His tone made her realize that he'd been expecting an answer.

"Of course not. I just didn't want to be any trouble to your...a...friend." She kept her gaze on the paper, afraid of what he might be able to read in her face.

"Sybil is Jackson's wife and a very good friend. She'll be happy to do it." His amused tone told her that he'd guessed the purpose of her words. "I'm not married or involved with anyone at the moment."

Yvonne felt the heat in her cheeks. Lordy, had she really been that obvious? She stole a glance at him and was relieved to see kindness rather than derision in his face. "I couldn't help wondering," she admitted. "It's so awful not knowing—about anything, I mean. Like existing in a vacuum."

"Would it help if I told you a little about myself?"

She nodded, her embarrassment fading. She'd never met a man so sensitive... at least not that she could remember. Yvonne rubbed the side of her head, finding another sore spot not far from the bullet wound. Had she hit her head when she fell into the ravine where Curt had found her?

"Let's order some food first," Curt suggested, distracting her. "How do you feel about pizza?"

"Just so you don't order anchovies."

"Ah, a woman after my own heart." Curt reached for the phone book. "Oh, why don't you make a list of what you need in the clothing line while I order the food, then I can call Sybil, too. Might as well get all this taken care of, then we can just relax and pig out."

Yvonne stared at the sheet of paper he'd handed her, then looked up at Curt. "Why are you doing this?" The question was out before she thought.

His grin seemed to congeal, then it was gone. She squirmed under his gaze, suddenly aware of just how her words had sounded, but unable to take them back. "I mean, it's not that I'm ungrateful, but I'm not really your responsibility, Curt. How do you know I can repay you for these clothes? And you've lost your cabin because you helped me. I just keep wondering..." She let it trail off, suddenly wishing she hadn't brought this up now.

Curt looked away from her probing gaze to write down the number of the nearest pizza delivery place, using the time to think. He'd expected questions, of course, but not so soon. Not until he had time to decide exactly what he wanted to tell her—or more importantly, what he didn't want her to know.

She was still watching him when he looked up. Curt did his best to arrange his features in an easy grin. "Truth time, huh?" he began, choosing his words with care. "Well, like I told you, I'm an investment broker, but I used to be a cop and I miss it. When I heard a gunshot in the desert not too far from my cabin, I went to investigate and I found you.

"At the time, I figured you just needed protection until you woke up, but since you don't know who you are or where to turn, I'd like to help. What happened to you is a mystery that we can solve together." He hesitated for a moment, then went the rest of the way. "Unless you want me to call in the police or someone else?"

His grin was so charming, Yvonne found herself responding with a smile even before he began his explanation. She tried to concentrate on his words, wanting to believe them, yet afraid to. A cop and now an investment broker? If only she could remember enough about what happened to be sure. . . . Her head throbbed a warning and she closed her eyes, fighting the pain.

"Are you all right?" Curt took her hand, hating the way pain deepened the lines in her forehead. "Just think about the clothes now, we can sort out the rest of it later."

"Clothes." Yvonne focused her mind firmly on his words and felt the pain easing immediately. "But I have no idea what I'll need."

"Just think what you'd want to pack for say...a...long weekend in a private home." He grinned at her for real. It felt good to be taking care of someone else for a change. The eleven months since Genna's suicide had been busy, but now he realized that they'd also been empty. "Don't worry if you forget stuff. Sybil loves to shop, she'll welcome another excuse to invade the malls."

"Sounds like a woman I could like." Yvonne released his hand to pick up the pen, then started writing.

"You like to shop, too?" Curt kept the question casual.

"Only till I drop. I just wish I . . ." Yvonne stopped, shocked by her own words. She met Curt's gaze, then groaned in frustration. "It's gone. For just a second there, I almost thought of something, but now... Damn the pain."

"Hey, it's coming, that's all that matters. You can't force it, so don't even try. We'll just take our time and lay low until you get your memory back." Curt reached for the phone. "Meantime, I'm starved. Peanut butter sandwiches just aren't my idea of a meal."

"Now that you mention it, I could use something a bit more substantial myself." Yvonne managed to match his grin even though she couldn't help wondering how long it was going to take for her memory to return. And what awful things might she remember when the time came? It was scary not to know anything about herself.

The afternoon passed easily. Once they'd stuffed themselves with pizza, Yvonne gave Curt her list. He took one look at it, swallowed hard, then offered to introduce her to Sybil by telephone, stating firmly, "There's no way I could explain all this stuff to her."

"I could cut out some of it. It's just that I don't know how long..." Yvonne found herself caught between guilt and amusement. It was kind of nice to know that a tough guy like Curt could blush, too.

"Don't be silly, there's nothing wrong with your list, it's me. Besides, you'll like talking to Sybil. She's a real special lady." Curt picked up the phone and punched in the numbers before she could argue.

Oddly enough, he was right. After a few moments of feeling shy and tongue-tied, Yvonne found herself actually enjoying the conversation. She could tell from Sybil's comments, that Jackson had told her about Curt's rescue and about her amnesia, so she didn't have to explain why she needed such basic things as lingerie, shoes, lipstick, shampoo, hairspray, a brush and comb.

"Feel better now?" Curt asked when she finally hung up.

"She's terrific, but I feel guilty for giving her such a long list. It's weird how much we take for granted. Starting from scratch is hard."

Curt drained a bottle of soda and leaned back with a yawn. "Did she say anything about finding our house?" He'd enjoyed watching Yvonne while she talked on the phone. Her sparkling eyes and laughter during the animated conversation gave him a whole new perspective on her. She seemed disturbingly normal...not to mention desirable.

"Just that her husband was out checking prospects now." She shook her head. "He must think you're crazy for helping me this way."

Curt chuckled. "As a matter of fact, he has questioned my sanity from time to time, but that won't keep him from helping."

"You must be very good friends." Yvonne didn't bother to hide her curiosity. Since she was being forced to depend on strangers for help, she felt a need to know as much about them as possible. "Did you say you work together?"

Curt sighed, realizing that it was time to give her the promised facts about his life. "Jackson and I met in Vietnam. We were a couple of green kids, scared to death and even more terrified of admitting it. We kept each other alive over there and made it back to the States more or less in one piece, then went our separate ways.

"Jackson went to college, got a degree in finance. That's where he met and married Sybil. I went home to Nebraska, knocked around a while, ended up in the police academy. I was married for a couple of years, but it didn't work out." He stopped, watching her expression, hoping for some sign that his words were triggering memories for her.

Yvonne waited for him to go on, her curiosity growing as she absorbed his bare-bones recital of facts. When he didn't appear anxious to continue, she decided to push a little; wondering about his life was a whole lot more pleasant than worrying about her lack of a past...or a future. "So how did you go from a policeman in Nebraska to an investment firm in Arizona?"

"After Sherry and I split, I decided I'd had enough of the Midwest. My Uncle Bennett Macklin, the one who founded

BCM Investments, had settled in Phoenix and we'd kept in touch after my dad died, so I came for a visit. I was heading for California, but I liked it here, so I joined the local police force instead.''

Curt smiled, remembering the years on the force with Pete and some of his other friends. "Ben was always after me to come and work with him, but I didn't want to settle down to working in an office. Then he had a heart attack and he was afraid of losing control of the firm, so I decided to give him a hand for a while." He grinned wryly. "The rest, as they say, is history."

"Do you like it? The investment business, I mean?"

Her question surprised him. Most people, hearing that story, congratulated him on his golden opportunity—which it had been from a financial point of view. Yvonne, however, looked as though she really wanted to know how he felt.

"Better than I thought I would," he admitted. "Ben was a good teacher and once I introduced him to Jackson, things took off. Those two really spoke the same language—they'd make the long-term plans and I'd do all the investigative work necessary before we got involved in new ventures. When Ben died a couple of years ago, I offered Jackson a partnership. We've been growing ever since."

"But you still miss police work." Realizing that made her feel a little better about the way rescuing her seemed to be upsetting his life.

"Old habits die hard." He found her understanding oddly touching. Had she made similar compromises in her life, maybe given up a dream or two? He wished he could ask her without causing her pain.

"Is that why you were out in the desert?"

Curt stiffened at the unexpected change of subject. "What do you mean?"

Yvonne sensed his tension immediately. The casual tone of his question didn't fool her. She hesitated, not sure herself what she'd meant and uncomfortable with having asked what was obviously the wrong thing. "Getting away from it all—your business, I mean."

"Yeah, sometimes I need a little distance from the world of high finance." Curt got to his feet and began gathering up the remains of their meal. Was she really that perceptive or had she begun to remember something?

Depression swept away her feeling of contentment as Yvonne watched him. What had she said or done to change his expression from friendly to cautious? Was he hiding something from her, something important? Her need to know ached as fiercely as the wound on the side of her head. "I keep wondering what I was doing out there."

Curt glanced back at her and recognized the despair in her face. He couldn't doubt the genuineness of her suffering. "It'll come with time, don't worry."

"Are you sure?" Yvonne touched the wound on the side of her head lightly. "What if I never remember?"

"Then I'll do my best to find out who you are. I'd start an investigation now, but until we know exactly who shot you and why—well we don't want to give them another chance."

His calm words sent a shiver down her back. Her head throbbed and she had to fight a sudden need to close her eyes and escape into sleep. Instead, she forced herself to meet his gaze and ask, "You really think someone is after me, don't you?"

"I saw the men on horseback searching for you last night." He hesitated, then added, "And Pete Rodrigues, a cop friend of mine, told Jackson that someone was making discreet inquiries to local medical facilities yesterday afternoon. They wanted to know if an unidentified injured woman had been admitted."

"Me?" The chill and the pain grew stronger, setting her stomach to churning until she was forced to retreat to the bed so she could lie down.

"Don't think about it." Curt cursed, realizing too late what his words had triggered. "Just relax. Think about something soothing. Do you like the ocean? Or how about the mountains?" He fought an urge to pull her into his arms, to hold her close until the pain vanished and she felt safe again.

Yvonne closed her eyes, doing her best to obey him. She had to, she could sense the rising tide of panic that was sure to overwhelm her if she didn't. His words conjured up vivid memories of the ocean. She could hear the waves pounding as the tide rose. She felt the warmth of the sand on her bare feet as she wandered along just beyond the water's reach. It was heavenly to lose herself in the peaceful scene. The nausea faded along with the pain and fear.

"I love the beach. I could spend hours just walking in the sand and..." Yvonne gasped as she realized what the images were. Her eyes opened and she looked up into Curt's face as he sank onto the side of the bed. "Curt, I remember..." She frowned as the images faded as suddenly as they'd come.

Curt stroked her forehead, trying to smooth away the lines that formed there. "It's okay, don't worry, you'll remember more in a while. Just close your eyes and let yourself drift. You can't make the memories come. You just have to be receptive to them."

"But..." Her protest died unspoken as she surrendered to his hypnotic touch, but she didn't close her eyes. She was fascinated by the gentleness of his mouth, the tender glow that lit his dark eyes from deep within. Without thinking, she lifted a finger to touch his lips, tracing the softened contours as he smiled at her.

Her touch sent shock waves through him. What was going on here? It took all his self-control to hold back. Her lips were slightly parted, a sweet invitation that he suddenly wanted very much to accept. He forced himself to look past her mouth to the bruise that darkened her jaw, to remember the wound on the side of her head—the fact that she'd come from the Hanover Ranch.

"Feeling better now?" His voice sounded a little rusty, but he couldn't help that. He caught her fingers and gave them what he hoped would appear to be a friendly squeeze, then released them and got up.

"Much, thank you." Or she had been until his sudden retreat. Had she done the wrong thing, touching him like that? But what about her memories of being in his arms?

Was he the kind of man who resented a woman initiating any kind of contact? She closed her eyes again, wondering bitterly if anything would ever make sense to her again.

Curt turned back to her, sensing an undercurrent in her voice. Disappointment or relief? With her eyes closed, her face was a mask of composure, giving nothing away. He watched her for several moments, sure that she wasn't sleeping, hoping that she'd open her eyes and give him a chance to say something…anything that would bridge the awkwardness that seemed to be spreading between them. But she didn't and, after what seemed an eternity, her breathing slowed and deepened and he knew that she was asleep.

Curt stretched out on the other bed, but sleep refused to come. He was much too aware of her, remembering the beauty of her body, the way she'd laughed while she was talking to Sybil, the touch of her finger against his lips, the way she'd snuggled in his arms… He rolled over, cursing himself for a fool. Much more of that kind of thinking and he'd need a cold shower.

The phone rang, startling him, but bringing the sweet relief of a distraction. He grabbed it, hoping that Jackson had found a house. If he had to spend another night this close to Yvonne… He refused to even think about what might happen.

Curt drove slowly, squinting in the fading twilight as he tried to read the house numbers. The Mesa development was new to him, but promising. He liked the privacy offered by the large houses, set well back, most with block walls protecting them from the street as well as separating them from each other.

"That's the number there," Yvonne informed him, pointing to the handsome wrought-iron gate that stood open, welcoming them into a driveway that curved around stands of blooming oleander.

Yvonne caught her breath as the house came into view. It was quite a change from the cabin in the desert. If this was Curt's idea of a temporary rental, his business must be doing very well indeed. The cream-and-turquoise single-story house rambled in both directions from a handsome entry where a light burned in welcome.

"Looks like Jackson rented a car for us, too," Curt observed as he parked beside a white sedan he'd never seen before. He grinned at her. "I guess Sybil wants the van back."

"It's hers?" Yvonne frowned. "But I thought..."

Curt explained about Jackson's visit to their hideaway as he helped her out of the van and gathered his few possessions to carry up to the house. If getting her memory back took very long, he was going to need clothes, too.

They were halfway along the flagstone path that led from the driveway to the house when the massive, carved front door opened. Yvonne stopped, momentarily frightened by the brawny black man who seemed to fill the opening with his massive shoulders.

"I was about to start hunting for you," he said, his grin so friendly Yvonne's fear vanished as quickly as it had come. "Did you have trouble finding the place?"

Curt chuckled. "The way they disguise house numbers in this area, I'll bet the residents offer maps to their friends." He made the introductions as they entered the elegant foyer, then looked around. "I take it the Taj Mahal was booked this week."

Jackson's bellow of laughter seemed to echo as they entered the spacious living room. "Completely furnished with a security system and guaranteed privacy is a hard order to fill. Besides, I didn't have a whole lot of time to comparison shop. At least I found one with a pool." He grinned at Yvonne. "If he gets too grouchy, just push him in."

"Don't get started, you two." A feminine voice interrupted just as Curt was opening his mouth to retort.

Yvonne recognized Sybil's lighthearted tone from their telephone conversation and turned to greet her, then gasped. Though she hadn't consciously pictured Sybil, never in her wildest dreams would she have matched the friendly, no-nonsense voice to the elegantly sophisticated woman who came to shake her hand. "These two will carry on for hours if you let them get started.'' Sybil introduced herself, then continued, "Why don't I show you around while they get the teasing and insulting out of their systems.''

Yvonne nodded, too overwhelmed to speak. Fortunately Sybil seemed to understand; at least, she didn't appear to be bothered by Yvonne's lack of response as she showed her the dining room and the two large bedrooms, then the beautiful yellow-and-white kitchen, its spacious cupboards now littered with partially emptied sacks of groceries.

"I put away what needed to go in the refrigerator or freezer, but I thought you'd probably want to take care of the staples. That'll give you a chance to figure out what I forgot." Sybil's green eyes were compassionate in her golden-brown face as she met Yvonne's gaze. "It'll make it a little easier to feel at home here, too, I imagine."

Yvonne swallowed hard, touched by the sympathy in Sybil's face and words. She hadn't expected a stranger to understand how lost she felt. She had to blink back tears. "I can't believe you did all this. I didn't even think about groceries.''

"Actually I didn't, either. Jackson suggested we pick them up on the way over, so we just stopped at a supermarket and filled up the back seat of the rental car.'' Her grin softened her face and Yvonne recognized the glow of love in her eyes. "Trust a man to remember food.''

"I'm glad he did, since I don't seem able to remember anything." Yvonne fought back a wave of frustration that ambushed her. "Sometimes I feel so..." She lifted her hands, unable to find a word to describe the bleak emptiness of not knowing anything about herself. Of being afraid without knowing of whom or why.

"I hope you remembered beer.'' Curt's voice broke through her dark thoughts as the two men entered the kitchen through a door Yvonne hadn't noticed before. When his eyes met hers, she felt some of the burden shifting from her shoulders.

Jackson's chuckle eased the sudden silence. "When I shop for staples, I don't leave out the most important." He crossed to the refrigerator and got out a couple of bottles, then looked at Yvonne, lifting one dark brow questioningly. "Care for one?"

Yvonne shook her head, suddenly conscious of her disheveled appearance. She'd been so troubled by her loss of memory, she'd almost forgotten how awful she must look, but now she couldn't help contrasting her battered jumpsuit with Sybil's trim lime cotton slack suit. She hated having Curt's friends see her this way, looking like something the cat dragged in. A bone-deep weariness swept over her, staggering her. She leaned against the cupboard, doing her best to hide her weakness.

Curt frowned, his gaze telling her that she hadn't fooled him. "Are you all right, Yvonne?"

"Just a little tired." Yvonne felt the red rising in her cheeks, it was embarrassing to be so transparent, but the room was beginning to tilt and sway ominously. "I don't know..."

Yvonne tightened her hold on the cupboard and closed her eyes, fighting the sense of drifting. She'd never fainted in her life and there was no way she was going to start now.

Curt caught her as her knees gave way, lifting her easily against his chest. "Is it your head? Did something trigger the headache again?"

She sighed. "No, I just got tired all of a sudden. I'll be okay in a few minutes, really. Maybe if I could lie down for a little while..."

Curt muttered a curse, then headed back along the hall. "Which bedroom did you put her stuff in, Sybil?"

Yvonne tried to protest that she could walk, but no words came when she opened her mouth. Besides, Curt's embrace was so comforting, she really didn't want to argue. It was so hard being strong and brave; maybe it wouldn't hurt to lean on him for a few minutes. Just long enough to find herself again.

And if she never regained her memory? She pressed her cheek against Curt's chest, drawing strength from him. He believed that she'd remember and she would; it was just a matter of time before she knew what had happened to her and why. Then everything would be all right—wouldn't it?

Chapter 5

"So that's your little bird." Jackson sank onto one of the lounge chairs that were arranged around the concrete pool deck. "How come you never mentioned that she was beautiful?"

Curt took a long swallow from his beer bottle, then glared at the landscaped area beyond the pool, not really seeing it. "I didn't think it was important." At the moment he definitely didn't want to talk about Yvonne's looks. "What concerns me is whether or not I'm doing the right thing."

"About what?"

"Bringing her here without having her checked by a doctor."

"I expect something can be arranged, if you're worried about her." Jackson didn't sound particularly concerned.

"Don't you think I should be?" Curt studied his friend, wishing that he could read his mind. He knew how Jackson felt about his determination to find out the truth about Hanover, but he sensed there were other reservations behind his friend's bland tone.

"Depends on whether or not she's faking." Jackson's dark eyes challenged him.

"I don't think she is."

"She seemed fine when you got here. Why would she suddenly fold up the minute we came into the kitchen?"

"Head injuries can be tricky, you know that from Nam. Guys would seem perfectly normal, then suddenly come unglued or just collapse." Curt twisted on the plastic, wondering if he was being foolish. But, damn it, she couldn't be faking everything that he'd seen; she had to have amnesia.

"Maybe a doctor could tell you for sure." Jackson was studying the shadowy top of a silk oak that towered near the block wall on the far side of the yard.

"But any reputable doctor would have to report her head injury—it's obviously a bullet wound."

"Don't you know anyone you could trust to keep quiet? Say for a price?"

Curt sighed. "No one that wouldn't sell out for a higher price."

"You could take her out of state. Maybe down to Mexico."

"I don't have the connections there, plus I hate to put her through any more stress. According to what she says, every time she tries to remember her headache gets real bad. The minute she thinks about something else, the pain eases."

"Hmm." Jackson drained his beer, then stretched out, his hands behind his head. "You know what that sounds like?"

Curt nodded. "Traumatic amnesia, coming from what happened before the injury, rather than the injury itself. Which could make sense. I told you, she'd been battered."

"Enough to scare her into amnesia?" Jackson's tone reflected his skepticism.

"Who knows, depends on what they were threatening. We had an attempted rape case once—the guy never got beyond tearing off her blouse. She freaked, ran, fell and hit her head and woke up not knowing anything. Took months of treatment before we could even question her. It was a mess.''

"You think this is going to take months?" Jackson sat up. "You can't take months to hide out and play shrink, Curt. We have a business to run and I could use some help.''

Curt sighed, knowing that Jackson was right; BCM Investments needed both of them full-time. "A couple of days, maybe a week. If she doesn't remember anything by then, I'll see about getting her some professional help. It's just that . . .''

"That she came from Hanover Ranch and you think she might know what really went on during the secret meeting.'' Jackson shook his head. "When did you take over Genna's obsession?''

The question hit him like a spur. Curt got up, hot anger pulsing through him. "What the hell difference does it make?''

Jackson didn't flinch away from Curt's glare. "It makes a lot of difference to me, if it gets you killed.''

Jackson's simple statement pulled the teeth from his anger, leaving only weary frustration. He knew he owed Jackson more of an explanation of his need to help Yvonne, since he expected him to take care of BCM while he watched over her, but what could he tell him? He wasn't sure himself why he'd gotten so involved.

"If I abandon her now, chances are, they'll try to finish what they started in the desert. I'm not ready to let that happen. Until she gets her memory back, she's a sitting duck. She has no way of knowing who her enemies are.''

"You haven't told her about Hanover?" Jackson sounded surprised.

"She passed out cold when I told her that she'd been shot. I thought maybe I'd wait a while before I gave her any more lurid details." Curt sank down, suddenly tired of the conversation; it was time to change the subject. "Enough about Yvonne. If you need my help, why don't you fill me in on what I've been missing at the office.''

Jackson sat up, his face suddenly animated. "Well, starting with the Fenster deal..."

Yvonne lay back against the pale blue sheets with a sigh of contentment. It was truly amazing how much difference a bath and a clean nightgown could make. Even her headache seemed better. Probably due to the fact that Sybil had helped her wash the blood out of her hair.

Thinking of Sybil brought a smile. It was nice to have a friend and she already thought of her as one. She was so real, talking on about Jackson and their two kids, J.J. and Cindy, and her job as a school counselor. The only thing that bothered Yvonne was the fact that she couldn't match Sybil's revelations with her own.

Did she have a family somewhere—a husband, a daughter or son, someone who would be worried about her? Her head throbbed, forcefully reminding her that she didn't dare probe for her own past. To distract herself, she looked across the room to the open closet, smiling at the colorful outfits hanging there. Though not precisely her taste, Sybil had done a terrific job of shopping for her.

A tap on the door interrupted her and Sybil came in carrying a tray. "I assured Curt that you were just tired and hungry, so you'd better eat every bite. I think he's feeling a little guilty about not getting a doctor to check you over."

"I really feel much better." Yvonne sat up. "I could have come to the kitchen to eat."

"You need rest and lots of it. You've been through a very traumatic experience, and with a head injury..." Sybil let it trail off. "How is your head now?"

"It feels much better. Thank you for helping me wash my hair. Curt tried to clean the wound when he found me, but..." She let it trail off, not wanting to remember that time.

"Men don't understand how important it is to feel clean." Sybil settled the tray on her lap. "I hope chicken noodle soup and a tuna fish sandwich are okay. My mom always fixed that for me when I was sick in bed. She said it would cure whatever was wrong with me."

Yvonne giggled as she picked up the spoon. "I think our mothers must have studied the same child-care books. That was pretty much Mom's standard remedy, too."

"You remember?" Sybil pulled up the navy plush boudoir chair and sat down.

Yvonne froze for a moment, trying to keep the images in her mind, but they faded. She sighed, aching with frustration. "Not really 'remember.' I get little, tiny flashes of my past, but the moment I realize they're memories, they disappear. It's driving me crazy."

"Well, they'll probably get clearer as time goes on. It hasn't even been forty-eight hours, you know."

Yvonne swallowed a bite of sandwich, then shook her head. "It seems like a lifetime to me." She laughed without humor. "Actually, in a way, it is my lifetime—since that's all I can remember."

She ate in silence for several minutes, not really tasting the food, but grateful to have something to occupy her hands and mind. She didn't want to think about anything right now, it was too depressing.

Sybil, obviously uncomfortable, got up and wandered to the closet. "So, have you decided what else you'd like me to get for you? Are there other colors you prefer? And what about shoes? Are white sandals and tennis shoes enough or would you like something dressy? And how about a bathing suit? Would you like a one piece or a bikini or..."

They were still debating her wardrobe needs when Curt tapped on the half-open door. "Jackson wondered how soon you'd be ready to go, Sybil?"

Startled, Yvonne pulled the sheet up before she met his gaze. Though the cotton gown covered her nearly as well as her jumpsuit had, she felt exposed and vulnerable lying in bed. She was instantly conscious of his gaze as it moved over her face. Awareness quivered through her and she licked her lips, which suddenly felt very dry.

"We were just making up another clothing list." Sybil flipped the small notebook closed. "I didn't know you'd have a pool, so now Yvonne needs a bathing suit and maybe a couple of sundresses. What do you think?"

"Whatever she wants." Curt's gaze never left Yvonne's face as he crossed the room to her bedside. He reached out to touch one of her still-damp curls. "How are you feeling now? No more dizziness? Headaches?"

"I'm fine, really. Sybil has been spoiling me with all the food and clean clothes. She even helped me wash my hair." She was babbling, but she couldn't seem to stop herself. Though she'd been sharing a room with Curt, had even slept in his arms, something had changed between them.

"Is there anything else you need, Yvonne?" Sybil's calm voice broke the spell. "What about food? Anything special?"

"You two can work out menus tomorrow," Curt said, before she could answer. "Jackson said something about it being past time to pick up the kids."

Sybil looked at her watch and gasped, then left in a flurry of explanations and promises to call or come by if the phone hadn't been hooked up by noon as promised. Yvonne smiled. It was the first time she'd seen her even slightly flustered and she liked knowing that Sybil could be as disorganized as she sometimes was.

Curt followed Sybil only as far as the bedroom door, waiting there until he heard the solid sound of the front door closing behind her and Jackson, then he turned back to Yvonne. She looked so different. He tried to convince himself that it was just the addition of makeup or having her hair curling around her face; but deep down, he knew he was kidding himself. Something basic had changed since they'd arrived here and he needed to know what it was.

"You feel up to a little talk?" He took the tray, pleased to note the empty dishes, and set it on the dressing table, then sat down in the chair Sybil had vacated. "What happened in the kitchen really scared me, made me wonder about getting a doctor to check you over. If you're having dizzy spells, it's possible you have a serious concussion."

Her eyes were mesmerizing, so clear and the deep blue of the evening sky; when he looked into them, he felt like he could see her soul. At least he had felt that way when her emotions had been reflected there, but now he found himself unable to read her feelings at all. He felt as though a door had been slammed in his face.

"I haven't been dizzy since. I think it was just too much all at once." She looked away from him, staring toward the open bedroom door. He sensed that she had more to say, so he waited. Finally she sighed and met his gaze again. "Besides, if he knew it was a bullet wound, wouldn't a doctor have to call in the police?"

Curt did his best not to show his shock and disappointment at the implications of her question. "Is that a problem?"

Yvonne sensed his withdrawal, though he hadn't moved. His gaze was cool now, almost clinical as it moved over her face. She swallowed hard, frightened at the feeling of abandonment that swept through her. She wanted to turn away from him, to close her eyes and shut out the confusion that threatened to overwhelm her; but she couldn't. She had to answer him, because without him she would be all alone. "I...I don't know. You said someone tried to kill me, but I don't know why. What if I did something awful and that's why I can't remember? What if the police arrest me for something I don't remember doing?"

For a moment her grasp of the situation amazed him, then the reality of her suffering hit him like a fist in the belly. Instinctively he moved to the bed and gathered her in his arms. She was trembling as he settled her head on his shoulder, but she stiffened when he tried to draw her even closer. "Don't be afraid," he whispered, remembering how she'd reacted other times. "I won't hurt you and I won't let anyone else hurt you, either."

She closed her eyes, losing herself in the comforting warmth of his embrace, feeling instead of thinking or worrying. Her fears were shadows, Curt was real, his slightly musky scent making her head spin in a way that had nothing to do with her injury. She wanted to cling to him forever... or at least until her memory returned.

That last thought chilled away the warmth and, suddenly fully conscious of what she was doing, Yvonne pulled away. She might not know her name, but instinct told her

that what she was doing was a mistake. She needed to be
strong, to stand on her own, not cling to a man who was
still a stranger.

Curt released her reluctantly, a little disturbed by how
much he'd enjoyed holding her in his arms. He might be
feeling protective now, but there was already an element of
desire in his need to hold her... a desire that he couldn't
afford to give in to, not so long as he suspected that Yvonne
was somehow tied to Hanover.

"That is why you brought me here, isn't it?" Yvonne's
question snapped his attention back to the present. "You
were afraid to take me to a hospital or a doctor."

Curt studied her, not sure how much he should tell her,
remembering what had happened when he'd explained
about the searchers. But they'd come a long way since then,
he reminded himself. "Not exactly afraid, but wary of it.
Since you have no memory of what led up to your being
shot, I felt you'd be safer if the people who shot you didn't
know what had happened to you."

"But they burned your cabin." She could feel his tension even though they were no longer touching. What was
he hiding from her? If only she could remember something... Her head throbbed its familiar warning, reminding her that she couldn't pursue the subject.

Seeing the pain reflected in her eyes was enough for Curt.
He got to his feet. "This isn't helping your head, is it?"

Yvonne shook her head, too sick with frustration to hide
her misery. "Every time I try to think about what happened, I crash into a blank wall. It's like something inside
me wants to keep me from knowing what happened that
night."

Though she'd spoken without thinking, her own words
chilled her and she looked up at Curt as the horror of realization swept through her. This time even the hammering inside her head couldn't force the truth away. In the
instant before she closed her eyes, she saw her realization
reflected in Curt's face.

As she slumped back against the pillows, her face twisted
with pain, Curt looked around desperately for something

to distract her. No matter how much he wanted to discuss her revelation with her, he couldn't now. The clothes in the closet caught his eye. "So, did you like the stuff Sybil bought for you?"

A part of her screamed in frustration at the change of subject, but the blinding agony in her head began to ease the moment she focused on the present. She took a couple of deep breaths to control the nausea that burned in her throat, then opened her eyes. It was hard to believe the world around her was unchanged by the explosion inside her head.

"You okay?" Curt's worried gaze made it clear that he, at least, was aware of what had happened.

"Thanks for pulling me back." Though the words made no sense, they were the best she could offer in explanation of what was happening to her.

Needing to touch her, Curt trailed his fingers down her smooth cheek, reassured by the warmth of her skin, the easing of the lines in her forehead. "You can't force it. Whatever is stopping your memory is stronger than your need to know, so you just have to wait. The memories are there, but they won't come through until you feel safe enough to accept them."

Yvonne lay very still, fearing the return of the pain; but it didn't come. "How do you know that?"

"I took quite a bit of psychology in college. After Nam, I had a lot of questions that needed answers and I thought I might find them that way." Curt pulled the chair closer to the bed and sat down, surprised at his own confession. He rarely mentioned Vietnam to anyone but Jackson or someone else who'd shared the nightmare.

"Did you? Find the answers, I mean?"

Curt shook his head. "Not in a classroom, but time helps. And distraction. Plus the stuff I learned helped me understand some of the ugly things that happen to a cop." Unfortunately nothing he'd ever read had helped him understand what Genna had done to herself. Or his failure to see her suicide coming in time to stop her.

"Maybe you should get me some books on amnesia."

Curt brushed back a lock of midnight hair that had fallen over her pale forehead. "I think what you really need now is a good night's sleep. Everything will look better in the morning, I'm sure."

Yvonne met his gaze, wanting to believe him, but unable to. At the moment it took all her concentration to keep from wondering what could be so horrible that she couldn't face the memory. What could possibly be worse than the emptiness of not knowing who she was or what she'd done?

"Sleep. Let it all go. Nightmares fade in the sunlight." Curt spoke softly, fighting his longing to hold her in his arms again. If he held her, he could protect her from the nightmares. If he held her, she'd be safe—from everyone but him.

He ignored the throb of desire, staying still and watching over her until her breathing slowed and her face relaxed. Only then did he allow himself to study the delicate perfection of her features. Even bruised, her face marked by the stress of all that had happened to her, she projected strength and character as well as seductive beauty. Whatever else she might be, Yvonne was definitely a woman with depth and intelligence.

So what was she doing at Hanover Ranch on the night he had a secret meeting? Window dressing? A party girl out for thrills? He shook his head, unable to accept that explanation. Even without memories, that wasn't Yvonne's image. A player in whatever power deal Hanover was working on? He had a sickening feeling that was the only logical explanation. And if he was right, that meant she wasn't just an innocent victim caught up in whatever Hanover was plotting.

Not liking the direction of his thoughts, Curt got to his feet. He turned on the light in the bathroom that opened off her bedroom, leaving the door slightly ajar so she wouldn't wake in the dark and be afraid. He left her bedroom door partly open also, wanting to be able to hear her if she needed him during the night.

Though he took his time, first fixing himself a snack, then checking the windows and doors of the house before activating the alarm system, he was still wide-awake when he came back down the hall that separated the two bedrooms. He paused at her door, listened for a moment to her soft breathing, then entered the room across the hall.

His bedroom was similar to hers only done in shades of beige and green instead of blue and cream. Not that it mattered. The house was handsome and comfortable and much better suited to Yvonne's needs than his condominium would have been. Still, he missed the feeling of home. After so many years of rented apartments, he'd really enjoyed furnishing his own place.

"You're just getting old and set in your ways," he informed his reflection in the bathroom mirror as he laid out his shaving kit. He sighed, feeling every one of his thirty-eight years even though his stern features didn't seem changed by all that had happened. He still just looked tough and hard; a man without soft edges or sensitivity.

His belly knotted as he remembered the pain that came from letting anyone get behind that facade. Genna had discovered his soft spots and losing her had torn something out of him. He'd believed in her strength and courage and in the end she'd failed him and herself. Or had he failed her?

He shook off the questions, aware that he had no answers. He needed sleep, whether he felt like it or not. Tomorrow he'd have to tackle the enigma of Yvonne and figure out how to help her regain her memory. Worrying about the past wasn't going to make that any easier.

Curt stripped to his shorts and settled himself in bed with the spy novel he'd been reading. Though he usually enjoyed the fast-paced books, he found himself unable to concentrate on the words. He kept seeing Yvonne's face, her eyes full of pain and pleading; seeking answers that he couldn't give her without letting her know that he'd been in the desert watching Hanover.

He twisted on the cool sheets. She was damned bright, even fighting pain and confusion, she'd begun to figure out what was wrong with her. Once he mentioned seeing the cars leave the ranch, it wouldn't take her long to realize what he'd been up to and if she was involved with Hanover... Then when she started getting her memory back, she'd never tell him anything he needed to know.

Curt closed his eyes, trying unsuccessfully to banish all thoughts of her. Her face filled his mind and memories of her warm body snuggled close in his arms brought an all-too-familiar ache. To combat the seductive images, he tried to concentrate on the various problems Jackson had discussed with him. Yvonne might keep him awake, but the Fenster deal didn't.

"No, you can't... Please, I don't... Don't kill me, please. Stop! No..." The screams brought him out of bed on a run. He was in the hall, pushing her door open before he even realized that it was Yvonne's voice.

Heart pounding, he forced himself to slow as he crossed the dim bedroom. She was thrashing wildly, fighting the sheet that was wrapped around her and moaning, though he couldn't be sure whether it was with pain or terror.

"It's all right, Yvonne," he whispered, touching her cheek very lightly, though he wanted to gather her into his arms and cradle her as he had before. "It's just a bad dream. I'm here now, you're safe."

For a moment, she seemed to freeze, not even breathing, then she caught his hand and clung to it, her nails digging into his flesh. She was shaking so hard, her teeth were chattering. Since he could see that her eyes were closed tight, he eased down onto the bed beside her, slipping his free arm around her.

"Don't be afraid, baby, it's okay. They aren't going to find you here. You're safe." He wasn't sure exactly what he was whispering, knew that it really didn't matter. It was his tone that would reassure her, not the words.

Whimpering, she snuggled against his chest, her panting breath hot against his cool skin, tickling through the thick mat of hair as she buried her face in it. One final shudder seemed to rattle her very bones, then she collapsed, relaxing completely in his arms.

Curt held his breath, not sure whether she was asleep or unconscious. Her even breathing was reassuring, as was the way she responded when he moved his hand gently along her arm. She sighed and shifted even closer to him, her fingers sliding lightly over the hard muscles of his waist.

Suddenly he was very conscious of his own nearly nude body. If she woke up now, he had a hunch she'd do some screaming for real. But what should he do? He tried to ease away from her, but she moved with him, digging her fingers into the small of his back. He smothered a groan of pure frustration as his body responded to the enticing closeness of hers.

Her hair smelled of lemon blossoms and tickled his chin. When she moved, he could feel the soft fullness of her breast against his chest. Erotic fantasies filled his mind, adding to his pain and no amount of telling himself that she was a suspect had any effect at all.

After what seemed an eternity, she stirred and he tried moving away again. This time, she settled back on her pillow with a sigh, offering no resistance as he left her bed, carefully pulling the sheet and blanket over her. Curt leaned against the wall for a moment, looking down at her, wanting her, aching for her with every muscle and nerve in his body.

Thinking painfully of a cold shower, he forced his gaze away from her soft lips, her warm curves, still visible through the covers. There were times when having ethics was damned inconvenient!

Yvonne stretched and opened her eyes. Where was she? Not the cabin. She frowned at the sunlit room. No, the cabin had burned down. And they'd left the motel... It was the house, the one that Jackson had rented for them. Memories of meeting him and Sybil flooded in, followed by what had happened between her and Curt after they left.

Since those memories brought twinges of pain from the side of her head, she decided not to worry about them now. Besides, there had been something else, something that had happened later. She'd been in the desert and someone was hurting her, then a car had come screeching up and . . . The pain increased.

Her nightmare. Yvonne got up, fleeing the memory but she sensed that there was more. The nightmare had stopped. Someone had saved her. That memory wasn't very clear, but the pain faded when she probed at it. She'd been safe in someone's arms, protected from all the pain and terror.

She padded to her door, which Curt had left open, and peeked out. The hall was empty and she heard soft snores from the room across the hall. Curt's room. Had he come to her in the night? She closed and locked her door, suddenly frightened by the implications of her fragmented memory.

Time she took a bath and got dressed in one of the bright shorts sets Sybil had bought for her. Nightmares were a part of the darkness and it was obviously morning. Maybe if she got busy and fixed breakfast she could escape this unhealthy fantasy about being in Curt's arms. A woman without a memory had no business having sensual feelings about a man she barely knew or anyone else for that matter. What if she had a husband somewhere?

The blue and white checked shirt and blue walking shorts fit perfectly and she felt much better as she padded through the house to the kitchen. Everything was pretty much as it had been last night, except for some dishes in the sink. Probably Curt had fixed himself something to eat before he went to bed.

Just picturing him eating alone here gave her a feeling of intimacy. To distract herself, she began emptying the grocery sacks, putting almost everything away. She was surprised to discover dishes and glassware in the cupboards, silver in one of the drawers. She'd never seen a house so completely furnished. Or had she? Once again, she couldn't be sure.

Thinking about her missing memory destroyed the illusion of normalcy that she'd felt as she tidied the kitchen and set out a box of pancake mix for breakfast. Her stomach rumbled, but a quick trip down the hall told her that Curt was still sleeping. Knowing how much sleep he'd lost since he found her in the desert, she decided breakfast could wait a little longer.

Returning to the kitchen, she put on the coffeepot, then poured herself a glass of orange juice from the container in the refrigerator and headed for the arcadia door. She'd been too tired to explore last night, but now she was eager to see what the backyard held. Sybil had said something about a swimming pool.

The moment she opened the arcadia door, the alarm began to wail. Terrified, she dropped her glass, which splintered on the tile floor. Hearing running feet, she turned to see Curt racing across the kitchen and through the door on the far side...the one she'd noticed last night when he and Jackson came through it. A moment later the alarm stopped. She sank into the nearest chair, suddenly wondering if Curt had really been naked.

Chapter 6

Curt closed his eyes as he leaned against the washing machine, trying to catch his breath. His own heartbeat pounded in his ears now that he'd shut off the blasted alarm and punched in the code that would tell the security company that everything was all right.

Relief brought anger. She'd damned near scared him to death waking him up with that racket. Of all the careless... Then reality banished his anger as he realized that he'd neglected to tell Yvonne about the alarm system last night. So it had probably scared the heck out of her, too. Which meant he owed her an apology, he decided as he pried his behind off the cool metal and headed for the door.

He stopped in the doorway, surprised to see Yvonne just sitting at the kitchen table, her full attention apparently on a shattered glass and spreading puddle of orange juice near the arcadia door. "Are you all right?" he asked as she looked up.

Her eyes seemed slightly dazed as they met his, but he had only a brief glimpse of them before her gaze moved from his face. "I'm sorry, I...a...sort of forgot to warn you about the alarm system. You have to deactivate it before you open any of the doors or windows. Otherwise, it sets off the ... uh ... alarm.''

Her gaze seemed to be traveling down his body to the floor then it returned slowly to his face. An odd little smile lifted the corners of her mouth as she met his gaze. "I figured that out. Just a little late. I'm sorry if it frightened you."

"Oh, no problem. I should have remembered to tell you after Jackson showed me the setup. It's real simple, but..." He let it trail off. Her little smile seemed to be growing. Was she going to be hysterical? He decided to try to distract her. "I could show you the setup now, if you..."

Yvonne couldn't keep the giggle back any longer. Under other circumstances, Curt's nearly naked form would have been either highly seductive or acutely embarrassing but for some reason the contrast between his serious expression and the red candy canes that trimmed his white briefs struck her funny.

Curt stiffened, irritation warring with his concern. "What the hell is so funny?"

Yvonne tried to answer, but she had trouble finding the right words, so she simply shook her head, waving a hand at him. After a moment, she managed to say, "The alarm system isn't the only thing you forgot, Curt."

It took exactly one second for him to realize where her gaze was directed. As he looked down, Curt felt a chill that had nothing to do with his lack of clothing. For a moment after he realized what he was wearing, his embarrassment nearly overwhelmed him, then the ridiculousness of the entire situation struck him. Suddenly he was laughing so hard he had to sit down at the table with her.

It took him several minutes to catch his breath enough to explain. "I'm sorry, but I don't own any pajamas and I didn't pack a robe to take to the cabin, so..." He let it trail off. "When the alarm sounded, I just hit the ground running."

She tried to resist, but the temptation was too great. "They're a bit out of season, but really adorable."

"They were a joke gift at the office Christmas party last year." He met her gaze, suddenly aware of a certain electricity in the air. "I'll go pull on my clothes. You can go outside now, if you want." He didn't move from the chair.

"Would you like some juice first?" Her giggles had died, probably from lack of oxygen, since she seemed to be having difficulty breathing when she looked into Curt's eyes. "I put the coffee on, but I don't think it's quite ready yet."

"Juice sounds great." He couldn't take his eyes off her as she got up and walked to the cupboard for glasses, then poured the juice. The shorts emphasized the length and flawless contours of her beautiful legs, while the blue intensified the shade of her eyes. She looked wonderful here, natural, right. Except that her hand was shaking as she handed him his juice.

"I'd better clean up the glass I dropped." Yvonne set her juice down on the table, then turned away, heading for the cupboard where she'd put the paper towels. With the ebbing of her amusement, she was suddenly much too aware of his body. His shoulders seemed broader without a shirt to cover them and the thick mat of golden brown hair was altogether too inviting. Her fingers itched to explore the elegantly sculpted muscles of his back and his arms and...

She swallowed hard, shocked at the thoughts that seemed to fill her mind. For a person with no memories, she certainly had an active imagination. Or was it all imagination? Once again, she was haunted by the shadowy memories of being in Curt's arms last night.

"What is it?" Curt's worried tone forced her attention back to the present and she realized that she'd been standing with the paper towels in her hand for some time. "Is something wrong?"

"I was just trying to figure out what I'm going to do with the glass when I pick it up," she murmured, doing her best to cover her lapse of attention. "I don't remember seeing a wastebasket anywhere, do you?"

"As a matter of fact, I think there's one in the laundry room." Curt grinned at her, suddenly sure that her discomfort had more to do with his lack of clothing than anything else. "Would you like me to get it for you?"

"Oh, no, I'll go get it." She hurried from the room so quickly, he knew he was right.

For a moment, he enjoyed the sense of power that came from the realization, then memories of last night filled his mind and he felt an unmistakable jolt of desire. Well aware that he wouldn't be able to hide his response, he took a quick swallow of the cold juice, then got to his feet. "I'll go shower and dress while you clean up, then we can discuss breakfast. I'm starving."

Yvonne returned to the kitchen in time to catch a quick glimpse of his elegant buns as he disappeared down the hall toward the bedrooms. Her heart rate rose instantly. The man had a gorgeous body, no two ways about it.

"Just clean up the juice," she told herself firmly. This was no time to be indulging in an attack of hormones. Until she knew exactly who she was and what had happened to her in the desert, she couldn't afford the distraction of getting involved with anyone—least of all the man who'd saved her life.

By the time Curt returned, clean-shaven, his hair still darkly damp from the shower, she had the pancake batter ready and the sausage frying. "Hey, I didn't know you could cook." His tone was teasing as he paused in the doorway, looking perfectly at home in his well-worn cotton slacks and a bright red knit shirt.

"Neither did I," Yvonne admitted, "but so far everything seems to be coming naturally, so if you don't mind taking the risk..."

"Hey, if I can eat my own cooking, I can survive anything. You want me to do the eggs while you take care of the pancakes?"

"Sounds good to me." It seemed wonderfully natural to work with him and even nicer to sit across the table from him while they ate. Maybe too natural, she told herself as she poured some more coffee into their cups. It could be habit-forming.

The rest of the morning was equally pleasant as they explored the house and grounds, making lists of the various things they would be needing. It was just before noon when the world intruded again. The telephone rang, startling Yvonne so that she nearly dropped the glass of iced tea she'd been about to take out to the pool.

"Don't answer it," Curt ordered as he moved past her to the wall phone. "We don't want anyone to know you're here."

"Jackson." Curt waved Yvonne on her way as he leaned on the counter. He was glad that the phone had been hooked up, but at the same time, he realized it could give Yvonne access to the outside world, something he feared.

He sounded relieved, Yvonne realized as she made her way outside, leaving him to his conversation. Probably because he had a life outside the house. For a moment, resentment stirred within her, then it faded as she settled in the shade of the umbrella table, extending only her legs to the sun. She had plenty of bruises, she definitely didn't need a sunburn.

"So, have you talked to Pete? Is there anything new going on?"

"I haven't heard a word from Pete, but there is one thing." Jackson's tone was businesslike. "We've had two calls now from Murray Kaufman over at Textron, Inc."

Curt swallowed a sigh. Since Yvonne had invaded his life, he was finding it increasingly difficult to concentrate on business matters, still he owed it to Jackson to try. "Are they looking for a new investment possibility?"

"I wouldn't know."

"What do you mean?"

"Mr. Kaufman insists on speaking only with you. Yesterday, I had Cheryl tell him that you were out of town and not expected back for several days. When he called today, I thought perhaps he'd decided to talk to me but he just asked if you could be reached over the weekend. Claimed it wouldn't wait."

Curt frowned. "Are we handling anything special for Textron?"

"Just the usual investments. And the last reports we sent reflected their normal profit margin. He was very pleased with our efforts the last time I talked with him." There was a slight undercurrent of anger in Jackson's tone.

"And I've never discussed his investments with him." Curt felt a tingle of suspicion, then a flash of memory validated it. "In fact, the only time I ever really talked with the man was at a fund-raising party that Hanover hosted about a year ago."

"Hanover. I should have known." Jackson sighed. "As a matter of fact, I did suspect it, so I ran a quick check before I called but I couldn't find any connection between Textron and any of Hanover's holdings."

"I doubt that you would, but I can't figure any other reason for Kaufman's insistence on speaking only to me. He was singing your praises loud and clear the last I heard."

"So what do you want me to do?"

"Ignore him for the moment. See what he does. I'd really like to know how far Hanover is willing to push this."

"I suppose that means your guest didn't wake up with her memory intact." Jackson sounded mollified, but not happy.

"No such luck."

"You know, there is another way we could play this."

"What do you mean?" Curt shifted his stance, turning slightly away from the open arcadia door. He didn't want Yvonne to know he was talking about her.

"If they're this anxious to find her, why not use her as bait? We could make sure she's protected, but something real interesting might shake loose. And, of course, if she is faking her amnesia, we'd probably get a miracle cure once she discovered she was in danger."

"No way!" The words were out almost before Jackson finished speaking and he barely contained the curses that threatened to follow.

"Hey, it was just a possibility." Jackson didn't sound apologetic. "This is your game, so we'll play it any way you want to."

Curt reined in his temper, realizing that he was over-reacting. No doubt as a result of the heated dreams that had haunted him following his late-night visit to Yvonne's room. "It would never work, anyway. Hanover wouldn't dirty his own hands cleaning up his mess and the kind of people he'd send would never roll over on him."

"So what do you want to do?"

"Give her a chance to remember. Once she does, she can tell us why he's after her. She has to know something that is a real danger to him or he wouldn't be this anxious to find her."

"Question is, if she's involved with him, why should she tell you?" There was no malice in Jackson's tone, Curt noted. He was just doing what he did best—playing devil's advocate as they worked out a plan.

"Because I'll protect her and he's already sent men after her to kill her." Curt stated that firmly; he had to believe it.

"Okay. What do you need me to do?"

The plans were quickly set in motion, but after he finished his calls, Curt found himself reluctant to join Yvonne by the pool. Talking to Jackson had forced him to remember exactly how Yvonne had come into his life and he didn't like the suspicions that accompanied the memories. He was going to have to be extra careful from now on. He couldn't let her appeal as a woman cloud his judgment or they might both end up dead.

He watched her as she got up and moved her lounge chair out of the sunlight entirely. Her dark hair rippled seductively over her shoulders and the shirt and shorts revealed her curves nicely as she settled herself again. Was ignoring her sensual appeal even possible when they were sharing a house? he asked himself. The ache in his body was an answer he couldn't ignore.

Okay, so he wanted her—a lot. What did he do about it? Cold showers weren't as effective as his mother had promised a lifetime ago. So should he go the other way? What would it hurt if he followed his instincts? She certainly hadn't shown any signs of reluctance to accepting his embrace. It was even possible that sex could trigger...

Curt closed his eyes, cursing his weakness. Since when did he take advantage of a woman? What would that make him? Yvonne's very vulnerability and dependence demanded that he protect her—even from himself. No matter what her involvement with Hanover was, the woman he'd spent the past couple of days with was someone he was coming to like and respect.

A friend? The idea was bittersweet, but he had to admit it felt right. He genuinely liked Yvonne, her humor, her quick intelligence, the way she'd come through this horrible experience without falling apart. That commanded his respect. The code of ethics that he'd hammered out for himself through the painful years of his life said you didn't take advantage of your friends and he knew he had to stick to that—no matter how difficult it proved to be.

Sighing, he helped himself from the pitcher of tea in the refrigerator, then went out to join her. One of the things he definitely needed to do was go by the condo and pick up some clothes and his swim trunks. Swimming in the unheated pool would probably be more effective than a cold shower—if he swam enough laps, anyway.

"Business problems?" Yvonne asked, sensing Curt's tension as he settled himself on the other lounge chair.

Curt started to deny it, then changed his mind. If he accepted the fact that Yvonne was involved with Hanover, it was probably in some business way, which meant discussing business could possibly trigger memories. He dredged up the details of the discussion he and Jackson had conducted out here last night and began describing the Fenster account for her.

Yvonne watched Curt's face as he explained how the possible merger could effect his client. At first, she was intrigued by the way the strain lines around his eyes eased as he talked but once his words caught her attention, she discovered an interest in the plan itself. Soon she was eagerly debating the feasibility of expansion while the local economy was still struggling. When the phone summoned him back into the kitchen, she resented the interruption.

Sighing, she stretched, realizing that she was getting hungry again. Though she had no watch, she knew it had to be well past noon, definitely time to be thinking about lunch. She got up, collected their glasses and headed inside.

"That's great. I'll need you to stay maybe an hour or two. Long enough for me to pack up some clothes and pick up the papers and files I've left at the condo." Curt was still on the phone, his back to the arcadia door.

Yvonne started across the kitchen, then stopped. Stay where? Who was he talking to? She felt like an eavesdropper though she hadn't really thought anything about his phone conversations earlier.

"So, did you find everything on the lists I gave you?" Curt's question answered hers. He had to be talking to Sybil and she'd be willing to bet he was asking her to come and spend an hour or two here, baby-sitting her.

"Oh, that's great. I'm sure she . . ." Curt turned toward her as he spoke and the guilty look on his face as he let the sentence trail off confirmed her suspicions. "She's right here, Sybil—why don't I let you tell her what you found."

Resentment rose in her throat like bile. All that friendly concern and consideration didn't fool her for a moment. He wanted Sybil here to watch her, to play guard while he was away. For a heartbeat, she considered just walking back outside and ignoring the proffered receiver.

"It's Sybil. She called to see if there was anything else we needed from the grocery store. She said she could stop and pick it up on her way over." Curt's familiar easy grin was in place when she met his gaze again.

As she accepted the phone, Yvonne couldn't help wondering if she could have imagined the flash of guilt. Maybe she'd just startled him. Or misunderstood what she'd thought she overheard. The warmth in Sybil's greeting seemed genuine enough and there was no mistaking the enthusiasm in her voice as she described her latest purchases.

By the time she hung up the receiver, Curt was elbow deep in sandwich fixings and Yvonne discovered she no longer wanted to confront him about asking someone to stay with her. The prospect of being here alone wasn't all that alluring, anyway. Besides, Sybil had promised to bring her some paperbacks, and magazines, which she hoped would help stimulate her memories.

Still, the overheard conversation returned to her mind as she put the dishes into the dishwasher, bugging her until she could think of nothing else. She also sensed Curt's growing restlessness as he wandered in and out of the kitchen, seemingly unable to settle down anywhere.

Once she finished in the kitchen, Yvonne went looking for him. She found him in the small den that opened off the living room. He was standing at the window, staring toward the street, which was hidden from view by the trees and the high block wall. He looked so miserable, she felt guilty.

"You can leave anytime, Curt. You don't have to wait for Sybil. I'll be fine by myself."

"What?" He spun around so fast he had to grab the lamp to keep it from falling off the table he'd bumped.

"I heard you tell Sybil that you needed to go to your condo to pick up some clothes. I just wanted you to know that I'll be fine here alone. I don't need a *baby-sitter.*" She emphasized the last sentence, suddenly angry at the burden his impatience had imposed on her.

"A baby-sitter? I'm sure Sybil would be pleased to know you think so highly of her company." Curt's gaze was unreadable, but definitely not friendly.

Yvonne began to wish that she'd kept quiet, but of course, it was too late to take back her impulsive words. Besides, she didn't really want to, since she'd spoken the truth. "I enjoy Sybil's company very much and I'm glad she's coming, but I don't want to be a burden to you, Curt. You didn't ask to find me in the desert and I've already caused you a lot of trouble, so..." She ran out of words.

Curt looked deep into her eyes, trying to gauge the truth of her words, then studied her body language. Unless she was the world's greatest actress, she was concerned, a bit uncertain and telling him exactly what she was feeling. He wished he could be as honest, but there was no way that he could admit that being close to her was driving him crazy.

"I swear I never thought of Sybil as a baby-sitter. I was just worried about leaving you alone. After a head trauma, there's always a possibility of your having another dizzy spell like you had last night. That's why I wanted someone with you." He was glad it was the truth, since he suspected it would be very hard to lie to her. When he met her gaze, he had trouble remembering that she could be working for Hanover.

"Oh, I hadn't thought of that." Yvonne found it hard to think about anything when he looked at her that way. She was dizzy now, but the feeling had nothing to do with her head injury.

Her gaze was irresistibly drawn to his mouth. How could she ever have thought his lips hard? She wondered how they would feel on hers. Would his kiss be tender or fiercely demanding? Even thinking about it sent a quiver of heat through her, drying her mouth and setting her pulse to racing.

"Anyway, there's no rush about my going to the condo. We do have a washer here and you've already seen the most colorful part of my wardrobe." His teasing reference to the candy cane briefs added fuel to the fire growing within her.

"I just feel like I'm keeping you from your life." She spoke quickly, afraid that she might be tempted to say something else if he kept looking at her so intently.

"You mean by forcing me to spend the weekend in this slum?" A mischievous light sparkled in his eyes. "With an ugly hag like you to keep me company? You've really messed things up for me."

Her grin refused to be controlled. He was so blasted charming and sexy and... She did her best to bring her chaotic thoughts into order so she could answer him. "Well, I'll admit this place is pretty hard to take, but I don't imagine your weekends are ever dull."

"I doubt this one will be." His gaze moved caressingly over her face, finally focusing on her lips.

The quiver of heat inside her began to swell, overpowering the small voice deep within her that warned her to run, to resist, to remember that someone wanted her dead. The room faded, time lost all meaning; so long as she looked at him, nothing else existed. There was only this moment, the wonder of being here, of seeing her desire reflected in his dark eyes.

Curt felt his control melting away. All he had to do was reach out to her and... A distant sound jarred the erotic images in his mind. He tried to ignore it, to block it out by concentrating on the realization that Yvonne wanted him as much as he wanted her. Then he heard it again, the sound of a car door slamming. He took a deep shuddering breath and tore his gaze from Yvonne's face so he could look out the window.

"Sybil's here." His voice sounded as though it was coming from a great distance. "I'll go help her carry stuff in." He fled the den as though Yvonne were in hot pursuit.

Sybil? Yvonne blinked, confused by Curt's abrupt exit. She slumped against the wall, her knees suddenly refusing to support her full weight. The wild spinning heat drained from her body, leaving her chilled in the artificial coolness of the air-conditioning. Shivering, she shook her head, feeling nearly as lost and disoriented as she had been that first day at the cabin.

Only this time it had nothing to do with her injury. She rubbed her hands over her cheeks, shattered as she remembered the flaming desire that had just swept through her. What in the world was happening to her? How could she be so emotionally drawn to someone she scarcely knew?

Or did she? When she closed her eyes, she remembered the tenderness of his touch, the gentle way he'd held her when she was afraid. How was it that she knew the warm strength of his arms, the comfort of resting her cheek against the tickling hair of his chest?

Had she known Curt before? She tried to remember, to see past the veil of darkness, but the clamp of pain held it shut and forced her to abandon the effort. Still, it was frightening to realize that it was possible. Thanks to her amnesia, she had only his word about what had happened, how she'd been injured. And she knew that he had a gun—she'd seen it at the cabin.

"Yvonne, aren't you going to come see what Sybil brought?" Curt's voice broke through the frightening tapestry she was weaving around herself.

"Be right there." She shook herself, not wanting to believe the ugly pictures that had filled her mind. Not Curt, he couldn't be the one who'd hurt her. He'd saved her from the men searching the desert and his cabin had been burned and . . . And she had only his word for everything that had happened. She fled from the den and the frightening suspicions. If she couldn't trust Curt, there was no one.

Sybil was in the living room with a half-dozen boxes and packages, her smile of greeting bright and friendly. "Curt's bringing in the groceries, but I couldn't wait to show you the dresses and bathing suits I found."

For a moment, Yvonne hesitated, still caught in the web of her suspicions, then she looked into Sybil's eyes and the last of the shadows faded. "I'm dying to see everything. You did such a super job on the rest of my clothes."

Suddenly she was caught by a memory. She and Suzanne, in their dorm room, the twin beds piled high with packages as they compared the fruits of their wild shopping spree. They'd laughed and daydreamed about the coming spring break, then . . . The memory faded into darkness as the side of her head throbbed a warning.

"Are you all right?" Sybil's warm hand touched her arm, recalling her to reality. "You're not dizzy again?"

Yvonne shook her head. "No, I just had one of my memory flashes. A shopping spree with my best friend in college."

Sybil's smile returned. "That's great. The more little flashes you have, the sooner you'll be able to start piecing them all together."

"You've remembered something?" Curt appeared in the doorway, his arms full of sacks. "What is it?"

"Just my college roommate." Yvonne met his gaze, the last of her doubts about him fading as she watched the hope change to disappointment. If he'd been lying to her, he wouldn't want her to get her memory back, would he?

"Well, at least you're getting more flashes," he echoed Sybil's words. "I'll go put these in the kitchen, then I'd better be on my way. I'd like to get in and out before too many of my neighbors get home. Don't want to make them curious."

Sybil chuckled as he disappeared in the direction of the kitchen. "He's probably afraid the sexy blonde that moved in last month will try to trail him over here. Not that I blame her. Curt's got to look like a terrific catch to any red-blooded woman."

Yvonne forced herself to concentrate on opening the box that Sybil had handed her, but her thoughts weren't on clothes any longer. Thoughts of a gorgeous, but predatory woman in hot pursuit of Curt twisted like a knife inside her. If he'd looked at the blonde the way he'd looked at her . . .

"You hate it." The disappointment in Sybil's voice forced Yvonne's attention back to what she was doing.

"How could I?" she gasped, suddenly aware that she was holding a dress in her hands. The sheer blue, pink, lavender and white print shimmered through her fingers as she shook it out. "It's absolutely gorgeous."

"It looked like it was meant for you," Sybil agreed, taking the dress and holding it up for Yvonne's inspection. The delicate fabric formed a draped neckline, cut fairly low both back and front, narrowed to the belted waist, then flared out in a full skirt made for dancing.

For a heartbeat, Yvonne lost herself in a daydream of moving to seductive rhythms in Curt's strong embrace, dancing the night away in some romantic... She shook her head. "It's perfect, but I can't accept something like this. I just need casual things to wear while I'm trying to get my memory back."

"You want me to take it back?" Sybil sounded shocked.

"Take what back?" Curt came into the living room.

"I was just explaining that I don't need something so dressy." Yvonne kept her gaze on the dress, not trusting herself to meet Curt's eyes while she was still under the spell of her fantasy. After what had happened in the den, she was afraid of what he might read in her expression.

"You have to keep it, that's your dress. You'll need it when we celebrate the return of your memory." He spoke lightly, but the promise of his words forced her to face him.

Did he mean it? Would they really be together once her memory came back? Or was he just trying to keep her spirits up? His easy grin charmed her, but she could read nothing beyond kindness in his gaze.

"Both of you be careful while I'm gone," he said, turning away abruptly. "I'll try not to be too long."

Yvonne stared at the empty doorway after he left. What had happened? Where was the intensity, the desire she'd seen in his eyes in the den? Had she dreamed the whole thing? Was that possible? Or was he trying to hide his feelings from Sybil? Her head throbbed as she tried to concentrate on the contents of the box Sybil was opening. How could she be sure of anything when she had no memories to help her judge?

Chapter 7

Now why the devil had he done that? Curt asked himself as he drove the rented sedan along the quiet streets of the posh neighborhood. He was anxious for Yvonne to remember everything that had happened to her, but *celebrate?* Whether they did or not would depend on what she remembered. And how much celebrating would he want to do if those memories linked her to some of Hanover's more questionable activities?

He sighed, realizing that, once again, he'd fallen into the trap of thinking of Yvonne only as the person he was getting to know. A risky proposition, since he had no idea what sort of person she'd been before he found her in the desert. The woman he'd just left seemed much too smart to be buying into any of Hanover's schemes, but what if she had a major part in it?

His belly tightened. That was what he was counting on, wasn't it? If she was just an innocent bystander somehow caught in the fallout from whatever secret meeting Hanover was holding at the ranch, her regaining her memory wouldn't help him. He needed an insider's information to figure out what Hanover was involved in. To learn once and

for all what the man had been trying to hide when he
framed Genna and so relentlessly drove her to her final
desperate act.

So why didn't he focus on what he wanted and needed
instead of remembering that moment in the den, the heart-
stopping invitation in Yvonne's eyes? She certainly wasn't
the first woman he'd been physically attracted to since
Genna's suicide. Maybe it was only her proximity. Having
her warm and willing and just across the hall was enough
to make any man eager to fall under her spell.

Having decided that, Curt turned his attention to the cars
parked along the streets near his town house. He'd have to
be careful. Yvonne's safety depended on no one finding out
about the house, so he'd have to slip in and out of the
condo without being spotted. It would be just like Hanover to have someone watching his town house. Which
meant he couldn't just pull up in front and let himself in.

After two passes around the quiet area of Scottsdale
where his town house was located, Curt pulled the sedan
into a shady spot one street over. He walked briskly between two of the large buildings, each of which contained
four of the two-story town houses. He paused in the shadows and studied the rear area of his building. As he'd
hoped, the area was almost deserted and he recognized both
of the women walking across the private roadway and
heading for the recreation area that served the complex.

Not wanting to be seen, he stayed behind the hibiscus
bush until they were past, then made his way to the locked
gate that led into his small rear yard. Since he generally
drove into the underground parking area beneath his unit
and used the inside entrance, the lock was hard to open. He
barely managed to get inside before a car came driving
along the road.

Maybe waiting until dark would have been smarter, but
then who would have stayed with Yvonne? He didn't want
to ask Jackson or Sybil to get any more involved. Yvonne
was his problem, not theirs. He started to fit the back-door
key into the lock, then realized that the door wasn't locked.

Curt froze. When he'd left for the cabin Tuesday morning, he'd locked up tight and set the alarm system. If anyone had broken in, the security company should have notified the police immediately. He was glad that he hadn't felt safe leaving his revolver at the house with Yvonne. At the moment, it felt pretty comfortable in his hand.

He moved through the rooms slowly, following his police training, every sense alert for a sound or a movement, but there was none. The air was musty and undisturbed dust lay on tables and countertops, reminding him that he'd forgotten to arrange for someone to admit the cleaning service people yesterday.

Once he was sure the town house was empty, Curt made a second tour of the rooms, this time checking to see what was missing. It took a while, since whoever had been here hadn't been very neat with his search, but in the end, he couldn't think of anything that might have been taken.

So what was he going to do? he asked himself, angry at the violation of his privacy. His first instinct was to call Pete and get an investigative team out here to dust for prints and to canvas his neighbors to find out if anyone had seen the intruder. After a moment's thought, however, he rejected the idea, realizing that he might be doing exactly what the intruder wanted him to. Besides, anyone with the knowhow to so efficiently disarm his security system, would be too smart to be seen or to leave fingerprints.

So where did that leave him, besides mad as hell with no one to slug? He studied the mess, then grinned as he got his suitcase. After he finished packing, he double-checked for bugging devices, then called Pete to set up a meeting. That accomplished, he arranged for the cleaning service to arrive bright and early tomorrow morning—so they could "discover" the break-in. That way if Hanover had someone watching the place, he'd have no way of knowing that Curt had stopped by.

Curt was even more careful leaving than he had been when he arrived. And once he was in the rental car, he spent an extra half hour practicing all the "lose the tail" routines he'd perfected during his years on the force. Not that he thought anyone was following him, but it paid to be careful. Feeling sure he was alone, he drove to the little neighborhood bar to meet Pete.

Pete's lazy grin greeted him as he slid into the dim back booth. "This had better be good. I'm off duty and I've got a date with a redhead who ain't gonna wait forever. She's not that crazy about cops, anyway."

"Don't give me that, I remember how they always seem to wait for you. Never could understand the attraction myself." Curt chuckled, relaxing for the first time since he'd left the condo. With his dark eyes, black hair and stocky good looks, Pete Rodrigues drew women like moths to a flame. The fact that he wasn't much inclined to resist had ended his marriage not long after he and Curt became partners.

"So what's up? You sounded a little hot on the phone. Has your woman come up with something? And where is she, anyway? Don't tell me you lost her?"

"No, she's safely tucked away with Sybil baby-sitting at the moment. And she hasn't come up with anything yet. That's not what I wanted to talk to you about." Curt signaled the barmaid for a beer, then began to describe exactly what he'd found at his condo.

"Well, well, sounds like you might have hit the jackpot this time. You're definitely right about her being wanted— big time."

"What do you mean?" Curt felt a chill. "Has something else happened?"

"Since I didn't know where to reach you, I was going to call Jackson tonight, fill him in. One of my snitches told me there's a high-level rumor going around that someone is contacting all the lowlife cut-and-stitch boys with a big money offer for a woman that might be brought in for medical help." Pete leaned back. "No name, just a description—five-seven, good-looking, long black hair, blue eyes, early thirties. Possibly with a bullet wound. Does that ring a bell?"

"Damn." Curt nodded.

"Someone is apparently very eager to find out where you've stashed the lady." Pete's eyes were full of curiosity. "What do you think she knows?"

"At the moment, I haven't a clue. Maybe the identity of Hanover's midnight visitor. Or better yet, what was discussed at this secret meeting. Is Hanover the one behind the money offer?"

"I don't think so. That was my first guess, so I ran a check, but I haven't been able to trace the inquiry back to anyone that would be a part of his organization. This seems to be coming from someone new on the scene."

"The visitor?" Curt frowned, not liking this at all. Hanover was dangerous enough, but if he'd brought in powerful outsiders, it could be far worse. What the hell was Yvonne involved in?

Pete shrugged. "How do you want me to handle the break-in at your condo once it's reported?"

"Just like I was out of town and couldn't be reached."

"Will you get back to me?" Pete didn't look happy.

"As soon as I know anything. Meantime, will you check me out for a tail when I leave? If they're that anxious to find her, I sure don't want to lead them to her."

Pete nodded. "You be careful. And tell Jackson to keep an eye out. If they figure out how close you two are, they could be watching him, too."

Curt sighed. "I hadn't thought of that."

"You're out of practice, man. All that corporate stuff has killed your instincts." Pete's grin widened. "Or maybe you're just getting old."

Since Pete was less than six months his junior, Curt just drained his beer. "If I didn't figure I'd be depriving the redhead of a night to remember, I might challenge you to a little one-on-one just to prove how wrong you are."

"I'll take a rain check. Meantime, I think you'd better get back to your lady." The laughter vanished from his face. "And I gotta tell you, I don't think this is going to wait long. If you can't get her to remember by the first of the week, I think you'd better turn her over to a shrink.

Someone who can use drugs or hypnosis or something else to bring her out of it.''

"I don't want to do that. She's already been through enough.'' Curt spoke without thinking, then wished he'd kept quiet. He definitely didn't like the speculative gleam in Pete's eyes.

"She's that good-looking, huh.'' Pete shrugged. "Well, just bear in mind that time is your enemy. These boys don't handle frustration very well. If she knows something real damaging, they'll just turn up the heat. They never give up looking.''

Curt nodded, aware that Pete was right. "I'll try pushing her a little, see what happens.''

Yvonne moved restlessly around the living room. After dinner Curt had holed up in the den with the phone and the briefcase full of papers he'd brought from his condo and he was still in there nearly an hour later. Not that she blamed him. She knew how it was when the business was your own: you didn't get to quit at five like everybody else.

She gasped, waiting for the pain of memory, but this time it didn't come. Instead, she remembered the office from her dream, the stacks of papers and phone messages she always found on her desk. Realty Specialists, Inc.—that was her company! Yvonne sank onto the couch, closing her eyes, trying hard to dredge up more memories, but nothing came.

Frustrated, she leaped to her feet. How long was she supposed to endure this crazy jigsaw puzzle in her head? What was happening at her company without her? Why wasn't someone looking for her? Or were they? She wanted to scream. No, she wanted to interrupt Curt and demand that he help her make sense of her new memories.

She got all the way to the closed door before she lost her nerve. He'd been so strange since he got back, that's what made her hesitate. Instead of the charming and exciting man she'd spent so much time with, he'd been cold and withdrawn, troubled. Yet when she'd asked him if something had happened, he'd claimed nothing was wrong.

Yvonne sighed and wandered back through the living room and into the kitchen. She might have believed him, except that she'd overheard him telling Sybil that it might be better if she stayed away from now on, just in case someone was watching her. Someone like who... or was it whom?

A wail of frustration caught in her throat. What difference did her English make when someone wanted her dead? And if he knew what was going on, why didn't Curt tell her? What was he hiding? And why couldn't she remember? She stared out at the glow of the setting sun and wondered if she'd ever know the answers.

A light breeze stirred the trees and rippled the water in the pool, like an invitation; one she decided to accept. Maybe she just needed exercise. She was used to... Flashes of an aerobics class filled her mind—friendly faces, smiling and greeting her, the pounding rhythm of the music, the wonderful healing power of a good workout.

More pieces to the jigsaw, but nothing that gave her even a tiny idea of what the whole picture would be like. Yvonne sighed, then headed for her room to change into one of the bathing suits Sybil had bought for her. Swimming laps and trying a few dives had to be better than sitting around here waiting for Curt to finish his work or her memory to suddenly show up.

Curt slammed his briefcase shut with a curse. So much for working. He'd checked the details on the Kaufman deal three times and he still couldn't remember what he'd read. Which was proof positive that he was in here avoiding Yvonne, not working. Only he hadn't succeeded in avoiding her, either, since her image intruded at every opportunity.

The trouble was, he wanted to be with her, but not as an investigator. How could he push her to remember? He'd seen her pain too often to want to intentionally cause it. Maybe it would be better to just get her out of here, take her somewhere safe. He could hide her until... Until she remembered the deal that had brought her to Phoenix.

That thought twisted in his gut like a knife. Logic told him that she had to be involved with Hanover, but when he looked into her eyes and saw confusion and pain... Or the beginning flames of a desire that matched his own... When he held her trembling body close in the darkness of the night... He felt the pulsing heat rising inside him.

"Damnation!" He got to his feet. About thirty laps of the pool ought to be enough to cool even his ardor. And maybe then he'd be tired enough to sleep without the erotic dreams that had tormented him last night and every night since he'd found her. He got up and stretched, aware of the tension that knotted his shoulder muscles. Maybe he should have asked Pete if the redhead had a friend.

The living room was empty as was the kitchen, but the door to Yvonne's room was closed, so he wasn't worried. She was probably hiding out from his bad mood, he decided, feeling guilty as he remembered the way he'd behaved since he returned from the condo. Maybe if he swam enough, he'd even figure out what questions to ask her.

He padded barefoot through the quiet house and out the open arcadia door, not bothering to switch on the pool lights. After what Pete had told him, he didn't want to be in the spotlight, even in his own backyard. So long as people were looking for Yvonne, he'd be safer swimming in the dark.

Yvonne gasped as she looked up to see Curt standing in the kitchen doorway, his magnificent body outlined by the light behind him. He was going to join her. She opened her mouth to call a greeting, but before she could say a word, he was racing toward the pool. His dive wasn't elegant, but he cut the water smoothly, then disappeared into the darkness beneath the surface. The waves he generated washed over her.

Why hadn't he turned on the pool lights? It had still been light when she came out, but now she realized just how dark it had become. She wasn't used to the lack of twilight in the desert. Here one minute it was light, the next it was dark and with all the trees and bushes back here...

Curt came up for air and crashed into something soft and warm that clung to him for just a heartbeat. A feminine squeal startled him so that he swallowed a gulp of water as he sank beneath the surface again. He came up choking and gasping. "Yvonne?" he managed, once he'd caught his breath.

He looked so shocked in the light reflected from the kitchen, she couldn't help laughing. "You were expecting a mermaid?"

"I...uh...thought you were in your room. I mean, I didn't know you were out here swimming." His brain seemed waterlogged or maybe he was still suffering the aftershock from his impact with her softly curved body.

"You mean you didn't look before you dived." Yvonne moved her feet lazily, keeping just her head and shoulders above the water, enjoying his discomfort. "Isn't the water heavenly? I looked out and I just couldn't resist."

"No reason why you should." Curt reined in his scattered thoughts and managed a smile. "Sorry about the collision. I really thought I was alone."

"Why didn't you turn on the pool lights?"

He hesitated, knowing this was an opening he could use, but he found himself unwilling to burden her with his fears right now. He opted for a half-truth. "Old cop phobia, I don't like being in the light when I can't see who's in the dark."

"Do you really think someone might be out there watching us?" Yvonne felt a chill that had nothing to do with the water or the breeze blowing over it.

"It pays to be careful." His eyes adjusted to the darkness and he could see the pale perfection of her shoulders as she paddled just enough to stay upright. Her long hair floated free, a sleek dark cap on her head, a veil behind her shoulders. It was several minutes before he became aware of the silence growing between them. "Have you been out here long?"

"About fifteen, twenty minutes, I guess. I really miss my watch. It seems like I'm forever wondering what time it is." She spoke more to distract herself from the quivering anticipation that seemed to be spreading through her, than because she really cared about the time. Once the words were out, however, she gasped, realizing what she'd said.

"What kind of watch did you have?" Curt's tone was casual, but she sensed that his tension matched hers.

"A gold one, with tiny diamonds around the face. It was special, a gift from—" The quick stab of pain stopped her for a moment, but she was determined to continue. "It was a gift, but I lost it." The pain intensified and she felt herself sinking.

"Yvonne." He caught her waist, lifting her easily, pulling her close so that her head could rest against his shoulder as he kept treading water to support them both. "It's okay, you don't have to remember. Just think about something else."

Like the feel of his hot hands on her naked skin? The pain receded quickly as the new sensations rippled through her body. Every inch of skin he touched seemed to quiver with electricity and anticipation. Her arms slipped around his broad back easily, her fingers exploring the sculpted muscles that supported her.

"I want to remember," she murmured. "I really need to remember, but I can't."

"I know you're trying." He felt the swell of her breasts brushing against his chest as she lifted her head and her legs began to move, touching his as she kept herself afloat. He should let her go. He should be swimming laps and trying to forget the heat that burned through him, then settled into an all-too-familiar ache.

"I keep getting bits and pieces, but when I try to find the pattern..." Her lips were only inches from his and that nearness dried her mouth. She licked her lips as she stared at his mouth, wondering again how it would feel against her own. If she just moved a little... Her eyes were drifting shut.

Mesmerized by the way her tongue moved over her lips, he felt the tightening bands of desire. Her lips were slightly parted, an invitation. He fought it for a moment, then he gave in, seeking her lips with a hunger that he couldn't deny any longer.

His lips were cool from the water as they claimed hers, but when he slanted his mouth over hers deepening the kiss, a surge of heat blazed between them. She dug her nails into his back as her lips parted under his assault and she surrendered eagerly to his questing tongue. Instinctively she moved closer, wanting to feel the heat of his body against her own, wanting...

Yvonne stiffened, suddenly aware of exactly what she wanted. The sensations pulsing through her were familiar, the wanting, the hunger to be ever closer, to fuse her body to his. For just a heartbeat, her mind was filled with images of someone... of a lover whose touch had taught her the meaning of the feelings that now made her ache inside.

She couldn't do this! That realization muted the wild need slightly. No way could she explore this magic feeling with Curt when she had no idea who had made love to her before. What if she had a husband somewhere, someone who was desperately searching for her? Tears burning in her eyes, she forced herself to let go of Curt. She brought her hands around to press against the firm wall of his chest, not to push him away, but to separate herself from the temptation he offered.

"What is it?" Though every fiber of his body ached to keep her close, Curt forced himself to release her. Something must have happened since he knew she wanted him! She'd answered his kiss with too much passion for her to deny it. Yet now... It had to be her internal censor, the thing that sent the pain to keep her from remembering. "Are you in pain, Yvonne?"

Yvonne closed her eyes, forcing herself to tread water and breathe deeply as she tried to calm her pounding heart and fight the desperate longing that grew with every inch of water that separated them. In pain? That was a mild description for what she was feeling. She needed his embrace; she wanted his lips on hers and she wanted so much more.

Cursing her own desperate desire, she forced herself to meet his gaze and guilt flooded through her as she saw the worry there. He thought it was her head wound! For a moment, she considered letting him believe that; it would be far easier than admitting the truth. But she knew she couldn't betray him that way. The attraction between them was too strong to be denied and because of that she owed him the truth.

"My head's fine," she began, then stopped, not sure how to explain.

"Then what's the problem?" He sounded hurt and that cut more deeply than anger would have.

"What if I have a husband, Curt?" The words came out closer to a sob than a question.

Curt felt the impact like a fist in his belly. The thought of her having a family had occurred to him before, but somehow he'd managed to put the idea of a husband out of his mind since they'd been sharing the house. Now a faceless shadow loomed like an ugly threat between them. "Have you remembered something that makes you think you do?"

Again Yvonne hesitated, not sure she wanted to admit her vulnerability, but unable to find another way to explain her feelings. "Not really. It's just my emotions, the way I react. I know there was someone that I loved before. That's what scares me." She closed her eyes, seeking more, but there was nothing, just a strong throb of warning from her wound.

Curt did his best to control a flash of jealousy. Discussing her past lovers wasn't exactly what he'd had in mind for tonight. Still, he had to accept and pursue any path into her memory—her very life might depend on it. "That's not surprising, that you've been in love, I mean. You're a beautiful woman. That doesn't mean that you're currently involved with anyone." He reached out to touch her cheek, smoothing back a dark tendril of hair.

A shiver of desire swept through her, nearly swamping her resolve to fight her attraction while she still could. "But don't you see, I can't get involved with you when I don't know if there is someone else."

Get involved? The words should have sent a chill through him, but they didn't. Curt realized that a part of him had already accepted the fact that Yvonne wasn't a woman given to casual affairs. Which was one of the reasons that, despite his logic, he couldn't quite accept the idea of her being involved in anything illegal. And why he still ached to have her back safe in his arms. "You weren't wearing a ring."

"I'm not wearing a watch, either, but I know I had one." It was a bitter reminder and brought still another throb of pain, but she had to voice it, anyway. She needed the pain to keep her from swimming back into his embrace.

"Do you remember a ring?"

The image of a diamond-encrusted band came into her mind for just a moment before the pain overwhelmed her, but even as she sank into unconsciousness, she realized that what she felt about the image wasn't love, but anger and hurt. And there was so much despair, she welcomed the darkness that freed her from it.

"Yvonne!" Curt grabbed her the moment he realized she was sinking. Anger at himself and the faceless people hunting her warred with his anguish as he pulled her unresisting weight toward the steps. He'd almost reached them, when she came alive in his embrace, fighting him.

"Take it easy," he murmured, releasing his lifesaving hold, but catching both her arms to steady her. "You fainted out in the deep end. Are you all right now?"

Yvonne caught her breath, suddenly realizing that the man she'd been fighting was Curt, not some nightmare enemy. The whole episode flashed into her mind as her feet touched the solid bottom of the pool and the last ripples of fear fled. She'd done it again—almost remembered something, then lost it to the pain. For a moment she just wanted to cry out her frustration, then she focused on Curt's face and the worry that lined it.

He really cared! That wonderful realization tempered her despair and gave her the strength to believe she could defeat it. She managed a shaky smile as she sank onto one of the concrete steps. "I'm fine, really. And I'm sorry if I scared you. The pain came when I tried to remember about a ring.''

The pain and something else—he could read a new awareness in her expressive features. Curt felt a thrill of hope as he sat down beside her, but he controlled it with a heavy hand, not wanting to hurt her again with his questions. He needed more information. "Does the pain come with every memory flash?"

"Not really. When I remember things from the more distant past, nothing much happens. And I've thought some about my business and that wasn't so bad, either. Mostly it seems to flare up when I try to remember something specific, like the night I..." Her eyes narrowed against the pain. "The night before you found me."

Wanting to distract her before the pain overwhelmed her again, Curt asked, "What business is that?"

"Realty Specialists, Inc." Yvonne relaxed slightly. "We handle the development of small malls, mostly specializing in craft and antique shops, though our plans usually include compatible tenants to broaden the appeal of the malls. We've done quite well in the L.A. area and—" She stopped, shock robbing her of breath.

Memories flooded into her mind, not in tidy order, but in waves of images—people, places, occasions—all jumbled together. She closed her eyes, terrified of losing the memories to the pain or to her own confusion, but this time they didn't fade.

"It's coming back, isn't it?" Curt's arms slipped around her and she couldn't resist relaxing against the warm strength of his chest. The night breeze felt chilly as it brushed over her wet skin, but touching Curt banished the cold with a wave of heat that radiated from deep inside her.

"My name is Worthington, Yvonne Worthington. I have an apartment at..." She reeled off the address of her apartment, her office, even the most recent of the malls she'd helped to develop, glorying in the details that flooded past the veil that had hidden her memories.

Curt did his best to keep track of her words, wishing mightily for either pen and paper or a tape recorder. When she finally paused for breath, he got to his feet. "What do you say we move this inside? That breeze is getting a little cool."

Yvonne shivered as she got up. "I could use some coffee," she admitted, feeling a little disoriented as she returned to the present. "Why don't I put it on before we go change?"

Much as he hated to let her out of his sight now that she was remembering, Curt nodded, well aware that they could be facing a long night. And an important one. He tried not to go too fast with his plans, but for a moment hope blazed nearly as hot as his passion had. He needed to get to the truth quickly, before it was too late. If it wasn't already. Memories of holding her in his arms rose in his mind, letting him know that he was already having trouble seeing the situation objectively.

He left her fixing the coffee and headed for the den. He had a small tape recorder in his briefcase and he wanted to make a note of what she'd told him so far. This had to be the breakthrough they were waiting for. Now that she'd started to get her memory back, it was just a matter of time before she remembered everything.

Then it would be all over. So why didn't he feel the glow of anticipation or the familiar excitement at the prospect of finally settling with Hanover? The answer formed in his mind as he remembered the way Yvonne had looked just before he kissed her. What if finding her memory meant losing Yvonne forever?

Chapter 8

Yvonne wrapped herself in the terry robe, then sank onto the bed. The swirling pictures continued to fill her mind, making little sense, but reminding her of so many people and places in her past. Some brought smiles, others a touch of concern, but oddly enough, nothing seemed urgent.

Because none of it was recent? Her memories didn't exactly have dates attached, but she had a distinct feeling that most of them came from several years ago. Was that why she was being allowed to remember? If so, what could have happened since that was too painful for her to recall?

Probing in that direction brought a swift slash of pain, reminding her forcefully that her own mind was still hiding things from her. She switched her attention to another question that was bothering her. If she was in Arizona, who was taking care of her company? Surely she hadn't sold it?

A memory slipped into her mind. There'd been a time when she'd considered selling, when she'd gotten involved in several real estate ventures at the same time and it had all threatened to come unraveled when a bankruptcy had stalled a sale. But Gwen had come to her rescue and...and become a partner.

Relief renewed her energy and she got up to pull on a pair of artistically faded jeans and a bright red cotton sweater. Gwen was undoubtedly wondering where she was, but at least she could handle Realty Specialists, Inc. until Curt helped her sort things out enough to return.

Thinking of Curt brought a smile. She tied a white scarf around her still damp hair, then headed for the kitchen, eager to tell him everything she'd remembered. If there were any clues in the memories, she was sure—

Her joy drained away abruptly. What was she thinking? Nothing she'd remembered could have anything to do with someone wanting her dead. And nothing explained what she'd been doing in Arizona, anyway. Her frustration returned full force.

Curt looked up as she entered the kitchen, his grin warming her before he turned his attention back to the cookies he was piling on a plate and the two mugs of coffee he'd poured. "How's it going? Are you remembering more?"

"Lots, actually, but nothing recent. It's strange. I get bits and pieces of everything, but I keep feeling like there are big time gaps. Only I have no idea why. I'm not even positive when anything happened."

"So, just tell me about Yvonne Worthington, maybe that will help you sort things out." Curt put the mugs and cookies on the glass-topped kitchen table, then produced a small tape recorder. "Would you mind if I tape what you say? I thought it might make it easier for you to fill in the blanks if you had something you could go over and over."

Yvonne shrugged, not really comfortable with the idea, but unable to say why. "I suppose it might help." She grinned at him. "And if it doesn't, I expect it'll make a great insomnia cure."

Curt chuckled. "I'm glad your memories haven't hurt your sense of humor."

"I haven't remembered anything important enough to do that." The admission came without thought, sobering her immediately. She sighed. "Where do you want me to start?"

Curt flipped on the recorder. "How about your business? Is it doing well? Could it be the reason you were in Phoenix?"

"I don't remember, but I could call and find out. Everyone is probably wondering about me, since I've been out of touch since at least last Tuesday."

"I rather you didn't call anyone just yet." Curt's words held an edge of steel that stopped her impulsive movement toward the phone.

"Why not?"

Curt recognized the stubborn gleam of independence in her blue eyes and he couldn't really blame her. She had no reason to fear her friends, not while her memory of recent events was still hidden from her. "I know that sounds arbitrary, but until we find out who tried to kill you, we can't let anyone know where you are. In fact, I'm hoping that the person who shot you will eventually decide that you died in the desert."

His words sent a shiver down her spine. "That's a terrible thing to say. Besides, Gwen has to be worried sick, she's my friend. I can certainly trust her."

Curt could hear the resentment in her tone, but he didn't react to it. This was no time to challenge her. Instead, he simply asked, "Who is this Gwen and what's her last name?"

"Gwen Verona. We met when..." She hesitated, feeling the warning pang. "I've known her for years, but we didn't get close until I had a serious cash flow problem. It turned out that she was looking for a new challenge at that time, so I offered her an opportunity to buy into the company and she jumped at the chance."

"She's your partner, then." That surprised him, though he wasn't sure why. Maybe because he hadn't wanted to picture her with a full life that didn't include him?

"She's terrific at scaring up financing, which is my weakest point. With her handling the money end of our business, I have more time to do what I do best, which is develop the properties."

"Sounds a little like the arrangement Jackson and I have," Curt admitted, his mind already busy with theories. Financing could involve a power broker like Hanover, but why would he be interested in what sounded like a small company? From what Curt had observed, Hanover was into megamalls or high-rise business complexes; crafts and antiques wouldn't be his style.

Though he continued asking questions about her work and her family, before he'd finished his second cup of coffee, it was obvious that her traumatic amnesia was far from cured. Whatever was keeping her from remembering who'd shot her was also holding back all her recent memories.

"This isn't helping, is it?" Yvonne slumped in her chair, looking every bit as miserable as he felt. "If only I knew why I was in Phoenix, maybe I could remember something. That's why you should let me call Gwen. I wouldn't have to tell her where I am or anything about what happened to me. I could just ask her about whatever I was working on."

Curt studied her, aware that she was making sense. If a word could trigger... His gut knotted, every instinct warning him of danger. He forced a lazy grin he was far from feeling, then switched off the tape recorder. "Hey, it's Friday night, there's no point in trying to call her now. What say we give it until Monday? Who knows, by then maybe you'll have remembered on your own."

"Do you really think that's possible?" Her longing to believe was written all over her face.

He shrugged. "Look how much you remember tonight. More will come, it just takes time." Which he hoped they had.

His words soothed away the knots in her stomach. As long as he believed in her, it would be all right. "So what do you think we should do now?"

Curt looked at her, several erotic images filling his mind. Picking up where they'd left off in the pool sounded like a terrific idea, but he rejected it firmly. Yvonne had already made her feelings about that clear and he wasn't going to add to her stress by pressuring her into something she wasn't ready to accept. "I think maybe I'll go swim some laps. I haven't been getting enough exercise lately and . . ." He let it trail off, not sure she needed to know about his need for a cold shower. "What about you?"

"I think I'll go start one of the books Sybil brought me. I love escaping into a big, thick historical romance. Right after I was—" Her voice broke and he saw the white rim of pain around her tightly compressed lips.

"I like to read, too, but I'm more into complicated spy novels. You know, the kind where you never can figure out what's going on until the last chapter." He watched her, waiting until her mouth softened and her eyes focused again. "You okay?"

Yvonne nodded, getting to her feet. "I just wish I knew what it was I almost remembered. Sybil and I talked about books this afternoon and I didn't have a pang, so it has to be something else, but what? I wasn't even trying to remember."

"We'll try some more tomorrow." Curt rose, too, aching to take her in his arms and comfort her, but well aware that he couldn't trust himself to let her go again. "Now that you've started to remember, maybe it will come easier."

And maybe he could help it along—like by asking her about Hanover. If she recognized the name, it might trigger some memories. Or some pain, which would be a clue in itself. Meanwhile, he was going to swim laps until he was too tired to even remember what it felt like to kiss her.

Yvonne closed the paperback novel and rubbed her burning eyes, wishing again for a clock. It had to be late, though. She'd heard Curt come in several chapters ago. She shivered, remembering the way his footsteps had stopped outside her door as though he might be thinking of coming in. She'd held her breath, caught between fear and anticipation, then he'd gone on to his own room, leaving her awash in disappointment.

Which was why she'd kept reading until her eyes were ready to fall out. She'd wanted him to come in and sweep her up in his arms just the way the swashbuckling hero of the novel had. She didn't want the questions and the doubts and fears to stop him; she wanted it all to disappear so that they could simply make love the whole night through.

The ache inside her intensified as she remembered every burning moment she's spent in Curt's arms. One kiss and he'd reduced her to quivering jelly; how long had it been since she'd wanted a man with such intensity? Or had she ever felt this bone-deep longing? She turned out the light, aware that reading about the long-ago lovers wasn't helping. She needed warm arms around her tonight; but they had to be Curt's arms, no one else's would do.

Curt woke early in spite of his restless night. Aware that sleep wasn't hanging around waiting to relieve his suffering, he dressed and headed for the den. Listening to the tape didn't provide him with any new clues, but he made a list of the names that Yvonne had remembered. Once he had a few more, he'd call Jackson and Pete and ask them to run a check on each one. You never could tell what might turn up.

Yvonne came out yawning and sleepy-eyed just as the coffee was ready. "Rough night?" he asked, noting the dark circles under her eyes.

"I read too late." She kept her eyes on the English muffins she was putting in the toaster. No way was she going to admit that thoughts of him had kept her awake long after she turned off the lights.

"I hope you weren't worrying about remembering." He really sounded concerned.

"It is kind of scary. I mean, it's bad enough not being able to remember, but it's worse not knowing why I can't." She shook her head. "If that makes any sense."

"I understand. According to what I learned in college psych, though, it just means that a part of your brain is protecting your conscious mind from something that was very traumatic. When you are emotionally able to deal with whatever it is, your memory should return."

Yvonne rubbed the healing wound on the side of her head. "I suppose getting shot is pretty traumatic, but I keep wondering why I don't remember everything else. Why is my memory so selective? What else could I be blocking out?''

Curt studied her. She was suffering, there was no doubt about that. But would remembering make it better? He wished he could be sure.

"Don't you have any idea?" Her eyes, dark with pleading, met his. "I keep thinking that there must be some little clue that will start more memories."

Curt sat very still, wanting to wait, afraid of what he might learn, yet unable to ignore the opportunity she was offering him. "Does the name Hanover mean anything to you?"

"Hanover?" Yvonne took the muffins out of the toaster and buttered them. "Would that be Keenan Hanover?"

Curt nodded, afraid of betraying his animosity toward Hanover if he spoke. He'd noticed how sensitive Yvonne was to the nuances of his moods, he didn't want to distract her now. He accepted a muffin, even took a bite as he waited for her to go on. It might as well have been cardboard for all the taste he was aware of.

Yvonne's little frown stayed in place for several minutes, then it smoothed out and her eyes lit with excitement. "That's it, Curt! I came to Phoenix to meet with Mr. Hanover to discuss expanding our interests into the area."

"Hanover is interested in a craft and antique mall?" He tried to hide his skepticism, but it wasn't easy. The answer was too pat. Besides, he couldn't believe that the secret meeting at the ranch had anything to do with a legitimate real estate investment.

"I guess so." Her frown returned and her gaze was troubled, reminding him of how delicate her memories could be.

"I'm sorry, I was just surprised. Why don't you tell me what you do remember." Curt made a show of adding jam to his muffin, doing his best to project calm and only casual interest. If Hanover was involved in the shooting, why was she able to remember coming to see him?

"I'm afraid there isn't too much. I flew in Monday, I think. I remember renting a car, checking into the Scottsdale Desert Resort, making some business calls, then..." She shook her head. "There's just nothing. No pain or not much, anyway, but I can't seem to remember anything else."

"What about the people you called? Do you remember who they were?" Frustration gnawed viciously making him long to shake her until the memories broke free of the darkness that hid them.

This time he could see that she was hurting, but he didn't interrupt or try to distract her. If they were ever going to find the answers, she had to penetrate the veil her mind had erected. Eventually, however, she just shook her head and slumped back in her chair. "Nothing. And it does hurt now."

"So we'll let it go for a while. At least you know you were here on business and who you may have contacted, that's a start."

"Do you know Hanover?"

The question startled him, though he realized at once that it shouldn't have. Yvonne had displayed her logical mind before. He kept his answer short and simple. "I've met him. You can't be in business here without knowing him."

"Is that why you asked about him?" Again the question was a logical one.

"Actually I asked because I know he has a ranch in the area where I found you. Your visiting there seemed a logical reason for you to be in that part of the desert." Curt watched her closely, not sure what he expected...or feared.

Yvonne ignored the tingles of pain in the side of her head as she set her muffin down and picked up her coffee. What was going on here? One glance at Curt told her how tense he was, his grip on his juice glass threatened to crush it, yet he seemed to be trying to project calm—as though this was just an ordinary conversation. Why?

Anger edged the pain further from her consciousness. "If you knew about this ranch, why didn't you mention it before?"

Curt hesitated, well aware of the sharpness of her tone, the fire in her eyes. He was treading through a mine field, that was sure. If he lost her confidence and trust, she might run and if she did, she'd never survive. "I was hoping you'd remember on your own and I was afraid of causing you pain or setting off another of your panic attacks...like what happened when I told you that you'd been shot."

He forced himself to relax under her scrutiny. What he'd said was the truth, which helped. It was just the guilt of knowing that it was only one of his reasons that haunted him as he waited for her reaction.

"Why didn't you call Hanover and ask him what happened?" Her tone told him she hadn't totally bought his explanation, but at least the anger had faded.

"Because someone shot you and I had no idea if Hanover was involved."

"But if I was just out there discussing a business deal, why would anyone..." She let it trail off, her eyes glazing with pain.

"Forget it for now." Curt took her hand, shocked at how cold her fingers felt in his warm palm. A sudden surge of rage nearly swept away his carefully formed plans. Hanover was responsible for her suffering, just as he'd been responsible for what Genna had done to herself. The man was like a plague, spreading death without even having to touch the people he killed.

"Curt, are you all right?" Yvonne's question forced him back to reality and he realized that he'd nearly crushed her fingers.

"Just worried about you and angry at whoever did this to you." He forced a reassuring grin. "I'm letting my 'white knight' urges get the better of me. Fact is, I'd like to pound the bastard to a nice satisfying pulp."

"When we find out who it was, I'll be happy to help. I'd really enjoy sharing this headache with him." The glowing warmth in her eyes banished his anger, replacing it with a much more enjoyable emotion.

"We'll see what we can do when the time comes. Meanwhile, why don't we forget discovering your past for now and just enjoy ourselves?" Curt forced himself to settle back in his chair, talking of other things to help ease Yvonne's pain, while he battled his own ache of desire.

Yvonne found it much easier to ignore her past than it was to forget the way she'd felt when he held her hand. She gave off sparks every time he touched her. While he meant only to comfort her, she got weak all over even when their knees touched under the table.

Though he'd laughed about being a protective "white knight," as far as she was concerned, he fit the bill perfectly. Besides, in all the romances she'd read, when the knight saved the fair maiden, he swept her off to his bed and made love to her for hours. Even thinking about it had her squirming in her chair.

Yvonne took a deep breath. If she sat here much longer, he was going to be able to read her feelings on her face. She'd always been lousy at hiding her emotions. When she and... Pain bit through her, slamming the door on her memories and at the same time killing the heat of desire.

"What is it, Yvonne?" Curt was holding her hand again, but this time her head hurt too much to enjoy the contact. "Is it your head?"

She nodded, too nauseated by the pain to speak.

"Maybe you should go lie down for a while. If you didn't sleep well, a nap..." The concern in his face touched her deeply, easing the pain a little.

"I think you're right." She forced the words past the lump in her throat. What she really wanted was to lie in the protection of his arms. She'd felt safe there before and she ached for that now. It seemed that she'd been afraid and lost forever. Aware that she'd cry and beg if she didn't get away from him, she stumbled to her feet and fled the kitchen without a backward glance.

Once out of his mesmerizing presence, she slowed, troubled by her own emotions. This wasn't like her at all. She'd always been an independent woman, not some clinging vine who felt incomplete without a man's arms around her. Why should losing her memory make her so eager to surrender that independence to Curt Macklin?

Aching with confusion, Yvonne slammed the bedroom door and collapsed on the unmade bed, burying her face in her pillow so he wouldn't hear her sobs. If she could remember that much about herself, why couldn't she remember more? And if she was as emotionally strong as she believed she was, how could anything that had happened to her be so awful she couldn't face it?

Her courage revived once her sobs stopped. She *was* strong, a survivor. She'd made a good life for herself in Los Angeles, built up her own business. As her self-confidence grew, her curiosity returned, stronger than ever. Why should anyone want to kill her? Since she couldn't believe she'd done anything to merit such violence, there had to be another explanation—but what? A dozen possible scenarios filled her mind, then the most logical occurred to her. Maybe she'd seen something she shouldn't.

Feeling much better, she got up and washed her face, added a touch of fresh makeup, then brushed her hair. She needed to talk to Curt about that. Maybe they were pursuing the wrong course by thinking that she was directly involved in whatever had happened. She could remember plenty of movies and television shows where the heroine had gotten into trouble simply because she was a witness to someone else's evil deeds.

The house seemed extra quiet when she emerged from her room. Sure that she'd find Curt out by the pool, she hurried to the kitchen. The rear yard was deserted. Disappointed, she headed through the house to the living room. This time, she'd interrupt him even if he was holed up in the den working, she decided. This was too important to wait. She was just ready to knock on the door when she heard his voice.

"That's right, Pete, she's definitely tied to Hanover. I just don't know how yet. I thought maybe you could find out more by checking out the telephone records at the resort, see who else she might have contacted. And I need you to run a thorough background check on her and her partner Gwen Verona. You can coordinate with Jackson, he's going to look into her business records for me.''

There was a pause, then a chuckle. ''Hey, it's not that I don't trust you to check out the business, I just figured Jackson had the kind of contacts who would tell him things that they wouldn't want the police to know.''

Her stomach knotted so tight she almost cried out with the pain. He'd called the police! After all he'd said about her not trusting anyone, he hadn't been protecting her at all. He'd just been waiting for her to tell him something so he could start an investigation on his own. All his gentleness, all his kindness had just been a way of getting her to trust him.

The agony of Curt's betrayal nearly swamped her, yet even as she suffered through it, she had a strange sense that it had all happened before. Someone else had made her care deeply, then he'd... The stabbing in the side of her head stopped that train of thought and forced her back from the brink of despair. Healing anger flowed in to fill the hollowness that had come from what she'd overheard. She didn't bother to knock before she opened the door.

''Yvonne.'' One glance at her face made it sickeningly clear that she'd overheard at least part of what he'd just said to Pete. Hoping to calm her, Curt stayed at the desk, trying to look as though he'd been working. ''How are you feeling now?''

''I was feeling pretty good until I heard you asking someone to run a background check on me, my friends and my business.'' Her eyes blazed with fury as they met his.

So much for keeping her in the dark, Curt decided, oddly relieved. He'd never been comfortable keeping secrets from the people he cared about and after last night, it was clear that he had strong feelings for Yvonne. He just hoped he could come up with the right words to explain what he'd been doing.

''Well?'' Her tone warned him that her patience was running thin.

"I was talking to a friend of mine, Pete Rodrigues. He was my partner while I was on the police force here. I didn't want to make any official report about you because it would put you in more danger, but since you'd started to remember names and places, I knew he could run a discreet check that might give us some more pieces of the puzzle."

"What happened to 'wait until Monday and see if you remember on your own'?" Her glare didn't waver as she quoted his words back to him and she ignored his gesture inviting her to sit down. "Did it ever occur to you to ask me before you set something like this in motion?"

"Why, do you have something to hide?" Guilt goaded him into the quick question and he regretted it the moment the words were out.

For a heartbeat, she just stared at him, not wanting to believe that she'd heard him correctly. Then, slowly, the fury that had given her strength ebbed away and she had to sink onto the love seat. "Is that really what you think?" Her throat was so tight that even saying the words hurt. "I thought you believed me."

Watching the spirit drain from her face tore at him as nothing else could. Without thinking, Curt leaped to his feet and hurried around the desk. "No, it's not what I think. I do believe you, Yvonne. I know you can't remember what happened. That's why I'm afraid for you. I need to find out who is hunting for you before it's too late."

"Hunting for me?" She'd pulled away from him as he sank onto the love seat beside her, but now he felt her trembling. "What are you saying, Curt?"

Sighing, he explained what he'd found at his condo, then described the meeting with Pete, hating the way the last of her color drained from her fragile features, leaving her ghostly pale. Though he ached to pull her into his arms, he hesitated, afraid that she'd reject him now. He was shocked to discover how much that prospect hurt.

"You really think all this is happening because of me?" Her frown was back, but he sensed that it was no longer directed at him.

"According to Pete, they're still looking for you. They've been checking with the more unscrupulous doctors in the area, offering a reward for information about you." He eased a little closer, then reached for her hand, cradling it gently between both of his. "I planned to tell you. I just hated to frighten you when you seemed to be getting better."

She wanted to pull away, to reject both his terrifying words and the comfort his touch offered, but she couldn't. Though a little voice deep inside her warned that she had no proof that he was telling the truth, a stronger force drowned it out with a dozen memories of his tenderness and caring.

But what he said couldn't be true! It had to be some kind of mistake. There was nothing in her life that would make someone want her dead—was there? She closed her eyes, trying to remember, to see beyond the veil of blackness, but the only memories she had were those that she'd already described for Curt.

Despair swelled inside her, bringing tears to her eyes and a lump to her throat. How could she fight them, if she couldn't remember who they were? Where could she turn? What could she do?

"I know it's scary, Yvonne, but I promise we're going to find out what happened. That's why I called Pete and asked for his help. The more we know about you, the better chance we have of finding out who is behind all this. Please try to trust me just a little longer."

One arm slipped around her shoulders, drawing her closer until she was safe in the protection of his embrace. For a moment she held herself stiff, refusing to surrender to her own need; but the temptation was too great. As she snuggled against his chest, however, she knew that it wasn't fear that had weakened her resolve. When she breathed in the spicy scent of his after-shave and rubbed her cheek against his chest, she knew she was exactly where she wanted to be.

The moment she relaxed against him, Curt realized his mistake. He'd meant to comfort and reassure her, but just touching her made that a mockery. Desire knifed through him with the same force he'd felt last night in the pool. Never had a woman affected him so quickly and so deeply. It was more than lust, more than desire even; it was ...

It was a damned mistake. He couldn't be falling under her spell. Not now, now when he wasn't even sure what kind of person she was going to be when she got her memory back. No way in hell could he let himself get involved with a woman who was tied to Hanover.

But he couldn't let her go...not yet, not while she needed him to hold her and keep her safe. Even as he thought that, he could hear the cynical laughter echoing in his mind and he knew he wasn't even fooling himself with his excuses. He was holding her because it felt right and good and he didn't want to let her go.

Chapter 9

Sensing that Yvonne shared his growing passion, Curt ran his fingers through the heavy curtain of her hair, enjoying the sensuous scent that rose from the thick black waves. "What brought you to the den?" he asked, more to distract himself from her soft curves than because he really wanted to know.

She sighed, rubbing her head against his fingers much like a cat seeking further caresses. "I was trying to figure out what could have happened to me and nothing made sense. Then I got to wondering if maybe I was just an innocent bystander to whatever happened out there in the desert. I mean, do you think maybe I saw something I wasn't supposed to see and that's why someone wants to kill me?" Her voice faltered slightly on the last two words, but she didn't move away from him.

Could that be it? He closed his eyes, remembering clearly the events of that night, the first car leaving the ranch, the other coming after it. Could she have been running away? But why would she have stopped? He was quite sure both cars had been parked before he heard the single shot that had come so close to ending her life.

"Don't you think that could be what happened?" This time she pulled away enough to look up at him and he wanted very much to agree with her, but he just couldn't.

A chill intruded on the warmth she'd been feeling and suddenly his arms seemed restricting. Had she trusted too easily? Were her instincts as confused as her memories? She didn't want to doubt him, but . . . "What is it, Curt? What else do you know that you haven't told me?"

Confusion made her head spin, then she remembered the first words she'd overheard and a whole new set of questions filled her mind. She pulled away, no longer drawing comfort from being in his arms. "You said something to your cop friend about Hanover. What do you know about him that you haven't told me?" She felt the sudden tension in his muscles as his body reacted to her question and that forced her to ask another. "What were you doing in the desert and how did you happen to find me, anyway?"

He was losing her again. He could feel it as surely as if her skin had shivered away from his touch. But how could he give her the answers she demanded without telling her everything? He met her gaze, willing her to trust him even though he knew she couldn't, not as long as he denied her the truth.

"Why won't you tell me, Curt? Don't you trust me? What do you know that could be worse than all the horrible possibilities that haunt me now?" The quiet courage that shone from her eyes was a challenge he had to meet.

"I was in the desert because I was watching the Hanover Ranch."

"Watching it? You mean like a stakeout? But I thought you said you'd left the police department."

Curt winced at her quick perceptions, aware that, now he'd started along this path, he'd be able to hold nothing back. "I was watching him for my own reasons."

"Business reasons?" Her frown deepened, but he could hear the doubt in her voice. "But I thought he was . . . Is there something going on with his companies that I should know about? He's not in financial trouble, is he?"

"Not that I know of." Curt shifted uncomfortably, feeling oddly bereft now that he no longer had his arms around her. "This was personal."

Her gaze didn't waver from his and he knew that she was waiting for him to explain. He took a deep breath and plunged in, hoping that he wasn't making a mistake.

"It had to do with a woman, Genna Lindquist. She was a cop. Actually I met her through Pete and we, well, we fell in love." He found the words easier to say than he'd expected. Not that he'd tried before. His friends already knew all about Genna and there hadn't been anyone else he'd cared enough about to tell them.

"Genna was working with a special task force investigating money laundering in the area. She had some background in the accounting field and the kind of mind that could come up with new possibilities where the rest of us just saw facts." He felt a pang of regret, remembering his envy of her efforts. "She was a damned good cop, one of the best."

"Was?" Yvonne's voice was so soft he hardly heard it.

"We were engaged, planning our wedding, but she wanted to finish up the case she was putting together. She'd followed a money trail through a half-dozen paper companies and was closing in on the man she was sure was investing the funds in legitimate enterprises. That man was Keenan Hanover."

"Hanover? Are you sure? I dimly remember Gwen telling me that he was a respected financier with an excellent reputation for making good business choices." Her words rubbed over his memories like sandpaper.

"That's what everyone said. Nobody could believe it, but Genna was so sure. She said she just needed one final link in her chain of evidence to make the connection and she was sure she knew how to get it. That's why she wouldn't give up on the case." Not even when he'd urged her to set a wedding date.

Yvonne watched him, mesmerized by the emotions she could read in his face. Anger, pain, even confusion shone from his dark eyes for her to read. Curt definitely wasn't

the stone-faced man with no feelings he'd appeared to be in
the beginning. Something horrible must have happened to
him or to the woman Genna. The woman he'd loved. That
thought hurt a little, but she endured the pang gladly in
exchange for this new insight into his feelings.

She waited for him to go on, but he didn't. Instead, he
stared off into space, shutting her out of the pain that
deepened the lines in his face. Though she wasn't sure she
wanted to know the rest of the story, she couldn't let him
suffer alone. "What happened?"

Her question forced him to abandon the ugly memories
that haunted him. "Genna was trying to develop a source,
someone she believed was deeply involved in the dark side
of Hanover's business. The trouble was, everything she did
sucked her in deeper and deeper. Pete warned her and I
tried to talk her into turning the investigation over to
someone else, but it was like she couldn't bear to let go."

Curt ran his fingers through his hair wishing again for a
cigarette or enough booze to blot out the memories of all
the broken promises. How many times had she said, "Just
another couple of weeks, then I'll have him"? And how
many times had he agreed, caught up in the excitement of
her investigation?

Not sure what had happened, but feeling his pain all too
easily, Yvonne reached out to take his hand. He'd comforted her, held her until the nameless terror passed; she
only wished she could help him as he'd helped her. His fingers tightened around hers painfully, but she didn't try to
pull away. Instead, she used her other hand to gently caress his fingers.

"She wouldn't let go. The brass finally got fed up and
ordered her off the case, but she wouldn't listen. She swore
that Hanover had bought them off." He stopped, fighting
the anger that seemed to build up inside him. "We had one
hell of a fight about it. She broke our engagement and
stormed out, promising that she'd prove them and me
wrong."

"Did she?" Her fingers were numb, but she didn't care.
Though she had no proof, every instinct told her that this

was something Curt hadn't told anyone before. She longed to put her arms around him, to drive his pain away with kisses, but she couldn't, not until he'd said it all.

"I don't know. That's what kills me, Yvonne. I'd done everything I could to help her and she'd told me stuff about her investigation that she never put in her reports, but after that, she wouldn't even talk to me about what she was doing. Then she was busted on a narcotics charge—possession with intent to sell."

"What?"

"She swore it was a frame and I believed her. She hated the stuff, that was what got her into the money laundering investigation in the first place. She wanted to get the people behind the drug trade. She always said that busting pushers and users was just treating the symptoms. To fight the disease, you have to kill the infecting agent and that means cutting off the money that drugs produce."

He slumped back, releasing his hold on her hand, rubbing his fingers across his eyes as though trying to erase images that she couldn't see, then his expression changed. The pain vanished and with it the vulnerability that had touched her heart.

"Couldn't you help her?"

Curt turned to her and she felt a chill as his dark gaze moved coldly over her face. "She wouldn't let me. She refused to talk to the lawyer I hired. She wouldn't work with the private investigators I brought in. Pete tried, too, but she just laughed at him and told him she was going to prove everybody wrong." Fury burned in his eyes.

Yvonne trembled at the force of his anger, yet she sensed the pain that fueled it. Somewhere, sometime, she'd known that kind of pain and the anger it produced. "You tried to help her anyway, didn't you?" It wasn't even a question, deep down, she knew instinctively that he'd never let someone he loved fight such a desperate battle alone.

His anger flared for a moment longer, then all expression seemed to drain from his face, leaving a cold emptiness that chilled her. "I tried, but she just kept pulling further and further away. Finally I gave up, then one night

I came home to find a message from her on my answering machine. She sounded hyper, demanding that I come by her house.'' He closed his eyes. "I thought maybe she'd finally found something that would help her case, but when I got there, the place was dark.''

He stopped, but this time Yvonne didn't press him to go on. Even though they were no longer touching, she could feel the terrible tension in his body, hear it in the ragged sound of his breathing. She waited, expecting the worst.

"I went around to look in the garage to see if her car was there, that's when I heard it running—inside a closed garage.'' Curt clenched his teeth, enduring the memories that swept through him. The terrible fear as he'd kicked in the garage door. The acrid burn in his lungs as he'd broken into the locked car and pulled her out. He even remembered the weary sadness in the face of the paramedic who'd pulled him away from her after what seemed hours of CPR.

"She committed suicide?" Yvonne couldn't hide her shock. Nothing he'd said had prepared her for that. "Oh, Curt, I'm so sorry.'' Without thinking, she held out her arms to him.

For just a heartbeat, Curt resisted the temptation to accept her comfort. He couldn't lean on Yvonne; he couldn't lean on anyone. But the depth of understanding he could read in her eyes was irresistible. He'd stood alone for so long that he felt something deep inside him tearing loose as he surrendered to her arms. He had to blink back the tears he hadn't been able to shed even when it happened.

Yvonne tightened her embrace as his trembling communicated his suffering to her. "Losing someone you love is always such a tragedy, but when they take their own life…''

"I couldn't believe it then. After almost a year, I still have trouble accepting the fact that she would do something so desperate. Genna was always so strong and determined. But Pete headed up the official investigation and he swore that they checked every possible angle and couldn't find anything to suggest that it wasn't suicide.'' Just saying the words eased a little of the tightness in his chest.

Some of his bone-deep anger faded into sorrow as Yvonne's gentle fingers caressed the back of his neck.

She held him tenderly, sharing his pain, yet a part of her mind was still caught by her own questions. The story, horrible though it was, really didn't explain what he'd been doing in the desert last week. Unless . . . Shocked, Yvonne blurted out the question without thinking. "Were you out there watching Hanover because you're trying to carry out the investigation she started?"

Her words pulled him from the past, reminding him forcefully of just whose arms were comforting him. Yet even as he remembered the suspicions he'd held about Yvonne's connection to Hanover, he refused to heed them. They'd shared so much in the short time they'd been together and there was so much more he wanted to share with her.

Mastering his emotions, he sat back so that he could watch her face as he answered her question. "In a way, I suppose that is what I've been doing. But it's more personal than that. You see, I honestly believe that Genna was right, that she got too close to linking Hanover to the money laundering. I'm sure he set up the drug frame, used it as a way to get her kicked off the force. When that didn't stop her, I think he did something else."

"What?" The sharp blaze of comprehension was in her eyes even as she asked the question. "You don't think he killed her?"

Curt squirmed under her gaze, aware that he'd had this conversation with Pete—too many times. "I don't think he put her in the car and turned on the engine, but I can't shake the feeling that he had a hand in it. If he didn't have her murdered, he did something else to her, something so awful that it drove her over the edge. That's why I don't accept the official finding of suicide and why I can't give up. I want him to pay for what happened to her."

Yvonne's lack of reaction chilled away the cobwebs of his grief. He hadn't expected her to argue against his theory the way Pete did, but at the same time, she should feel something, shouldn't she? All that marred her serene features was a little frown and a slight narrowing of her lovely eyes.

"What did you see that night, Curt? What made you search the area where you found me?"

Relief warmed him as he realized that her apparent coldness came from her preoccupation with her own problems, not a lack of belief in his theory. Knowing it was time to tell her the full story, he described the activity he'd observed from his cliff top, watching her closely, hoping for some sign of returning memory.

Her frown had deepened by the time he finished, but there'd been no flicker of memory in her eyes. "That's it? You just saw two cars going out, heard a single gunshot, then saw two cars coming back?" She didn't bother to hide the depths of her disappointment. Why didn't his description mean anything? Why couldn't she remember being in the car? What had happened? Why had she been at the ranch, anyway?

"It made me curious. I wondered what they were doing out along the road that they couldn't have done more safely within the confines of the ranch." He drew her gently into his arms, reading despair in her eyes. Obviously she'd counted heavily on remembering everything once he filled in some of the blanks. And why hadn't she? What could be horrible enough to hold her memory prisoner now?

"You didn't see anything else? Maybe they were chasing me and I..." She tried to come up with a scenario that would explain everything, but instead the warning pain began to throb in the side of her head. She closed her eyes, wanting to fight the agony, to see beyond its veil, but the darkness loomed there, threatening to close over her.

Curt tightened his embrace, wanting to fight the pain for her, to shield her as he hadn't been able to shield Genna. "Let it go, Yvonne. You'll remember everything when you're ready. Meantime, you're safe here. I'll protect you."

For a moment, she clung to him, wanting to avoid the battle, then she pulled away abruptly. She couldn't surrender, not even to the pain. The fact that she even wanted to scared and infuriated her. "Don't you see, that's what I can't do, Curt. I can't wait. I can't keep leaning on you. I need to know what happened. I have to find out who shot me and why." She was shouting, her anger raging out of control.

Her furious determination to handle this herself irritated and worried him, yet at the same time, he had to admire her fight. She might look fragile, but there was obviously steel beneath her softness. Unfortunately determination and courage wouldn't protect her from the evil that stalked her. Weariness swept through him. "If I knew any way to help you remember, believe me, I would."

Yvonne recognized the shadow of despair looking back at her from his dark eyes and her anger fled. He wasn't the one keeping her from remembering; it was some flaw within her that kept the past hidden. "I know you would." She reached out a finger to trace the marks that caring and sorrow had left in his face. "I just get so frustrated sometimes."

The lines in his face suddenly softened as a gentle grin lifted the corners of his mouth and humor replaced the sadness in his expression. "No, kidding. You're frustrated? I never would have guessed."

She felt herself responding to the teasing gleam in his eyes, even giggling as she let go of the last of her anger and fear. "That's because I cover it so well."

His chuckle was like a healing salve on her raw nerves and when he turned his head and touched his lips to her fingers, she found it very easy to forget her worries about the past. His lips were sweetly erotic as they nibbled down her fingers, then brushed her hand. Shivers of desire traced down her spine as she felt the tip of his tongue lightly tickling the center of her palm.

For a moment, she simply enjoyed the sensations, then the shivers moved deep inside her and she began to find it hard to breathe. Her eyelids felt heavy, though it wasn't sleep she craved, and when his gaze focused on her lips, she grew dizzy with longing. Slowly, as though mesmerized, she slipped her hand around so she could bury her fingers in the thick hair on the back of his neck. No longer conscious of anything beyond the way he'd made her feel, she leaned forward slightly, offering him her mouth.

He brushed his lips over hers lightly, his hands cupping her face as his tongue slowly traced the outline of her mouth, probing delicately at the corners. The promise of his touch made her quiver, but he seemed oblivious to her hunger as he moved on, raining light kisses on her eyes, the tip of her nose, everywhere but her longing lips.

Unable to endure the torment of wanting, Yvonne strained to catch his lips, eagerly pressing her mouth to his. She felt the shudder that shook his body as his arms tightened around her and his lips claimed hers with a hunger that more than matched hers. His hands moved over her back, restlessly exploring the curve of her waist, the line of her spine. His power enveloped her as he deepened the kiss, eagerly tasting the sweetness of her mouth, caressing her tongue with his in a sensuous dance of desire.

Moaning as the tides of her own passion exploded within her, Yvonne clung tightly to him, her whole body throbbing with a raging desire to be even closer to him, to feel the hardness of his body pressing into the softness of hers. Yet it wasn't her body's hunger that fueled the flames; even without memory, she knew the difference between physical hunger and the deeper, sweeter fire that now burned within her.

Never had she felt so close to any man. Today when he'd shared his feelings about Genna with her, she'd actually felt his pain, his grief, his anger over the loss of the woman he'd once loved. But even before his obviously painful confession, she'd explored the depths of his kindness, felt the tender wonder of his caring, actually survived because he'd given her his protection against the evil that stalked her. Now she ached to give herself to him, to love him.

Curt gasped as he freed her mouth for a moment. Her fiery response was rapidly shattering his control as he shifted her tempting bottom into his lap, then lifted a hand to caress the swelling curve of her breast through the soft knit of her sweater. He left a trail of kisses down the side of her neck, then came back to taste her ear as he lightly rubbed his thumb back and forth across her nipple, feeling it tighten with desire.

Her soft moan of pleasure moved through him like liquid fire, urging him to slide his hand beneath her sweater, to seek the satin skin hidden by it and a wisp of lacy bra. He wanted to feel her skin on his, to explore every inch of her body and make it his own. He needed to bury himself in her warmth; once she was his, everything would be all right.

Her body was on fire. Everywhere he touched, he ignited new flashes of heat. Yvonne rubbed against him, blindly seeking the proof of his desire, aching for more. A sweet, tender madness swept through her as his lips returned to claim hers again. His kiss triggered even more sparks in her quivering body. Never had she known that it could be like this, that she could want someone so completely, could need him with every fiber of her body. Before she'd only...

"Curt," she gasped, her mind spinning as she floundered between memory and the shimmering magic of this precious moment. "Oh, Curt, I remember..." She might have said more, but his lips covered hers and nothing else seemed important.

As he ravaged her mouth, Curt did his best to ignore the implications of what Yvonne had started to say. He didn't want to think about anything that had happened before; he only wanted to celebrate the passion that filled him with such wonder and such anticipation. He wanted to make her his own, then he'd listen and...

But the spell of their lovemaking was broken. Even as he tried to cling to the magic, he knew it was too late. If Yvonne had actually remembered something important enough to make her speak at a time like this, he knew he had to listen. Feeling as though he was giving up a part of himself, he reluctantly lifted his lips from hers, studying her face as he tried to catch his breath.

"You don't have to stop." Her gaze was languorous as she looked up at him, her beautiful eyes half-closed, her lips bruised and swollen from his kisses. "I remember now. There isn't anyone else."

Though he ached to try to recapture the special magic they'd been sharing, Curt controlled his desire firmly. "I think maybe we need to take a breather—this is going pretty fast."

"Afraid?" Yvonne's eyes were fully open now, the glow fading as she straightened, sliding off his lap. She left a chill behind, though his body still throbbed with his wanting.

"Maybe I am a little scared," he admitted. "I don't want to hurt you." Nor did he want to make himself vulnerable to the kind of pain that came when love was betrayed. Curt's passion ebbed further at that thought—since when had love come into this? He liked Yvonne and he definitely wanted her, but he'd been around long enough to know that sexual attraction had little to do with love.

"You weren't hurting me." Yvonne smoothed down her sweater, evading his gaze now, though he could see that her hands were shaking and spots of color were burning in her cheeks.

"Last night you asked me to stop," he reminded her, suddenly aware that she looked hurt, but not sure why she should be.

"Last night I thought that I might have a husband or lover somewhere, now I know that I don't." Her voice held no emotion and her thick lashes kept him from looking into her eyes.

"Are you sure?" The sharpness of his need to know told him that his interest had nothing to do with what had happened at Hanover Ranch. He wanted to know that she was free because of what was blazing between them. Another fact that did little to ease his mind.

"I was married while I was still in college, but it only lasted four years. David and I were divorced five years ago."

Though she'd spoken calmly, he sensed a new tension in her body, a slight flicker of something else in her eyes. A feeling very close to jealousy cut through him. "And there's been no one since?"

Yvonne started to shake her head, then frowned, suddenly aware of all the gaps in her memory. Had there been other lovers since her divorce? She tried to probe the darkness, but there was nothing, not even the familiar pain. "I don't think so. I'm sure I would have remembered."

Five years alone? He found that hard to believe, especially when he remembered the fiery way she'd responded to his touch. Then another memory clicked in his mind. "David . . . that was your husband's name?"

Yvonne nodded, startled by the sudden excitement she could read in Curt's face. Though her memories of David were still rather hazy, they came with a deep sense of betrayal. What if there was some connection between David and Curt? Her stomach knotted at the very idea. "Did you know David?"

Curt shook his head. "It's something you said when I found you. You were barely unconscious, but you cried out the name David. With everything else that happened, I'd totally forgotten about it." Or hadn't wanted to remember it? He hated to think that he'd been that unprofessional, but he had been attracted almost from the first moment he'd seen her.

"That doesn't make any sense." Waves of confused memories made her head hurt, but she ignored the pain. "David's been dead for four years, Curt. He was killed in a boating accident somewhere in the Caribbean. Not that I would have called out for him, anyway. Believe me, our parting was anything but friendly."

"I'm sorry." Sensing her pain, he reached out to her, drawing her into the warm protection of his embrace. Though touching her brought a throb of desire, he held her gently, wanting only to offer comfort as she'd offered it to him when he told her about Genna. "I'm sorry the memories hurt, but at least they are coming back, Yvonne. That's the important thing."

Was it? She rested her head against his chest, feeling his warm breath stirring her tangled hair as he spoke. What was so wonderful about remembering the absolute worst time in her life? "Maybe some things are better forgotten." The words were out before she could stop them.

"Only if they don't keep the power to hurt you." His stern tone reminded her of all that she'd been through recently.

Yvonne sighed. "I know you're right, but my marriage was really a disaster."

"What happened?"

"Reality. I guess I was naive, but when I met David Rogers, I thought he was the most exciting, sophisticated, wonderful man in the world. He swept me off my feet. After he graduated from law school, we moved to Los Angeles and started living the American dream and for a while, it was great."

She expected him to ask questions, but he seemed content just to hold her. Or maybe he didn't want to press her, she remembered well his gentle consideration. A sensitive man lay hidden behind his tough facade and she was grateful she'd been permitted to see that side of him. She sighed, deciding that she might as well tell him everything she'd remembered.

"David's career demanded more and more of his time and soon I was spending most of my days alone. I got bored. That's when I discovered my interest in real estate and developed the first of my craft and antique malls." She hesitated, not really wanting to go on. In spite of what Curt had said, there were things that were better off forgotten.

"Did he resent your success?"

"Not really." Yvonne looked up at Curt, remembering all that he'd told her about Genna. She'd seen his suffering as he explored his own memories, yet he hadn't hidden them from her. Perhaps she owed him the whole truth. "My sense of satisfaction was terrific, but by then David had begun to change. At first I blamed myself, my fascination with my own career, but after a while, I discovered that he had a whole life that I knew nothing about. He was a high-stakes gambler and he'd come to love that a whole lot more than he'd ever loved me."

"So your marriage broke up." It wasn't a question.

Yvonne nodded. It hadn't been that simple and it certainly had been painful at the time, but now it all seemed a very long time ago, something without the power to touch the person she had become. She snuggled closer in his arms. "Anyway, you can see why it couldn't have been David that I was calling out to."

"Not that David, anyway." Though his tone wasn't argumentative, he didn't sound convinced, she realized. But should he be? Suddenly she wasn't sure. What if some sinister man named David had entered her life—a man whose identity was still hidden behind the dark veil that concealed so much of her past? Though she was sure that her memory loss didn't conceal any lovers, she knew for sure that it still hid someone who wanted her dead. That thought chilled her and she was grateful for the tender security of Curt's embrace.

Chapter 10

In spite of her fears that all they'd revealed to each other would somehow strain their relationship, the day drifted on with a special kind of ease. It was as though revealing the secrets of their pasts had somehow freed them. They laughed and teased through a late lunch, then moved outside to relax by the pool as the afternoon drowsed slowly away.

Curt lost himself in watching Yvonne as they stretched out in the shade after a brief dip. He found himself savoring each moment they shared. She fascinated him with her sparkling eyes, her slightly offbeat sense of humor, the incredible beauty of her smile, the graceful promise of her delicious body. Though he'd suggested the need for a breather from the intensity of their kisses, he now ached to hold her again.

There seemed to be something special growing between them, he couldn't deny it any longer. Nor could he casually label it simply physical attraction. His desire to make love to Yvonne had more to do with the person he'd come to know, than with her obvious beauty and sexy body. A fact that both disturbed and intrigued him even as it made him more determined to explore the depths of whatever emotion was burning inside him.

Yvonne stirred, feeling the heat of his gaze even as she tried to ignore his nearness. Despite her intention to keep a cool head, being this close to Curt was like standing outside just before a thunderstorm. She could feel the tingles of electricity on her skin whenever he looked at her and when he touched her... She swallowed hard, deciding it wasn't wise to even think about what his touch did to her.

So why hadn't he kissed her again? Was it because she'd remembered David? The memory of her dead ex-husband sent a chill down her spine and the side of her head throbbed. She didn't want to believe there could be any connection between what was happening now and the man who'd managed to hurt her so deeply so long ago.

"Dark thoughts, Yvonne?" Curt's voice was a welcome diversion from her memories.

Yvonne opened her eyes, happy to look into his familiar face. He seemed different since this morning, more relaxed, at ease with her and with himself. She remembered her intuitive feeling that he hadn't told anyone else the whole story about Genna. Could that be the reason he'd changed?

"You looked sad for a moment there." His words reminded her that he'd asked her a question.

Suddenly sure that she didn't want to waste any more time rehashing her dimly remembered past or his, she smiled lazily and stretched her arms above her head, well aware of how her bathing suit revealed her body. "How could anyone have dark thoughts or be sad on such a wonderful afternoon?"

The jolt of desire took his breath away. The seductive curve of her lips reminded him of the way they'd parted in response to his kisses and the look in her eyes... This was a new Yvonne, more seductive, enticing; it was a side of her that he hadn't experienced before, but one that he found incredibly exciting.

"You're right. The sun's shining, the pool is just the right temperature, we've got a refrigerator full of food and wine and nothing to do but enjoy ourselves." And he couldn't think of a single reason not to respond to the obvious invitation in her eyes.

Watching the flames of desire ignite the golden flecks in Curt's chocolate eyes, sent a current of heat radiating from the pit of her stomach. He wanted her! The instant sense of her own power was heady, yet slightly intimidating, too. She'd wanted to make love with him this morning, but then she'd been in his arms. Now distance gave her time to wonder about the cost.

A quivering deep inside her warned that if he reached out and touched her now, she'd go up in flames. And if he didn't reach out, how long would she be able to resist the invitation of his sleek, golden body? Her fingers tingled at the prospect of caressing him, of memorizing each elegantly etched muscle, of exploring the thick mat of hair that covered his chest, of...

Shuddering with longing, but not sure she was ready to handle her own emotions, she got to her feet, hoping that her knees would support her. "Think I'll test the waters," she murmured, then raced for the pool, diving into the cool water before she surrendered to the invitation in his gaze.

Curt lay still for exactly one second, confused by what he'd seen in her eyes, then he was on his feet. "Oh, no, you don't. You're not getting away from me that easily." He dived into the pool after her. If she wanted to play games, she was going to discover that he was no novice at seduction.

Yvonne stroked strongly underwater, hoping that the cool liquid caress would soothe the wild pulse that beat inside her. She didn't surface until she was nearly half the length of the pool away from Curt. Gasping for breath and shaking the water from her face and hair, she looked back. He was gone!

Suddenly strong arms closed around her, nearly taking her to the bottom before Curt's strong kick brought them both to the surface. "I think the temperature's great." His eyes gleamed wickedly, giving his words a subtly different meaning as he turned her so that she was facing him, her lips just inches from his. "Swimming is such good exercise."

She felt his strong legs moving, one sliding between hers as he kept them afloat. Her breasts tingled as they brushed against his chest. His hands now clasped her waist, sending shivers of awareness through her body.

"I always enjoyed a good swim." Her voice seemed to be coming from a great distance and she had a hunch her words weren't making a great deal of sense, but she couldn't concentrate on conversation when his lips were so close that she could see the tiny beads of water clinging to his skin. Slowly she moved close enough to taste the drops with the tip of her tongue.

His hands tightened convulsively, pressing her closer as his lips captured hers. Dizzy with the sensations his hungry mouth evoked, she pressed her breasts against the hard wall of his chest, feeling the wild pounding of his heart echoing her own racing pulse. Without her willing it, her hands found their way around him to caress the rippling muscles of his back.

Curt deepened the kiss, claiming the willing sweetness of her mouth as his own, then inviting her to do the same; until their tastes were mingled into one. Finally, lost in the shattering sensations, he forgot where they were and the water closed over them. Reluctantly he released her and they both bobbed back to the surface.

"You got the kind of kisses that could drown a fella," he teased, grinning at her as he tried to catch his breath.

"Maybe we need a designated water treader." Yvonne laughed with him.

"Or we could move this to the shallow end. Things might get even more interesting if I had both feet on the ground." The heated challenge in his eyes made breathing difficult and she nearly sank again as she forgot to move her legs.

This was going too fast. Panic warred with desire and she wasn't sure which she wanted to win. "I thought you wanted to swim." Her voice sounded a little squeaky, but that was because she couldn't catch her breath. Determined to be sure before she succumbed to her own desire,

Yvonne splashed him before she executed a surface dive and swam away from him.

Curt plunged after her, laughing. If she wanted to make war instead of love, it could be arranged. He'd already tasted the rewards that would come once they both surrendered to the power that drew them together. Waiting would only make it sweeter.

They churned up rippling waves as they chased each other around the pool, splashing and shouting like children. But each time Curt captured her, he stole a kiss or lightly caressed her thigh, the tender curve of her waist or the promising swell of her hip, always sending wild flares of desire through her body. Soon, she found herself slowing, not really trying to elude him.

"I think it's about time we called a truce," Curt said, leaning against the side of the pool to catch his breath. "I'd hate to see you turn into an albino prune."

Giggling, Yvonne collapsed on the concrete steps. "Be careful, your elegant compliments will turn my head."

"I'd much rather help you wash all this chlorine off in the shower." Curt's gaze moved over her slowly, like a caress.

"I just have a bathtub in my bathroom." Her mouth was suddenly so dry, she could hardly speak.

"Well, that could be nice, too. How big is it?"

She studied his long, muscular legs picturing them on either side of her in the tub, then shook her head. "Not that big."

"Showers are more fun, anyway." He was coming toward her, the shallow water moving down his chest to his waist as he reached the steps. He held out his hand. "What do you say?"

He was giving her a chance to retreat, to change her mind about what lay ahead, but even as she felt his fingers closing around hers, Yvonne knew she wouldn't refuse. She wanted to explore the limits of the attraction that blazed between them; she wanted to see where it led and what it might mean to love him, to be loved by him. She'd come into his life without memories; she had no intention of leaving the same way.

Curt watched the emotions that were so clearly revealed on her face, almost afraid of what he might see. If she was wary of him now... But there were no doubts in her eyes, only a fire that matched his and something that he hadn't counted on—trust. He felt ten feet tall as they stepped out of the water.

Because of the purring air conditioner, the house felt chilly as they made their way along the hall to his bedroom, but Yvonne was barely conscious of the goose bumps that rose beneath the beach towel she'd thrown around her shoulders after she dried off outside. Curt and the sensations his nearness caused within her consumed her whole attention.

"Want to wear the suits in and rinse them that way?" Curt's question sent a shiver down her spine.

"Sounds like a good idea." The quivering inside her intensified as she stepped into the bathroom and watched as he regulated the water. Though the shower was large and beautifully tiled, it still seemed small and very intimate.

"Ready?" He gently lifted the towel from her shoulders and tossed it into the corner.

Yvonne nodded, not trusting her voice. Though she'd been in his arms countless times in the pool, this was different. For some reason he seemed bigger now, filling the space around her, overwhelming her senses so that she was drifting, pliant, waiting only for his touch.

The warm water washed away the chill bumps and for a moment she was too busy turning this way and that, trying to rinse off the pool chemicals to really think, then she felt his hands lightly caressing her shoulders, sliding down to grip her arms. He turned her to face him, deflecting the spray with his broad shoulders. Using one finger, he tipped her head up so that she had to meet his gaze.

"May I?" he asked, his fingers moving to the narrow strap of her bathing suit.

A shiver traced down her spine in spite of the steam that surrounded her. She nodded again, beyond speech.

His hands were gentle as he slipped the straps over her shoulders and slid them slowly down her arms, carefully freeing her breasts to his gaze. His hands cupped her waist lightly as he bent down and tenderly kissed each rosy tip. "You are so exquisitely beautiful, Yvonne." He lifted his head to claim her lips, caressing her mouth with his, unhurried as his hands rose to her back to press her against him.

The tickling of his springy curls against the tips of her breasts tightened them to full arousal and started an ache deeper inside her. Unable to remain passive in his embrace, she moved her shoulders, rubbing her breasts through the thick mat of hair, thrilling to the sensations that weakened her knees and sent flames coursing through her veins.

Curt's hands slid lower, catching in the stretchy fabric of her suit as it clung to her waist and easing it down over the swell of her hips. His lips left hers just as her suit dropped to the floor. She met the challenge of his gaze without shyness or doubt.

"Your turn." His slight grin added heat to the challenge.

"My pleasure." She slid her hands slowly down his sleek, wet sides, feeling the ridges of muscle, lightly brushing over his taut belly, before she eased her fingers under the tight top of his trunks. "I'll try not to scratch you with my nails, but these are so tight."

Her concentration scattered as she felt his muscles flex against her fingers as she tried to force the fabric down. Her strength seemed to have melted away, leaving her with only enough control to stroke her fingers over his pale skin as he released his hold on her long enough to help. A second later, his trunks landed on the tile beside her suit.

"Let me get these out of here." He bent down, his shoulder lightly grazing her stomach as he picked up the two suits, opened the shower door slightly and tossed them expertly into the sink. He closed the door again and turned his dark, smoldering gaze her way. "Now we can concentrate on each other."

His gaze moved over her slowly, further heating her blood. Not that she needed any stimulation as she gazed mesmerized by his magnificent body. The ache inside her became more specific as she saw the proof of his desire.

"May I wash you?" His soft question forced her to notice that he now held soap and a washcloth in his hands.

She nodded, wondering how she'd ever be able to stay on her feet once he began touching her. At the moment she felt as though she might simply melt away.

His hands were shaking as he turned her around so he could start on her back. The depth of his need to bury himself in her took his breath away, making it clear that he couldn't wait much longer. He knew he'd explode once he began soaping her full breasts, or slid his hand down over the satiny skin of her stomach to... He pushed the incendiary images away, forcing himself to concentrate on washing the delicate line of her spine, the rounded curves of her hips, the sleek length of her thighs, even her toes.

When he turned her to face him, Yvonne sagged against the wall, the tremors of desire making her legs too weak to support her. She watched, dry-mouthed as he lathered the cloth and started at her neck, spreading the soap delicately over her shoulders and then her breasts. She rested her hands lightly on his arms as he moved the cloth lower. She felt the shudder that shook him.

Sensing that his need was every bit as deep as hers, she gently took the soap from his unresisting hand and placed it on its ledge. "I'm quite clean enough," she whispered as she lifted her lips to his, rising to her tiptoes to press her eager body against him.

His moan was lost in her mouth as his hands tightened around her waist and he lifted her. For a wild heartbeat, they were suspended on the cutting edge of anticipation, then he plunged into her welcoming softness, igniting the last of the fires, stoking them with each heated thrust. She clung tightly, dizzy as he lifted her beyond the bounds of earth into the star-burned world of lovers. She met each movement with her own, matching him in soul as well as body, giving and taking, reveling in the mystic union that made each of them complete.

The shivers of wanting changed to tides of ecstasy, swelling and filling her whole body until they exploded in a star burst that lit her from within. She collapsed against him, her legs firmly locked around him, her arms gripping him with the last of her strength.

Curt held her as his body shuddered with fulfillment. He cradled her close as the rocket ride settled slowly back to earth and he became aware of the water streaming down. Yvonne was trembling, but so was he, he realized as she finally relaxed, her legs sliding down until she stood once more on the tile.

"Are you all right?" he asked, aware that he hadn't exactly planned on making love to her in the shower. Teasing, playing out the games they'd begun in the pool maybe, but not surrendering all the way.

Her lazy smile answered him even before she spoke. "Oh, I'm more than all right, thank you. Now would you like me to wash your back?"

Something inside him seemed to shift, as though suddenly cut loose from its moorings and he felt an internal softening, a new warmth flooding through him. Suddenly he wanted to laugh and cry at the same time, yet neither seemed appropriate for what he was feeling. Not sure what was happening, he bent his head to capture her tantalizing lips, seeking an answer there.

Yvonne kissed him with great tenderness. Now that the sexual fog was clearing, she was far more aware of Curt's expression and it touched her deeply. When she'd first met his gaze, she'd seen his total vulnerability, the stunned confusion in his eyes and when she contrasted that with the powerful possessiveness of his lovemaking, it only deepened her feelings for him.

"You can wash anything you like, lady," Curt whispered as he traced a path of kisses down her neck.

Suddenly feeling much too vulnerable herself, Yvonne retreated to hide her feelings in their earlier teasing. "Now that's an offer I have no intention of refusing." She picked up the discarded washcloth and retrieved the soap, then ordered him to turn around so that he wouldn't see that her hands were trembling. She needed to get her emotions under control before she made a fool of herself, but as she began washing his golden brown shoulders, she knew that touching him wasn't going to help her do that.

Curt sensed the change in her mood. Had he rushed her too much? She'd wanted him as desperately as he'd wanted her, but still, this hadn't exactly gone according to plan. He'd wanted to take his time loving her, enjoy exploring her slowly, bringing her to the brink of madness. Unfortunately the madness had caught him, too, and carried them both away.

"You know what we need," he began as her hands slid seductively over his lean flanks.

"Some time out of the water?" Her chuckle made him feel better.

"That, too, but I was thinking about a romantic dinner, wine, good music, even dancing. Something special." He liked the images that filled his mind. A romantic evening, then a night filled with lovemaking. He felt the stirring of desire as she turned him around so she could continue her washing.

"I thought we had to stay here." From the luminous glow in her eyes, he could tell she was sharing his fantasy.

"We can't have a romantic dinner here?" Curt winced as her words reminded him of all the things he'd managed to forget for a few hours, then he forced reality away. They'd had more than enough of dealing with the real world since he'd found her. They deserved a reprieve at least for tonight. "I'll barbecue some steaks, we've got wine and candles and I brought some tapes from home, so that'll give us the music. What more do we need?"

Yvonne looked up at him, reading the need that shone naked in his eyes. Tough, hard-bitten ex-cop Curt needed a romantic evening? That thought truly intrigued her. "I can't think of anything else we need, except maybe to rinse away the soap and dry off. We really are turning into albino prunes."

Curt turned off the water, then lightly kissed the tip of her nose. "It was well worth a few wrinkles. You can share my shower anytime."

"I'll definitely keep that invitation in mind, but right now I'd better head for my blow dryer. A special evening demands something more than a drippy ponytail."

Curt chuckled, enjoying her easy banter as she wrapped herself in one of the big rust towels. "You look cute with your ponytail dripping."

The tenderness in his gaze brought a lump to her throat and she had to blink back a sudden burning of tears. It took all her self-control to walk away from him instead of running into his arms. But she couldn't let him know how she felt, not yet, not until she had time to sort out her emotions. Her damaged memories left her far too vulnerable to trust her heart. It would be so easy to fall in love with the man who'd saved her from the desert and given her back much of her life. So easy to fall in love with Curt!

If she'd expected the distance between their rooms to help her deal with her wild attraction to Curt, Yvonne quickly realized her mistake. The images and sensations of their lovemaking filled her mind as she dried and styled her hair. The wildness of the passion they'd shared excited her, but it was her memories of his gentle consideration from the very beginning at the cabin that touched her heart.

She closed her eyes, savoring everything they'd shared in the few days they'd been together. Laughter, sadness, her first memories, his description of what had happened to Genna; it all washed over her. Most of all, however, she kept remembering how he'd made her feel—the thrill of his touch, the sense of belonging when she was in his arms, the overpowering passion that...

She shook her head. It was far too easy to love him, but how could she expect him to love her? She was a woman without a reliable memory of her past; a woman who had, obviously, been somehow involved with the man he still blamed for Genna's death. That thought brought her back down to earth.

What they'd shared today had been wonderful and exciting, but it was just a moment out of time. A stolen afternoon of love and fun, but not something on which she could build a dream. Opening her heart to love had nearly destroyed her once; there was no way she could let it happen again.

She studied her image in the mirror, drawing strength from the fact that she wasn't the same person that David had so nearly destroyed. That naive girl had disappeared forever during the long months after she'd discovered the depth of his deception and betrayal. The Yvonne Worthington who'd emerged after the divorce knew better than to risk her heart for any man.

Her confidence renewed, she opened the closet and studied her limited wardrobe. Either of her two cotton print sundresses would probably be adequate, she told herself, but her gaze was drawn to the elegant pink, blue, lavender and white sheer dress that Curt has insisted she keep. A romantic evening, that's what he'd said he wanted tonight to be and that dress fairly radiated romance.

She stroked the silky sheer fabric, enjoying the sensation of it sliding through her fingers. He'd said she should wear it to celebrate the return of her memory, but she wanted to celebrate what they'd shared today... and what they might still share tonight. Her heart rate bounced up at the very thought of making love with Curt. Smiling, she lifted the dress from its hanger and slipped it over her head.

The house was quiet when she stepped out into the hall. Curt's door stood open and the room beyond was filled with evening shadows. Was he already outside starting the coals, preparing the grill? She hurried as she headed for the kitchen, eager to be with him again.

The kitchen was empty of more than human presence. The glass-topped wrought-iron table and two of its chairs had been removed. When she looked out at the backyard, smoke was drifting from the grill, but there was no sign of Curt. Soft music suddenly filled the air. Curious, Yvonne followed the sound to the living room.

Curt looked up from the tape deck as she walked through the archway, his grin almost sheepish. "I was planning to move all this out by the pool, but I decided it was too hot outside tonight. What do you think?"

His obvious desire to please her brought another quick welling of tears as she studied the candlelit scene he'd created. The heavy furniture had been moved back to the walls, leaving the center of the room clear for the table and two chairs. A single candle, surrounded by flowers from the garden was the centerpiece and the flickering light was reflected in the wineglasses and the silver he'd laid out.

"It's absolutely beautiful, better than any restaurant."

"I'm glad you kept the dress, you look stunning." His gaze moved over her with smoldering heat, making her feel beautiful and wanted and very special.

"Worthy of my debonair and exciting...escort." She caught herself before she said lover. The fantasy setting must be going to her head, she'd better be careful. She swallowed hard, realizing that she didn't really want to be careful. She wanted the fantasy. Fighting for an edge of reality, she asked, "What can I do to help with dinner?"

For a moment, she thought she saw a flicker of disappointment in his eyes, but he was still smiling as he said, "I've got the corn and potatoes cooking, but you could tear up a little salad while I do the steaks."

"You're pretty darn good at this cooking stuff. I'm impressed. Do you do these romantic dinners often?" She'd meant the words to be teasing, but halfway through, she'd remembered what Sybil had told her about the predatory blonde in his town house complex.

"Only when I want to please someone special." The intensity of his gaze made her forget the blonde and everything else, except the pounding of her pulse and the explosion of heat inside her.

He touched her cheek, sliding his fingertips lightly down to trace a circle around the bruise that still marked her jaw. "I just want to make up for all the bad things that happened to you, Yvonne. This afternoon was wonderful, but it was too fast. I want to take my time when I make love with you, to savor everything that's happening between us."

A tremor of desire quivered through her as she turned her head to touch her lips to his warm fingers. "I want that, too."

For a moment, they were suspended, time stilled by the magic that flared with the slightest touch, the heated gaze, then a distant sound broke the spell. Curt grinned. "Time to check the corn. I set the stove timer 'cause I thought I just might get distracted."

As the rising tide of her passion settled back to a manageable level, Yvonne chuckled. "I can't imagine how that would happen, but since things are progressing so well, I'd better start operating on the greenery. Wouldn't want your corn to be done before the salad."

"Oh, I'm sure we can fix it so everything comes out just right." The low purr in his voice made her knees weak, but she made it to the kitchen anyway.

Though the food was delicious and the wine perfect, Yvonne scarcely tasted either. Whenever their eyes met or their fingers brushed, the electricity between them dulled her tastebuds and she actually had to concentrate to remember how to chew and swallow. Not that she minded; the promise in Curt's eyes made it clear that he had plans for satisfying her ever-increasing hunger for him.

Oddly enough, the singing sexual tension between them had little effect on their dinner conversation. Once she asked him about his business, they found plenty to talk about. His interest in her real estate dealings also brought more memories about her own company and, along with them, a twinge of worry about what might be happening to the company without her guidance.

As she finished her steak, she studied Curt's expression, trying to decide how to broach the subject of calling Gwen. Though he'd rejected the idea before, his reasons didn't really make sense to her. Just making a call wouldn't give away where she was. And she really needed to know.

"More wine?" Curt broke into her thoughts and when she met his gaze, her worry ebbed as quickly as it had come.

Yvonne shook her head. Looking into his eyes made her dizzy enough, she didn't need wine. "Dinner was wonderful, but I couldn't eat or drink another thing."

"What no dessert?" The golden flecks of mischief were dancing in his dark eyes again.

Feeling the sizzling heat deep within her, Yvonne barely controlled a giggle of pure tension. "Please tell me you don't have some gooey chocolate confection hidden around here."

"I had a better idea." He got to his feet and held out a hand to her. "How about one dance, then I'll show you what I have in mind for the grand finale of our evening."

Yvonne rose slowly, her knees unsteady as her bones seemed to melt under the heat of his gaze and her own wild anticipation. "I love the way your mind works," she whispered as she stepped into his embrace.

The slow, sensuous rhythm of the ballad that was playing made it easy to follow his lead, but as his arms tightened, pressing her against him, she found it harder to move. Never had she been so passionately drawn to anyone. She wanted him, but not just with her body; her heart ached for the special completeness that came only when she was in his arms.

Curt gasped as an overwhelming surge of desire tightened his body. Taking it slow was turning out to be harder than he'd thought. Before this, he'd rarely had trouble controlling his passions, but where Yvonne was concerned, he responded like a hormone-driven teenager. He'd wanted to make love to her again fifteen minutes after she left his room this afternoon and every minute since.

Yvonne lifted her head from where it had rested against his neck, her eyes dark with passion, her lips parted, inviting his kiss. Curt claimed her mouth, losing himself gladly in the wild sweetness of her taste, the infinite delights offered by her willing body as she pressed ever closer to him. He was just ready to lift her in his arms and carry her off to the bedroom when the phone began to ring.

Chapter 11

Curt stiffened, closing his ears against the sound, but it refused to go away. Yvonne stirred in his arms, offering no objection as he lifted his lips from hers. "Of all the damned lousy timing," he began, heading for the den.

Yvonne sank onto the first piece of furniture she found, which proved to be one of the couches. Though she could hear Curt's voice through the door, which he apparently hadn't closed tightly, it was several seconds before she actually became aware of what he was saying.

"You're sure of that, Pete? Both numbers?... Yeah, that's not one that he hands out to casual acquaintances.... No, she still hasn't given me any answers. What did they have to say at the resort?" He cursed bitterly, then sighed. "So we're not going to learn anything there, either."

Her heartbeat, which had slowed after their kiss ended so abruptly, accelerated again. Curt was talking about her! A chill traced down her spine at the coldness of his tone and the ache of longing within her congealed as she remembered that he was talking to a cop—one he'd asked to investigate her.

As the glow of his touch faded, her doubts returned. He didn't sound like a lover now; he sounded like a man doing a job. Her stomach twisted and she had to swallow hard as nausea burned in her throat. That couldn't be all it was, not with Curt. His tenderness and concern, his caring and passion; he couldn't have faked it, could he? What had happened between them today...what had almost happened tonight...

Never! She fought the doubts even as a small voice deep within her whispered that she'd been betrayed again. That she'd trusted Curt, not because he was worthy of her trust, but because she wanted him. Sick at heart, she buried her face in her hands, hating herself because, more than anything, she still wanted to be in his arms.

"Yvonne, is something wrong?" Curt's worried voice jarred her out of her dismal thoughts. She looked up, realizing that she hadn't even heard him approaching.

"Maybe you should tell me." Pain put an edge of accusation in her tone and it was all she could do not to shrink away from him as he sank onto the couch beside her.

His frown deepened, yet she could read no guilt in his face. "I'm sorry about the interruption, but Pete thought you'd want to know that a tall brunette woman used your credit card to check you out of the resort. She evidently had the keys to your suite and packed up everything. She also turned in your rental car late Wednesday afternoon."

"My credit card, the keys to the car and my suite?" Yvonne frowned, diverted for the moment. "I suppose she must have gotten them from my purse." She lifted her hand to the side of her head, gently massaging the healing wound. "They must have taken it before they did this to me."

Curt nodded. "They probably had someone watching the resort, waiting to see if you'd show up. When you didn't, they figured it would be better for you to check out, then no one would be asking questions about why you hadn't come back from your evening out."

"Evening out?" She could hear an undercurrent of suspicion in his voice.

"According to several hotel employees, you came in late in the afternoon, had that gold jumpsuit of yours pressed, then left alone around six-thirty."

"Too bad I didn't file my itinerary for the evening." She couldn't hide the sharp edges of anger that tore away the last of her illusions of romance. Did he really think she knew where she'd gone, what she'd done? She was the victim of whatever had happened, not the one who'd... A throb of pain from the side of her head firmly derailed her thoughts.

"In a way you did." His gaze was assessing, as detached as his tone.

"What do you mean?"

"You asked how to find Indian Cliffs Road."

Though his scrutiny told her that he was expecting some sort of reaction, she felt nothing beyond confusion and sorrow. A few feet away the candle flickered in a wayward draft and soft music still spilled from the tape deck, all the touches of romance that he'd so carefully planned, and he was looking at her as though she were a stranger or a suspect. She met the challenge of his gaze without flinching, waiting for his accusation.

"You have no idea what I'm talking about, do you?" His voice softened slightly and she could read doubt in his eyes.

Yvonne shook her head. "Not a clue. Should I?"

"That's the name of the road that passes both the Hanover Ranch and what used to be my cabin. I found you about a hundred or so yards from it."

"Oh." She probed delicately at her memories, but nothing emerged. Her temper flared again. Why was he making so much of this? Just because his dead fiancée had suspected Hanover of being involved in money laundering didn't mean that she'd come to Phoenix to join the man in something shady. It wasn't fair.

Marshaling her anger, she challenged him. "So I went out there. I told you that I came here on business, maybe I was invited to the ranch to meet with some prospective investors. Hanover is a financier, after all."

"Not likely. That was one thing Genna was sure of, Hanover liked keeping his ranch private."

Genna. An unreasoning flash of jealousy burned through her. "What are you saying? That you think I was out there attending some illegal meeting? I develop craft and antique malls, Curt, not vast shopping centers or business complexes."

Looking deep into his eyes, she was chilled to see guilt there and sorrow. That was what he suspected! Shivers moved over her skin and her stomach knotted with pain. "You think I'm some kind of crook, don't you?" The words came out like a sob.

"No, I...when I found you I did have some doubts, but since I've come to know you and..."

She couldn't listen to his words, not after what she'd seen in his eyes. There was no way she could believe anything he said, not now. Stumbling to her feet, she fled to her room before the tears of betrayal spilled over and exposed her weakness. Now that she knew what he really thought of her, she couldn't let him know how vulnerable she'd become.

"Yvonne!" He followed her, shocked at the pain her accusation brought. Her door slammed before he reached it and he heard the sound of something being shoved in front of it. He slumped against the wall, cursing himself for letting down his defenses with her. Any first year rookie cop would have handled himself better. Rule one was always: you never allowed yourself to get emotionally involved with a suspect.

Pulling himself together, he knocked on her door. "Yvonne, we've got to talk about this."

"Go away." Her voice sounded rough, thick with pain, no doubt. A pain that knifed through him, too.

"I can't. You have to know that I don't suspect you of anything now. You were a victim of whatever Hanover was up to that night. I just want to help you remember what happened so you'll be safe."

"Go away, I can't talk to you now." Her voice was firmer, more determined.

Curt hesitated. He didn't doubt that he could force the door and drag her out, but he knew instinctively that she couldn't be bullied into trusting him again. She was too bright and intuitive. "Will you talk to me in the morning? I know you're hurt and angry, but you have to believe that I care about you. I never meant for you to be hurt. If we talk, I'm sure we can make it right again."

He waited, ear to the door, willing her to understand, to remember the drugging kisses, the violent explosion of their lovemaking. Surely that would convince her that they had found something too special to...

Curt swallowed a curse and controlled a strong desire to beat his head against the wall. What was wrong with him? His words were supposed to keep her from running, not lure her into his bed. He needed her trust so he could protect her from Hanover, but that didn't mean he was supposed to trust her. He couldn't do that until he was sure that she wasn't a part of whatever had brought the small jet to Hanover's ranch the same night she'd been there.

The silence from beyond the door grated on his nerves. What if she took it into her head to run? She'd be a sitting duck out there, a perfect target for whoever had missed the first time. "Please, Yvonne, promise me you'll listen tomorrow."

The note of pleading in his tone broke through her anger. She stared across the room at the chair she'd dragged over in front of the door, well aware that it wouldn't keep him out if he was truly determined to come in. But he hadn't tried to force the door. He'd never shown any sort of force toward her.

She swallowed a sigh. In all their time together, he'd never sounded so desperate, so truly worried. Could he possibly care about her? She hated herself for wanting so much to believe that he did. She wanted to be able to ignore him, to hate him, but she couldn't bear the thought that he was upset. "We'll talk in the morning," she called. "Just leave me alone now."

Curt stayed in the hall for several more minutes, then he shrugged and headed for the kitchen. She'd sounded sincere, but he was afraid to trust her. He locked the back door, then activated the security system. Once it was turned on, she couldn't open any door or window without his knowledge. Since he'd also taught her how to turn the system off, he locked the laundry room door and put the only key in his pocket. He'd keep her safe, whether she wanted him to or not.

Frustrated, Curt prowled the house, turning off the music, blowing out the candles, even carrying the table and chairs back to the kitchen. Each and every reminder of his romantic plans for this evening had to be removed because he couldn't bear to look at them. Not that it helped. The moment he stopped thinking like a cop, he ached for Yvonne.

Pete's words haunted him. "Most of the calls from her suite were made either to Hanover's office or to his private number at the ranch. Since the ranch number is unlisted, he had to have given it to her, Curt, and that means that he trusted her."

It made his gut ache to think of Hanover talking to Yvonne, inviting her out to his ranch. To do what? Not so he could invest in some small-time craft and antique mall, that was sure. Hanover didn't do projects that would only show a limited profit. Especially not now that he'd started being a political power broker. Unless there was more going on with her business than she'd remembered.

The itch of curiosity distracted him and he headed for the den and the telephone there. Maybe Jackson could fill him in. He'd had enough time to start digging into Yvonne's company.

Jackson answered on the second ring. "I was just wondering whether I should call you tonight or not."

"About what?" Curt settled in the chair behind the desk, wishing that he had a cigarette. "Did you turn up anything?"

"Maybe yes, maybe no." Jackson chuckled. "That's why I wasn't sure about calling. I need to do some more research."

"So why don't you give me what you have so far."

"Realty Specialists, Inc. has a good reputation, it has solid, though unspectacular, assets and a nice growth potential. On the surface, I'd say it was exactly the way your lady described it."

Curt waited, sure that Jackson had more to say, but his friend remained silent. Finally, when he could stand it no longer, he asked, "What about below the surface?"

"That's what I don't know. I've picked up hints from a couple of sources, but nobody seems willing to talk specifics. Since I know you need to protect the lady, I didn't want to do too much pushing, until I checked with you." The seriousness of Jackson's tone gave the vague words weight.

"What's your gut feeling?" Curt had trusted Jackson's instincts for too many years to doubt them now.

"My guess would be that they've used a multilevel approach. On the surface, we have a nice, stable business that shows good profit and growth. After a little creative bookkeeping, Realty Specialists gives birth to several other companies that make investments. Those companies create new companies to make more investments. Nobody gets into anything spectacular, they could have a string of bars, resorts, even car washes—any kind of business that deals in services rather than concrete products."

Curt swallowed hard. "Anything that can do a nice ordinary business without leaving a traceable paper trail. Each business proves extremely lucrative and their newly washed profits are carefully channeled into legal investments." It made sense.

Jackson sighed. "I'm not saying that's what is going on, because I really don't know. And, even if I did, I might have a hard time proving it."

"But it could be."

"To work well, a money laundering scheme has to start with a legitimate business through which the money can be funneled. When you add in someone with Hanover's power and ability to spread money around, you need a lot of channels. What was going on out at Hanover's could have been a recruitment meeting."

"With the man needing the laundering service flying in for the meeting." The logic of the scenario chilled him. "But how does that tie in with Yvonne being shot?"

"Maybe she said no."

For a moment, he was ready to accept that reason, but his own experience pointed out the flaw in the logic. "I don't see Hanover being foolish enough to set up a high-level meeting with anyone who might say no, do you?"

"We all misjudge people from time to time."

Curt leaned back in the chair, fighting a blaze of anger. He hadn't missed the implied warning in Jackson's words. But damn it, the Yvonne he knew wouldn't have been involved in something so blatantly illegal. Yet the question remained, if she was an innocent victim, why couldn't she remember? The very selectivity of her amnesia made it clear that she was blocking more than the terror of having someone shoot at her.

"So, do you want me to keep investigating or should I back off for the time being?"

Curt rubbed a hand over his eyes, fighting a headache of his own. "Go ahead, but be careful. I'd rather the investigation not be traced back to me."

"I'll do my best, but if Hanover's tied you to her disappearance, he's going to expect you to be poking around. A little pressure might even help. If he was desperate enough for funds to make a mistake with her, he might make a few more."

"What makes you think he's desperate for money?"

"Something I picked up at the local rumor mill. It seems our power broker isn't as good at picking candidates to back as he is at choosing corporations to invest in. A lot of his money has gone to waste recently. Which could explain his sudden need for midnight negotiations."

"I suppose you could be right. Things aren't too easy since the real estate market slumped, either. Lots of people have cash flow problems these days. Thanks, buddy."

"You watch yourself. If Hanover's trying to get into the laundering business with the big boys, they've got the kind of resources that can get real nasty."

As he assured Jackson of his caution, Curt's mind spun with this new tidbit of information. It increased the danger for Yvonne, but at the same time, he welcomed the possibility that she was an innocent victim. Though he ached with weariness, he stayed where he was after he broke the connection. Right now, he didn't want to face his bedroom. It was too close to Yvonne's and as for taking a shower... The sharp edge of his desire cut through everything, leaving him burning to relive what they'd shared. It was going to be a damned long night!

Yvonne paced the length of her room, feeling the walls closing in on her. She'd undressed and tried to read herself to sleep, but the words refused to make sense and every time she closed her eyes, images of Curt filled her mind. Unfortunately most of the images reminded her of the joy and wonder of their afternoon lovemaking and added to her misery.

How could the man who'd made love to her, doubt her? Or was the more appropriate question—how could he make love to her when he obviously suspected her of being involved in horrible things? And what about the romantic evening he'd planned? Why bother with all the special touches if he only meant to break down her defenses so she'd confess to... to whatever he thought she'd done?

Bitter tears burned in her eyes, but she blinked them away, realizing that her angry thoughts didn't make a whole lot of sense. Not unless there were two Curts. Even though her memory was still unreliable, she trusted her instincts and they told her that Curt wasn't at all like David.

The man who'd nursed her through the first nightmare hours after she'd been injured, kept her safe and hidden, brought her here to heal instead of abandoning her to the care of strangers, had come to care for her. And the man who'd played with her in the pool, kissed her senseless, then made powerful love to her in the shower, hadn't been thinking about trapping a money launderer. She'd bet her life on that.

A chill slipped down her spine as she realized that, in truth, she already had bet her life on Curt's protection. He was, after all, the only one who stood between her and whoever had shot her. Which left her where? She groaned as she rolled her eyes toward the ceiling. Confused, that was where.

Which meant he was right, she decided as she collapsed on the bed again. They did need to talk, if only so she didn't feel so shut out of her own life. She chewed her lip lightly, lost in thought, trying hard to understand why she'd been so angry at him, why she'd felt so betrayed.

Was it only because he had suspected her, perhaps still suspected her of some involvement with Hanover? Learning that had hurt, but when she thought about it objectively she had to admit that the evidence definitely pointed to some kind of relationship. Not anything illegal, of course, since her every instinct was revolted at the very idea of anyone taking advantage of her company, but a business deal . . .

The mall! She frowned, concentrating hard on bringing up the images that nibbled at the corners of her mind. Ocotillo Mall—that was what had brought her to Phoenix. The memories crowded in.

"It's not his usual thing, Yvonne," Gwen had bubbled after she finished her phone call. "Keenan Hanover does really big developments. You know, the kind that involve billions of dollars and scads of investors, but he got control of this property as a part of an investment package he took over and he thought of me—of us. Isn't that great! With him involved, we can be assured that the deal will be clear sailing and that will give us the start in a new market that we've been wanting."

There'd been a lot more, most of it details of how Gwen had become friendly with Hanover while she and her now ex-husband lived in Phoenix. Yvonne frowned, suddenly remembering that at the time, she'd had an odd feeling that Gwen had known Keenan Hanover far better than her words intimated.

Was that what had made her skeptical about the deal? But why should she have worried about that? Referrals from friends were legitimate sources for deals and this was just one of several good opportunities Gwen had brought to the company since she'd become a partner. Besides, she remembered Gwen insisting that she go to Phoenix to actually see the property before they went ahead with the details of the development. So she had.

As she relaxed, more memories came. She'd called Hanover's office as soon as she checked into the resort. He'd been charming on the phone, explaining that the mall had been built in Scottsdale just before the real estate market went flat, throwing the owner into deep financial difficulties. Though finished, none of the shop spaces had ever been rented. The only tenant in place was a chic and quite popular nightclub that occupied a freestanding building that shared the parking area of the property.

He'd made it sound so interesting, she'd eagerly accepted his suggestion that one of his associates call for her in the morning. Diane Collins had spent Tuesday with her, showing her around the mall, which was every bit as attractive as Mr. Hanover had said. After that, she'd introduced her to several of the prospective tenants, including a couple of up-and-coming young interior decorators that she'd really liked, and the representative of a group who wanted to open an elegant restaurant in the space that anchored one end of the strip-mall building.

Yvonne sat up, eager to tell Curt what she'd remembered. Maybe he could find out about the meeting at the ranch from Diane Collins, then he'd know... She sank back, suddenly sure that Diane hadn't known about the meeting. Not that she remembered anything specific, but she had this funny feeling that... Her headache flared sharply, forcing her to turn her thoughts away from whatever had happened at the ranch.

What did it mean? Why didn't any of it make sense? The development of the Ocotillo Mall into a craft and antique center seemed legitimate enough. Nothing she'd remembered so far was out of line with the mall projects she handled in the Los Angeles area. The cost of getting it up and running was actually quite a bit less than it would have been for the same development in California, but that was because the real estate market here was still depressed. The deal appeared to be exactly as Gwen had promised.

So why had someone shot her? And what couldn't she remember? The pain intensified again, reminding her that she couldn't force her brain to produce the answers. Not even if her life depended on it—which, unfortunately, it might. She buried her face in the pillow, wishing mightily that it was Curt's chest. Which probably meant that, in addition to amnesia, she had brain damage. If he didn't trust her, why should she be so sure that she could trust him?

After spending most of the night torn between erotic dreams and wide-awake fantasies, Curt slept late, waking to the enticing scent of coffee brewing and something baking. He stretched and yawned, smiling at the mental image of Yvonne in the kitchen fixing breakfast. Maybe she'd bring it to him here and then they could . . .

Reality slammed the door on that fantasy. Hurt and angry as she'd been last night, the only thing she'd carry in here was a grudge. Not that he'd blame her. Without her memories, she couldn't defend herself against his suspicions and since she didn't know about the secrecy that surrounded the meeting or the small jet he'd seen, she had no reason to think she'd been out there for anything but a business appointment.

Not sure whether he should tell her everything or not, he headed for the shower, wincing at the memory of making love to her there. Maybe if he told her everything, it would trigger more memories, something that he could use to . . .

To what? Prove that she'd been in league with Hanover? Did he really believe she could be? He shook his head. He'd done a lot of thinking about Yvonne last night and through the wee, small hours of the morning and nothing he'd come up with had convinced him that she would willingly be involved in anything illegal.

As a cop, he'd frequently depended on his instincts and in the past four days, he'd had an opportunity to get to know Yvonne in a way he'd never known any other person. He'd literally been able to watch her mind come alive as her memories slowly returned. He'd listened to her talk and observed her reactions to various situations. And he'd come to admire and like her as well as desire her. Maybe more than desire her.

He shied away from that thought. Passion could cloud the issues, which was why he'd been crazy to make love to her. But he sure didn't regret it. And once this was all cleared up, he was going to recreate the romantic evening that Pete's call had ended so abruptly. He cursed his body's enthusiastic response to that idea.

So how did he get this mess resolved? There had to be something he could do to shift the initiative from Hanover's hands to his. Jackson had been right about desperate men making mistakes, so they needed to make Hanover even more desperate—but how? He wiped the steam from the mirror and set about shaving.

Before he could do anything, he had to mend his fences with Yvonne and that might not be so easy. Experience told him that it would take more than an apology to erase the hurt from her lovely eyes. Maybe an explanation would help. More than once he'd been impressed by her ability to grasp someone else's point of view. If he could make her see how it had looked to him in the very beginning, she might forgive him for having doubts.

Holding firmly to that thought, he pulled on a clean pair of jeans and a red plaid Western shirt, then followed the delicious aromas to the kitchen. He stopped in the doorway, watching as Yvonne, who had her back to him, took something from the oven. Her peach-colored shorts displayed her elegant legs perfectly and when she turned he could see the glow from yesterday's sun in her cheeks and the deep V of her peach-and-white polka-dot blouse.

"Good morning." Her gaze was unreadable.

"Something smells terrific." He felt his body tighten with desire even as he tried to ignore the feelings that flooded through him.

"Since I couldn't get out to have an early swim, I decided I might as well try out the blueberry muffin mix." There was no accusation in her tone, but Curt felt a thrust of guilt as he looked toward the locked door of the laundry room.

Sighing, he crossed to pour himself a cup of coffee, then sat down at the table. "I'm sorry about that. It's just that you were so angry with me last night, I was afraid you might try to leave and I couldn't take a chance. Pete's sure they're still looking for you and since you don't know who they are…" He let it trail off, aware that her expression had softened slightly.

"If I'd discovered the locked door last night, I might have taken an ax to it, but I've cooled off a bit since then." Though she wasn't looking at him, his heart leaped as he caught the note of wry humor in her tone.

Taking a deep breath, he plunged in. "I know I hurt you last night, Yvonne, and I am sorry. There was a time when I suspected that you might be deeply involved with Hanover, but that time is past. I know you too well now. I just want to keep you safe and help you find out what happened out there."

"Why?" She put the plate of muffins on the table, then sat down opposite him. He sensed that her question was a test, yet he wasn't sure what she expected him to say.

"In the beginning, I wanted to keep you around because I thought you might be able to give me some valuable information about what was going on at the ranch. Then, when it became obvious that Hanover was desperate to finish what they'd done to you, I was sure you must be deeply involved." He paused, choosing his next words carefully. "As I got to know you better, however, what you do or don't know stopped being nearly as important to me as your survival."

He watched her eyes as she weighed his words and when she nodded, he felt as though a thousand pounds had been lifted from his shoulders. Her gaze was troubled as she asked, "But you still think I know something that will damage Hanover?"

"Someone wants you dead, Yvonne. It always comes back to that. Which is why it's so essential for you to remember what happened that night. Since neither of us believes you were out there to set up a channel for his money laundering efforts, it has to be something you saw or heard."

"I have remembered a little more." Yvonne picked up a muffin, split and buttered it as she described the memories that had come to her last night.

"That's it?" Frustration gnawed at him. More tiny pieces of a jigsaw puzzle that made no sense at all. After a day spent in perfectly normal procedures, she'd received a mysterious invitation to his ranch. Why? So he could ply her with charm before he made her an offer she couldn't refuse? Anger made it hard to swallow, turning the muffin to sawdust in his mouth.

"Whenever I try to think about anything involving the ranch, my head starts to hurt. Whatever is keeping me from remembering must have happened there." Her eyes reflected the pain brought on by even talking about it.

Curt forced away his impatience and reached across the table to take her hand. "It'll come in time, when you're strong enough to face whatever happened. Meantime, you need to relax and enjoy what we have here."

As she met his gaze, he knew that she was remembering yesterday and all they'd shared. Her lips softened and he sensed a longing that matched his own, then she looked down and her thick lashes shut him out. She might understand his doubts and suspicions, but she obviously wasn't ready to pick up where they'd left off last night. Something for which he should be grateful, but he wasn't, since he wanted nothing more than to hold her and kiss her until the questions no longer mattered.

Chapter 12

The day continued pleasantly enough, though with each passing hour, Yvonne found it harder to ignore the undercurrents of desire that continued to flare and sizzle each time Curt came near her. She might not be emotionally ready to accept his apology, but her body seemed to have its own agenda. The need to be in his arms ached inside her with such intensity, it made her shy away from touching him, from even getting too close to him when they passed each other in the kitchen or hall. She had a definite impression that she was going to explode if something didn't happen soon.

They were lying by the pool after dinner, enjoying the slight cooling of the air, when the telephone rang. Curt leaped up so quickly, she couldn't help wondering if he'd been as miserably tense as she was. Or had he been expecting a call? She closed her eyes, wishing mightily that she'd insisted on knowing everything he did about the night she'd been injured. When he came back out, she'd risk the pain and ask him.

Curt frowned as he listened to Pete's report. This didn't make any more sense than any of the other pieces of the puzzle. Still, it all had to mean something and the only person who could help him sort things out was lying on a lounge beside the pool.

"So what do you think?" Pete asked. "Should I pursue either of these when I get back?"

"Back from where?"

"I got to go to Flagstaff tomorrow. My sister is having some problems with her ex-husband harassing her and she figured a visit from a cop might cool his ardor a bit." Pete chuckled. "My guess is, he's figured out that she's got a good thing going with a professor at the university there and he's jealous. A case of I don't want her, but you can't have her."

Curt sighed, leaning against the wall. He'd always envied Pete his large, close family, but at the moment, he really wished they weren't claiming his free time. "Give me a call when you get back. I'll run all this stuff by Yvonne and see if it triggers anything, then we'll know more how to proceed."

"Will do, but keep a careful eye out. Hanover just may be getting a bit desperate. I'm hearing hints of high-level muscle being called in, which makes me wonder all the more about the passenger on that jet. If Hanover is increasing his involvement, that ain't good news for us."

"Don't worry, I'll take care of Yvonne."

"Take care of yourself, too." Pete broke the connection.

Curt stayed where he was for a moment, considering Pete's warning. Should he take Yvonne somewhere else? Out of state, maybe? But would she be any safer? The kind of money Hanover was capable of laundering could buy a lot of eyes and Curt knew from his days on the force that the men supplying the money wouldn't hesitate to arrange a hit if they knew where Yvonne was.

All of which meant that the only way out for her was to remember what she'd seen, so they could go after the men who were looking for her. It sounded so simple, but how the hell did he breach her mind's defenses? He got a cou-

ple of bottles of beer from the refrigerator and carried them
out to the pool.

"That was Pete. He had some information about David
Rogers's death."

Yvonne frowned. "You asked him to check on David?"

"I just gave Pete his name in passing, he's the one who
decided to follow up on it." He didn't add that he'd wanted
to be sure her memories of the man's death were accurate.

Yvonne seemed to consider his explanation for several
minutes, then she sighed. "I have to admit I've always
wondered exactly what happened to him. Did Pete tell
you?"

"According to his sources, your 'ex' was a guest on a
private yacht when it hit a reef during a storm in the Caribbean. No body was ever found, but three witnesses testified that Rogers was washed overboard and drowned."
Curt watched her face as he recited the facts. Though she'd
shown no sign of caring about the man, he needed to be
sure. Especially in light of the other factors Pete had mentioned.

Yvonne shook her head. "When I warned David that his
lust for life in the fast lane was going to kill him, a private
yacht wasn't exactly what I had in mind."

"What did you mean?" He couldn't ignore his instinc-
tive curiosity. She'd told him very little about the man she'd
once loved.

"Toward the end of our marriage, his gambling was getting out of hand. He even tried to sell my first mall development to pay his gambling debts. Actually that's when I
found out how serious his problem was. It was sad, really— I mean, he had changed so much. The man I divorced definitely wasn't the man I married."

"According to Pete, you could be right about his gambling killing him. He said one of his sources mentioned that
there were a lot of rumors about David just before the accident. The most reliable being that he'd come to the Caribbean seeking money to pay back some very unfriendly
men in Las Vegas. Since he was the only one who didn't

survive the boating accident, it's possible that he didn't find the money and they decided to make an example of him.''

Yvonne shuddered, then took a sip of beer to ease the tightening in her throat. She wasn't hurting for the man who'd died, but her heart ached for the young man she'd once loved. But she couldn't think of David now, this was the time when she should ask Curt the questions that were tormenting her. Still, she hesitated, not sure how to begin. "So what else did he have to tell you?" she asked, to fill the silence.

"He called your office yesterday, claiming to be a resort employee checking on your whereabouts because you'd left something behind when you checked out."

Yvonne glanced at him quickly, well aware of his change of tone, the sudden intensity of his scrutiny. There was definitely something bothering him. "What did he find out?"

"The secretary told him that following your business trip to Phoenix you were vacationing in the northwest and she had no way to contact you to find out if the earring was yours."

"What? I'm vacationing in the northwest? In the midst of negotiations for a new mall investment? Where in the world did she get that idea? Why didn't he talk to Gwen, she'd know that wasn't right." Her stomach knotted as the absurdity of the story struck her.

"Pete tried to get her, but the secretary informed him that Miss Verona had given her the information as soon as she received your telegram and suggested that if he wanted more details he should try calling Monday, when Miss Verona might be available." His frown deepened. "Pete suggested that whoever checked you out of the resort must have sent the telegram to keep your partner from starting a search for you when she couldn't reach you."

"I can't believe that Gwen would..." Yvonne let her protest die away, suddenly remembering a conversation she'd had with Gwen several weeks ago. "Unless she thought I'd finally taken her advice."

"What advice?" He'd settled back on his lounge chair, but she sensed that his tension hadn't abated.

"Oh, she's been after me to take a vacation for nearly six months. She claims I'm going to burn myself out, but every time I start looking at travel brochures, another deal comes up and, well, you know how it is when your own company is involved." Yvonne chuckled wryly. "Actually I've had more rest since you found me than anytime since I started Realty Specialists."

"So she might actually buy a telegram like that?" His doubt showed in his tone.

"I don't know. Maybe I should call her and . . ."

"No way, not till we know what's going on." Curt sat up, his grim expression matching his adamant tone.

"But she's the one person who might be able to tell us." Frustration sharpened her tone; damn it, she was getting a little sick of his rules. He called his partner and his cop buddy for information, so why shouldn't she check with her sources?

"Please, Yvonne, give it a little longer." His gaze was so full of concern, she found her need for action melting away.

"I'll make you a deal," she said, forcing herself to ignore the longing that threatened to overwhelm her. "I'll wait to call Gwen, if you'll tell me everything you know about the night I was shot. I can tell there's something that you haven't told me and I think I have a right to know what it is."

She was sharp, Curt acknowledged to himself as he fiddled with his beer to cover his surprise at her offer. Not that he should be shocked that she'd guessed that he was withholding information. In fact, he should be grateful that she was forcing the issue, since he'd been trying to decide when to tell her about the jet.

"Well, will you tell me?" Her question forced him to meet her gaze.

"Of course. There's really no reason why I haven't told you before, except that other things seemed more important."

"I think maybe it's time you let me decide what's important. After all, we are dealing with my life and my memories here."

If this hadn't been so serious, he would have smiled at her take-charge attitude. With her quick mind and good instincts, he'd bet she was terrific in tough negotiations. "You got it. No more secrets," He gave the promise willingly, hoping he wouldn't live to regret it.

"So what happened?" Yvonne's eyes were wide and dark as she looked into his. She might be firm in her demands, but she was scared, too, he could tell.

"Well, I told you I was watching the ranch from the cliffs. I was out there because I'd heard rumors about a secret meeting being planned for sometime during the week. Nothing had gone down Monday night, but things were obviously stirred up by Tuesday. Cars coming and going, Hanover out there from early in the morning."

"That must be why he asked Diane to show me around. She couldn't answer all my questions, though. I had to call him a couple of times to get specifics." Her fear seemed to have faded as she concentrated on what he was telling her.

"Anyway, there were several more arrivals around dusk, then nothing. I kept dozing off up there until I heard a plane circling around. It woke me up, but I didn't think too much about it until the lights went on about half a mile from the ranch house. Hanover has a desert landing strip out there. Pretty soon, a small jet came in."

"A plane?" Her frown deepened. "I have this feeling that I..." She winced and he knew immediately that her mental censor was once again blocking her memories with pain.

Though he hated the necessity of causing her more suffering, he continued, determined to say it all now that he'd started. "While I watched, a couple of cars went out to meet the plane. I couldn't see much, but I know at least two, maybe three people got off the plane and into the cars. They were driven to the ranch, entering through the rear, where I couldn't see them. That was about midnight."

Yvonne was rubbing the side of her head, her eyes closed. He waited several minutes, hoping that she'd say something, but she didn't. Finally he decided to go on.

"Nothing much happened from then until around two. That's when I watched the first car leave, then the second going after it. They stopped out of my view, I heard the shot, then both cars came back. It got quiet again until the jet left about four. I don't know how many people left with it. As soon as everything was dark at the ranch, I headed out to investigate the gunshot. That's when I found you."

Silence stretched out between them, but it was far from peaceful. Yvonne was lying still now, but he knew that she was fighting the pain and it killed him. He ached to take her in his arms and tell her to forget this whole mess. He wanted to kiss away the darkness, make her whole and free and . . .

He couldn't stand it any longer. He pried the sweat-beaded bottle from her tense fingers, then held her hand in his. "Are you all right, Yvonne? Can I do something for you?"

She took a deep breath and he felt the shudder that shook her whole body. "That's it? That's everything?" He could hear the despair in her voice.

"That's all I saw and heard."

"You're not keeping anything back, maybe trying to protect me?"

He shook his head. "That's all I know, beyond the stuff that Pete's told me about Hanover trying to find you since. Did anything I've told you help?"

"Not really. I have a sense that I knew about the plane, but when I try to remember. . . ." Her eyes narrowed from the pain. "I just can't fight my way through, Curt. When I try, I start to slip away and I'm scared to death that I won't wake up again."

"Oh, Yvonne, I'm sorry. I didn't want you to . . ." He pulled her into his arms, hating himself for what his words had done to her.

For a moment she was stiff, not resisting, but not accepting his embrace, either, then he felt the tension draining away as she curled into him, rubbing her head against his chest, her soft sigh stirring the hair that was exposed by his half-unbuttoned shirt. Suddenly he felt the dampness on his skin.

Tears. He felt her misery knifing through him, taking his breath away. He lifted her head gently so that he could look into her eyes. "It's all right, it doesn't matter. You don't have to remember. Just don't cry." He framed her face with his hands, wiping her tears away with his fingers.

"I was just so sure that you had the answers." Her voice was heavy with despair. "That's why I asked, Curt. I had to know. It's just that it doesn't help. That's what breaks my heart. I keep finding things out and none of them help."

"They will. You're remembering more all the time. We just have to be patient." He focused on her lips, remembering their taste, the fires they'd ignited.

"I've never been good at patience." Her tone reflected less sadness and tears no longer spilled down her cheeks. He lifted his gaze to her eyes and recognized the sensual awareness that glowed in their depths. Her arms slipped around him, her fingers coming up to tangle in the hair at the back of his neck.

"Me, either," he whispered just before he claimed her lips. The explosion of desire was instant and stunning. Twenty-four hours of denial had only made the banked fires hotter. He took the kiss deeper, delving into the sweetness of her mouth. Her tongue answered his caresses with matching enthusiasm as she moved over on the lounge chair, making room for him to stretch out beside her.

How could a kiss be so potent? Her whole body throbbed and ached with longing the moment his lips touched hers and now as she felt his body hard against hers, nothing else mattered. All day she'd told herself that she couldn't be falling in love with Curt, that it would be madness to even consider such a thing under the circumstances, but now she couldn't deny it. The wild current of emotion that flowed through her like a stream of lava came straight from her heart.

She moved her hands slowly, measuring the width of his shoulders, caressing his back, exploring the ripples of muscle that moved beneath her hands as he shifted slightly so that she rested on his chest, her breasts pressed tightly against him. She felt his heart pounding against the hard wall of his chest, its rhythm matching her own. His lips left hers to taste the skin of her cheek, then she felt his tongue lightly tickling the sensitive area below her ear. He nibbled her earlobe, then plunged his tongue into her ear making her moan as she tried to move even closer to him.

The wild hunger she'd felt in the shower had changed and expanded. The throbbing emptiness inside her ached, but only for him, for the overwhelming sense of completeness she'd felt the first time they'd made love. She quivered as his hand slipped beneath her T-shirt and found her breast. His light touch ignited more fires.

Wanting to give him the same magical feelings he was spreading through her body, she rubbed her face against the springy curls on his chest, seeking one of the tight male nipples that nestled there. Finding it, she touched it with her tongue, marveling at the salty male taste of his skin and the instant groan of pleasure that rumbled in his chest.

Curt shifted on the lounge chair, trying to fit his body more perfectly to hers, craving her closeness, the feel of her softness accepting the angles of his body. The chair creaked and rocked slightly, making it clear that it hadn't been designed for this sort of activity. A curse of frustration formed on his lips as he gave up his attempt to make their contact more intimate and contented himself with stroking the tightening crest of her breast through the lace of her bra.

"If we keep this up, we're going to end up falling off this blasted chair," he whispered trailing kisses across her cheek as she lifted her head, seeking his lips.

Her tongue touched his lips, tasting lightly before her mouth parted beneath his. He tightened his embrace, not caring what happened so long as she remained in his arms, safe and his. *His?* The realization of the implications of that thought forced back the drugging clouds of passion for a moment.

Yvonne sensed the change immediately. His lips had softened their sensual attack, moving tenderly now, caressing rather than demanding, savoring instead of ravaging. Was he beginning to regret his desire for her? Did he still have too many doubts? She grew still in his arms, afraid of her own vulnerability. Could she bear it if he walked away from her now? It scared her to realize that she honestly didn't know.

Something had changed. Even as their kiss ended, Curt tightened his arms, wanting to bring back the burning fire that had united them just seconds before, but this time Yvonne didn't respond. Though she didn't actually try to pull away, the closeness that had pulsed between them was gone. Curt reluctantly loosened his embrace.

Had he come on too strong, pushed her too fast after what had happened yesterday? Her response had seemed to match his—until now. Could it be that last night's debacle had made her afraid to trust him? That thought hurt more than his frustrated body. After what he'd just realized about his own feelings for her, he needed to know exactly what she was thinking and feeling.

Taking a deep breath, he pressed a kiss to her temple, then began, choosing his words with care. "I want to make love with you, Yvonne, but only if you want it as much as I do. I think something very special is happening between us and I don't want to destroy it by pushing you into more than you're ready for. I hurt you last night— I won't risk doing that again."

Yvonne lifted her head, needing to look into his eyes, afraid to trust her ears. He sounded so serious, so…almost unsure of what he was feeling. Since he'd always appeared to be a man very much in command of himself and his emotions, his vulnerability moved her as nothing else could.

His dark eyes met hers and even in the shadowy light from the kitchen, she could read the depth of his longing. The questions were there, too, and something very akin to fear. He looked like a person teetering on the edge of a decision that could change his life. She swallowed hard; that certainly was what she was feeling. Was it possible that he felt the same way? The very idea set her heart to pounding faster.

For a moment she hesitated, afraid to plunge into the uncharted waters of admitting her feelings. Her marriage had taught her that trust could bring pain, but could anything hurt worse than never knowing what might happen between them? If she turned away from this moment, she might never find out how Curt felt about her. Besides, no matter what lay ahead, she couldn't deny her own growing love and if there was even a chance that Curt could return it... It was her turn to be honest.

"I really do understand about last night and why you have doubts about me. Especially now that you've told me everything else that happened that night. That's one reason I want so much to remember exactly what happened to me. Deep inside, I'm sure I couldn't be mixed up in anything illegal, but until I can see beyond the dark veil in my mind, I can't prove it." She forced herself to continue meeting his gaze, exposing herself to his probing, letting him see the truth of her feelings even though it scared her to be so emotionally naked.

The gift of her trust spread over him like a lover's caress, warming away the last of his fears. He had to touch her cheek, caress the silky skin that surrounded her slightly swollen lips. He realized that he had no more doubts about the woman in his arms. "You don't have to prove anything to me, Yvonne. I trust the woman I know you are."

"Then make love to me." The words came out in a whisper before his lips closed over hers, sealing the moment and banishing everything but the magic that flowed so sweetly between them.

Several kisses later, Curt eased away from her. Yvonne moaned in protest, unwilling to be separated for even a moment now that she'd surrendered to the drugging wonder of his kisses.

"Let's move inside before this chair tosses us both onto the concrete," he whispered, shifting her into his lap, then getting to his feet with her in his arms.

"I could walk." She giggled and nipped at his ear. "At least I think I could."

"Keep that up and you may find out." His sexy growl didn't sound at all unhappy. "Can you get the door?"

It took all her concentration to open, then close and lock the arcadia door behind them. She felt as though she'd swallowed a whole bottle of champagne, though she had, in fact, drunk less than half a bottle of beer. Could she be intoxicated on kisses? Perhaps if they were Curt's she could.

She closed her eyes and pressed her lips to his neck, tasting his skin and drawing in heady lungfuls of his musky scent. As she trailed kisses along his jaw, she felt the spiky roughness of his sprouting whiskers. She ran her tongue over them, finding the sensation exciting.

"Why do I feel like an hors d'oeuvre?" Curt's chuckle rumbled against her breast as his arms tightened slightly.

"Well, you are pretty tasty." Yvonne opened her eyes to discover that they were now in her bedroom. She nipped daintily at his lower lip.

"Oh, you're getting dangerous. I think I'd better put you down." He released her legs, but tightened his hold on her waist, so that she slid very slowly down his body until her toes touched the floor.

"Don't tell me I'm too hot to handle." She transferred her tasting to the base of his throat, delighting in the sensation of his racing heartbeat as she pressed her tongue to that pulse point.

"Hot, yes, but too hot? No way. You're just right for me." He bent to capture her lips as his hands slid below her waist, pressing her body even more tightly against him. Her moan of pure delight was lost in the welcoming heat of his mouth.

Her body was melting and their confining clothes kept her from fusing with his burning body. Her hands shook as she helped Curt tug off her T-shirt, then tried to unbutton the last two buttons on his shirt so she could pull it out of his cutoffs and shove it out of her way. She longed to feel his skin touching hers, to lose herself in the sensation of becoming a part of him.

The rest of her clothes were easily stripped away as she rubbed the sensitive tips of her breasts against his chest, luxuriating in the tickling curls that covered his heated skin. Her knees were growing weak, she had to cling to him as he left a trail of kisses along the side of her throat, then nipped lightly at the point where her neck and shoulder met.

"We'd better lie down before we fall down," she gasped, dizzy with the sensations that quivered uncontrolled through her body each time his hands, lips or body touched hers.

"The world does seem to be whirling faster than usual, doesn't it?" His low voice sent more shivers through her as he guided her down on the cool sheets, then lowered himself beside her.

He was going to take it slow, he told himself as he began a careful exploration of her delicious curves and hollows. He wanted to learn everything about her, what made her gasp, what set her to trembling, what would truly make her his. Yesterday's fiery union had been sensational, but this time he wanted to make it perfect for Yvonne.

Was he trying to drive her mad? Yvonne writhed beneath his caresses, her body screaming for the ultimate union. He seemed to know her better than she knew herself, his touch setting off new and wonderful sensations that lifted her closer and closer to the heights. The waves of her desire swelled higher and higher, crashing wildly within her as he finally claimed her.

The fires blazed out of control, melting her body and fusing it to his as they rose together, borne on the crest of their own wild passion, reaching for the stars and streaking past them into the flaming heart of their oneness. Then holding tight together, they drifted slowly back from the heights, settling at last into the peace of total fulfillment, still locked in each other's arms.

Yvonne was only dimly aware of Curt's gentle movements as he eased his weight from her, turning so that she was still safe in his arms. The shattering impact of their

lovemaking left her too deliciously exhausted to do more
than snuggle closer to his now wonderfully familiar body.
She'd never known it could be like that. Never dreamed
that she could feel so totally and completely loved. She
closed her eyes and slipped into dreams that in no way
matched the wonder of reality.

Curt heard the change in her breathing and smiled.
Though he, too, was exhausted, he wasn't really sleepy.
Besides, there was so much to think about. Like how it felt
to touch Yvonne and feel her respond. Like the way she
tasted and the way she made him feel when she cried out for
him.

He felt his body stir and swallowed a groan. He couldn't
want her again, not already. If he'd made love to any other
woman, he would be satiated, ready to concentrate on other
things, but with Yvonne... His smile faded. Could he be
falling in love? The very thought was enough to cool his
passion—at least for the moment. Men in love made mistakes, dangerous ones and Yvonne was already in jeop-
ardy.

As he stared up at the ceiling, the house creaked, cooling with the night's drop in temperature... or was it? Suddenly he remembered the security system—the one they'd
been too busy kissing to set. A chill slipped down his spine.
What if they'd found the house? Any pro would be able to
get in with the alarm turned off and his gun was across the
hall under the pillow on his bed.

Cursing himself for a careless fool, he eased away from
Yvonne's tempting body. Of all the times to forget the ba-
sics of safety, this was the worst. He pulled on his cutoffs
and padded to the bedroom door, pausing to peer out.
Lordy, they'd left the kitchen light on, too. He crossed to
his room to get his revolver, then moved silently through the
hall to begin a thorough check of the house.

It was a very long half hour before he finally felt secure
enough to activate the alarm system and return to Yvonne's
room. They'd been lucky this time, but he was going to
have to be more careful from now on. Hanover wasn't going to wait much longer and Curt had no doubt that the

man would come up with something to force them out of hiding.

So now what? He wanted nothing more than to climb back into bed with Yvonne. Holding her safe in his arms until morning sounded like a terrific way to finish the night, but he hated to risk waking her. After the magic they'd shared, he didn't want to talk to her about danger or have her see his revolver.

Of course he could put the gun back where he'd left it before. With the alarm on, no one was going to come sneaking in now. And if she did happen to wake, he just might be able to find some way to distract her. That thought brought an unmistakable response, proving that he wasn't nearly as tired as he'd thought he was. If this was love, it obviously did a great deal for his energy level.

He put the gun back under his pillow, then headed for his bathroom to get a drink of water. He was just putting the glass down, when he heard the first sounds. Whimpers, cries, moans! He started to retrieve his revolver, then realized that he wouldn't need it. He couldn't shoot the villains in Yvonne's nightmares, but he sure could be there to hold her so she'd feel safe when she woke up.

Chapter 13

They were coming for her. She could hear the footsteps, the rattle of the key in the door, but she couldn't move. They didn't turn on the lights, so they were just silhouettes against the sudden brightness that made her headache worse.

"Please let me go. I only wanted my watch. Just let me leave and..."

The first man to enter the room slapped her. "Shut up, bitch."

"Let's gag her till we get her out of here, you know what the boss said about causing a fuss while he's got company." The second man's tone told her that he was enjoying her fear.

"With what?" The first man yanked her arms, which were bound behind her, lifting her painfully to her feet. "She ain't going to make a squeak, 'cause if she does, I'll break her arms." He jerked up on her bound wrists again making her gasp with pain. "You got that?"

She gritted her teeth to keep back a scream, then forced herself to answer. "I'll be quiet."

"Wouldn't do you no good to howl anyway. Nobody here gives a damn what happens to you." The second man's lazy tone confirmed her own suspicion. She'd felt like an outsider from the moment she'd arrived.

"Just take me out to my car and I'll go away."

"Shut up or I'll put another dent in your thick skull." The first man gave her arms another jerk, then jabbed what felt very much like a gun into her ribs as he pushed her toward the lighted hallway. *"We're going for a little ride, then you're going to tell us exactly what you were doing here."*

"You shoulda left when the boss told you to." The second man crowded close to her on the other side, so that she was sandwiched between the two of them as they walked along the hall, then started down the stairway.

Fear made her knees weak and she was dizzy from the pain. Suddenly the stairs seemed to shimmy and shift and she was falling. The man holding her arm jerked her back and the pain from her shoulders sent her screaming over the edge into the darkness.

"Yvonne, honey, it's okay. I'm here now. I won't let them hurt you again." Gentle fingers were stroking her forehead, soothing away the darkness, the terror.

"Curt?" She couldn't open her eyes, not yet, she was too afraid, but she could move toward his warmth. His arms closed around her as she buried her face against his chest.

"It was just a nightmare, love. You're safe here." His voice was soft, comforting.

She clung to him, still lost between the vivid memories of terror and the new images of Curt that flowed into her mind. Curt had saved her, he was protecting her. He was in her bed! That final thought opened her eyes and brought her to full consciousness. She took a long deep breath as the wonderful memories of their lovemaking forced the nightmare images away.

"You awake now?" His embrace eased a little.

Yvonne nodded against his chest. "I think so. Did I wake you?"

"No, I was up getting a drink of water. I heard you start to moan and cry out. That's when I knew you were having one of your nightmares.'' His hands moved lightly over her back and she realized that she was still naked from their lovemaking while he was now wearing his cutoffs.

Distracted, she touched the waistband. ''You put on your clothes to get a drink?''

Curt shifted so that she could see his face in the faint moonlight that spilled in through the window. ''I went out to turn off the lights and activate the security system.''

''Oh.'' A shiver traced down her spine as his words reminded her of the danger that still surrounded her. ''We forgot, didn't we?''

''We were a little busy when we came in. Are you all right now? You sounded terrified when you cried out.''

''It was a nightmare.'' Even as she spoke, the images from her dream came back to her, chillingly.

''The same one, about when you were shot?''

''No, this was different.'' She closed her eyes, half expecting the pain to crash into her skull as she tried to remember the details of her nightmare; but the pain remained slight, just a distant ache.

''How was it different?'' His intense interest showed in his voice.

''It was a memory from before. Oh, Curt!'' She gasped as more images began to flood her mind, overwhelming her for a moment as she tried to sort through them, to make sense of everything.

''What is it? Are you in pain?'' His concern warmed her.

''No, no, I remember things, lots of them. And it doesn't hurt.''

''Can you tell me what you remember?'' Even though his voice was soft, she could hear an excitement in it that matched hers.

''After my tour with Diane, I started going through my notes and there were some details on the financing for the Ocotillo Mall that didn't make sense to me, so I called Hanover to see if I'd gotten the wrong information. He told me that he had to check on my figures and he'd get back to me in a day or two, but I didn't want to wait.'' Yvonne paused, enjoying the sensation of being in command again, of actually knowing what she'd done and thought.

"Did you tell him that?"

"I explained that there was an old home that was going on the market in the L.A. area that I felt could be converted into a stunning office and showroom set up for a decorator and I needed to get back to my L.A. office to call some people who might be interested in the deal."

"How'd he take that?" Curt sounded amused.

Yvonne frowned. "Now that I think about it, he seemed almost angry at first, then he suggested that I come out to the ranch that evening. He said he had a few guests, but that he would take time from his entertaining to go over the deal with me and he was sure we could iron out any difficulties. He kept insisting that we needed to have the papers drawn up before I left town."

"So you went."

"Ocotillo Mall is a great property and the way he laid out the deal, it would be terrific for Realty Specialists. It would give us a whole new market to work in." Yvonne sighed, her eyes on the ceiling. "Actually I think that's what made me ask so many questions, it seemed almost too good to be true. Know what I mean?"

Curt nodded. "You have good instincts, you just should have listened to them and headed back to Los Angeles instead of going out to his ranch."

His words stung. "Which would you have done?"

There was a moment of silence, then Curt sighed. "I'd have gone out to the ranch. If it really sounded that good, I'd have to check it out."

"That's why I went." Yvonne snuggled closer, treasuring his honesty and his understanding. Just knowing that he would have done the same thing made her feel closer to him than she had before. She'd learned the hard way that few people felt as she did about their companies.

"So was he able to convince you that it was a legitimate deal?"

"Not exactly." Yvonne frowned. "There was a small party going on when I arrived. I was late— I got lost twice

before I found Indian Cliffs Road and then I almost turned
back before I finally reached the ranch. Anyway, he introduced me to several businessmen, then pretty much left me
on my own. Since I was the only woman guest there, it was
rather uncomfortable.''

She closed her eyes, remembering the slow crawling
hours as she sipped unwanted drinks and nibbled endlessly
from the buffet. Several of the guests had left during the
evening and she'd been ready to walk out herself, when
Hanover cornered her and turned on the charm, promising to spend some time with her in a few minutes.

''It must have been close to eleven when he finally invited me into his office. He had the papers there, and we
were just starting to discuss them, when a man came in and
told him that he had a phone call. Hanover ordered the
man to stay with me, while he went to another phone. Like
he thought I might listen in or something.'' She'd been irritated at the time, but now she could see why. An ordinary businessman might be guarding business secrets, but
from all Curt had told her, Hanover had a lot more to protect.

''Too bad you weren't able to listen,'' Curt murmured.
''We might be a lot closer to knowing what he's up to.''

''Well, when he came back, the charm was gone. He told
me flatly that he couldn't talk anymore, that I'd have to
leave. I was furious, but he didn't seem to give a damn. He
pretty much gave me the bum's rush. One of his men even
escorted me out to my car.''

''He must have gotten word that the plane was coming.''

''No doubt. At the time I just figured that he'd gotten a
better offer for the mall and was freezing us out. I definitely planned to let Gwen know what I thought of his tac-
tics.''

''So what happened? Did they come after you?''

''No. I drove maybe three or four miles from the ranch
house, then I realized that my watch was gone. It was my
parents' last gift to me before they were killed in a car accident, so it's very precious to me. Anyway, I stopped the

car and searched it, but the watch wasn't there. Since I'd been watching the time most of the evening, I knew I must have lost it somewhere in the ranch house.''

"You went back." It wasn't really a question.

"I couldn't just leave it there. After the way he'd treated me, I planned on getting the first flight out in the morning. Anyway, I had no intention of seeing Hanover again. I figured I'd just slip into the kitchen and ask one of the maids to go check around for my watch.''

She had no trouble remembering her drive back to the ranch, the sight of the well-lit building as she'd walked around to the rear. Why hadn't she realized then the significance of the fact that no one was visible through the windows? The answer was simple, she'd been too angry to think about anything but getting her watch and leaving Phoenix and Keenan Hanover in a cloud of dust.

"So what happened?"

"There was no one in the kitchen. At first, I just figured he'd sent his help home for the night, then I realized that the place looked more abandoned than anything. Food was sitting out on the counters, dishes were stacked everywhere." She sighed. "I should have guessed that something was definitely wrong, but I didn't.''

"He probably sent his help away so they wouldn't see his guest.''

"Hindsight is wonderful. At the time, I just figured everyone was closeted in some kind of private meeting. I'd looked in the windows as I went around the house, so I knew that no one was in the living room or dining room. Since that seemed the most likely place to look for my watch, that's what I did.''

"Did you find it?''

Yvonne shook her head, remembering her hurried search and her growing sense of urgency as she'd failed to find it in any of the downstairs rooms she'd been in. "It was kind of spooky, you know, looking through those rooms. Like something out of an old sci-fi film, where the people are taken by aliens in the middle of a meal or something.''

Curt's chuckle held little humor. "Aliens, huh? That might not be a bad description of the people our Mr. Hanover was entertaining."

"I should have left when I finished looking everywhere on the first floor, but I couldn't. If it wasn't there, I figured it had to be either in the upstairs bathroom or the bedroom where I'd gone to get my stole and purse. Since I still hadn't seen or heard anyone, it seemed safe enough."

She'd stopped at the guest bedroom first and had just begun her search when she heard the plane. "I was upstairs when the plane landed. In fact, I watched it come in from the bedroom window. That's when I realized where everyone from the house had gone." She paused, remembering clearly just how she'd felt. "And I got real curious."

Curt's arms tightened around her as though he wanted to shield her from what had happened next, but he said nothing.

"Three men got off the jet and there was a lot of handshaking before they got into the cars and headed back toward the house. That's when I decided that I had to leave, watch or no watch. Since I was sure they'd be coming up the front way, I went looking for the backstairs that I'd noticed while I was in the kitchen." She stopped as a sharp pain suddenly knifed into her brain.

"But they came in the back."

Yvonne nodded, fighting the pain. "I was at the top of the stairs when they started up."

"Did you get a good look at the men from the plane?"

She closed her eyes, trying to reconstruct the scene even as the throbbing seemed to be trying to drive the memory from her. "One was a tall man, in his late fifties, I'd guess, with a thick mane of silver hair and the meanest dark eyes I've ever seen. When he looked up at me, I felt like he was sucking the breath out of my lungs. The one next to him was younger, but I... It's all hazy and... Oh, Curt, the pain..." She dug her nails into his arm, trying to hold on as the pain overwhelmed her.

"Yvonne!" He felt her body stiffen and tightened his hold on her, willing the pain away, his heart pounding with fear for her. "Hold on, baby. Think about your company. Focus on that house in L.A. you wanted. Do you think it's too late now?"

He felt like a fool babbling about real estate while she writhed in pain, but it was the only way he knew to stop her suffering. If he could stop it! He trembled at the thought that he might have pushed her too far this time. But she'd seemed so excited with her memories and . . .

"Curt." She was relaxing, her body molding to his. "It's okay now, really. You can let go."

It took him a moment to realize what she meant and another heartbeat before he could force his muscles to relax and let her breathe normally. "You scared the hell out of me. I didn't even know you were having your pains."

"I wasn't, not until I tried to remember what I saw." She flinched, took another breath, then went on. "I remember turning and running back along the hall and down the front staircase. There was some shouting and a couple of men came after me. I got as far as my car before they caught me. Then I think they must have hit me." She shuddered.

He waited a while, not wanting to press her for more details, but frustrated by his strong suspicion that what she was remembering now could lead him directly to the people who wanted her dead. "Is that what your nightmare was about?"

Yvonne shifted in his arms, rubbing the side of her head as she met his gaze. "No, it was later. The men who caught me must have taken me back into the house. When I woke up, I was lying on the bed in the guest room. My hands were tied behind me and I was in the dark. I heard them coming for me. They were taking me out, down the stairs when I got dizzy and started to fall. I must have passed out then, because that's all I remember."

"Nothing about the desert?"

She shook her head.

"Were the men in your nightmare the ones from the plane?"

"No. They said something about their boss not wanting me to be noisy when he had company. They must work for Hanover. They were taking me somewhere to question me about why I was there." She began to tremble, then shiver. "Oh, Curt, they were taking me to the desert to kill me."

The agony in her voice cut through him, making him want to find Hanover and personally extract retribution. But that would have to wait. He fought back his craving for revenge, concentrating instead on helping Yvonne. "We'll make him pay for that, honey, but right now you just need to let it go. The worst is over and you survived. You're here and you're safe. Now that you're remembering, we can stop them and make sure they never hurt you again."

"Can we really stop them?" There was no way he could miss the fear in her voice.

"We're going to give it one hell of a try," he promised, wishing that he could guarantee their success. "And I'd say that a charge of attempted homicide against good old Keenan would be a nice way to start."

Yvonne snuggled closer. "I like the idea of him behind bars." She ran her hand down his side until she reached the waistband of his cutoffs. "Since you've got clothes on, why don't you go get us something cold to drink, then come back to bed." She paused, then raised her head from his chest to feather a few kisses around his mouth. "Unless you're sleepy?"

He captured her mouth and quickly showed her just how wide-awake he was.

Keenan glared at the receiver. Damn, but he resented being called at 5:00 a.m. as though he was some kind of hired help. Once he got this network up and running right, he'd make this jerk pay through the nose for the privilege of using his channels to launder his dirty money. His lovely, necessary money.

"I told you, I've come up with something that will bring Macklin out of hiding. Once we have him distracted, your man can take out the woman."

He held the receiver away from his ear as the caller shouted angrily. Dealing with filth never changed, not even when they came dressed up in thousand-dollar suits and bragged about sending their sons to Ivy League schools. When the tirade slowed, he took a deep breath and plunged in. "That kind of thinking is what got us into this mess. If you'd left well enough alone, she and her car would have been found in the desert—just another visitor to the valley who didn't realize the dangers of straying off the main highway."

His caller snarled again, demanding more answers, reminding him of past favors until Keenan considered just hanging up. Only the spectre of losing his power base to the sick local economy kept him from telling G.P. where he could park his complaints.

"Don't worry about Macklin," he advised when he could finally get a word in. "If he knew anything, he'd have launched an investigation. Either the woman was too badly injured to talk or she really has no idea what she saw. I'll find out which and I'll take care of Macklin in my own time. Trust me, we don't need a full-scale murder investigation just now. Accidents are much tidier."

And assassinations were even more enjoyable to plan, he thought, smiling as he finally replaced the receiver and sank back against his padded headboard. He'd already set his plan in motion, but G.P. didn't need to know that. Macklin was going to be far too busy trying to keep his company afloat and his friends alive to worry about what had happened at Hanover Ranch last Tuesday night.

He chuckled as he slid back under the covers. It had taken him nearly a year to create the perfect way to destroy Curt Macklin, but now he had it. It was just a matter of time until the last loose end was neatly tied up. He could hardly wait!

"What the hell!" Curt struggled up through the thick mists of sleep, driven by a shrilling sound that refused to stop.

"It's the telephone." Yvonne moaned and pulled the pillow over her head. "Make it go away."

Groaning, Curt scrambled out of bed and padded across the hall to his bedroom, cursing as he reached for the offending device. His greeting was less than cordial.

"Well, at least you're not dead." Jackson's tone matched his and the chill of it blew away the last of the cobwebs.

Curt sank onto the bed, suddenly very cold. "What's up."

"This is not turning out to be your run-of-the-mill Monday mornings. We got a serious situation brewing."

"What sort of situation?"

"Officially, I'm not sure, but the bomb squad just evacuated the entire office building."

"The bomb squad is there? Why?" Could Yvonne's nightmares be contagious? Maybe he was still asleep and... A sound made him look up. She was standing in the doorway, her blue eyes wide with fright, her long legs trembling below the hem of her short robe.

"I called them. I was at the reception desk talking to Cheryl when a messenger came in with a manila envelope for you. Nothing to sign, no return address. She was going to open it, but I..." Jackson sighed. "Call it flashback time, but something about it didn't feel right, so I shoved it in a metal file cabinet and called the cops."

"I take it there hasn't been a big bang yet."

"So far just a lot of people in protective gear traipsing in and out." There was no humor in Jackson's voice. "My guess is, somebody wants you to come out of hiding and they figured this was a great way to get your attention."

"That's insane."

"Maybe old Keenan ain't wrapped too tight."

Curt began to curse, then controlled his temper. "I'll be in as soon as I can."

"No way, that's why I called. To keep you from coming down when you heard about it on the news." Jackson's tone was sharp.

"We can't let him get away with something like that. If you or Cheryl or anybody else—" Anger closed his throat.

"If you come in, he gets what he wants."

"And if I don't what will he do next?"

"He'll have to think of something else, which buys time. Also, whatever was delivered this morning is going to merit an investigation and my guess is, Pete will be right on it."

"Pete's on his way to Flagstaff. Today's his day off and he's got some family stuff to take care of." Curt rubbed a hand over his stubbly chin, then beckoned to Yvonne. He felt better when her warm body was tucked close against his side. "You really think this was just a ploy?"

"Can you think of any other reason for something like this?" Jackson's tone was lighter now. "Businesswise we haven't done anything too offensive recently and unfortunately, I know your love life wouldn't rate a firecracker attack."

"Thanks a lot." The tight coils of anxiety loosened inside him. "For catching it before somebody got hurt."

"Some things you never forget and spotting booby traps happens to be one of them. Has your lady come through for you yet?"

"I think so. She's remembered one of the men who came off the jet. If he's a major player in the laundering business and she can place him with Hanover, the fallout should take care of Keenan Hanover for good."

"She actually saw the passengers?" Jackson's gasp told him that he realized the significance. "Does that mean she's got her memory back?"

"All but the final bit and I expect we'll get to it." Curt hugged Yvonne, then frowned as another thought crossed his mind. "You'd better call Sybil and warn her to be careful. If Hanover's getting that desperate, he could try to get to me through the people I care about."

"They'll be on their way to her parents the minute school's out. Sybil planned to wait until late June, but I got to worrying over the weekend and convinced her to change their reservations."

They talked for a moment more, then Curt hung up after Jackson promised to call back when he found out exactly what had been in the manila envelope. He turned to

Yvonne, wishing mightily that she hadn't followed him. After all that they'd shared last night, he hated having to tell her what Hanover was up to now. Still, for her own protection, she had to know.

"It's bad isn't it?" Her face was pale and her fingers were icy as they rested on his naked thigh.

"It could have been, but everything seems to be under control, thanks to Jackson." He took a deep breath and repeated what Jackson had told him.

Yvonne listened without interrupting, but once he finished, she got to her feet. "I will remember the rest of what happened to me, Curt, I swear I will. That man has to be stopped." Anger and determination brought color back to her cheeks and sparks of temper to her eyes. She'd never been more beautiful or precious to him.

"We're going to stop him." He loved her determination, but it frightened him, too. Genna had been just as sure that she could stop Hanover. He forced an easy grin. "But what do you say we have breakfast before we start plotting his downfall?"

Yvonne moved around the kitchen efficiently, even though her concentration wasn't on the omelet she was preparing. Not that she expected to be able to eat anything, anyway. She just didn't want Curt to worry—at least not about her.

She'd had plenty of time to think about Jackson's phone call as she bathed and dressed. Her initial anger had ebbed away as she realized the implications of what Curt had told her. Hanover had ordered a bomb to be delivered to BCM Investments! And it was all her fault. Hanover was willing to hurt or kill innocent people just to get at her.

She shivered, thinking of Sybil and Jackson. Their only crime had been helping a friend protect an injured stranger and now they could be in danger. And Curt! Her stomach knotted as the ugly images filled her mind. Knowing that she'd collapse in screaming hysteria if she let her imagination dwell on what Hanover might do to Curt for rescuing her, she did her best to force them away.

She had to do something to stop him, but what? Curt wasn't about to let her out of his sight and, truth be told, she didn't want him to. Yvonne leaned against the counter, staring out at the pool, but not seeing it. She'd known Curt such a short time, yet they'd shared so much, she felt as though she'd known him all her life.

"Hey, lady, if I'd wanted burned eggs, I'd have done the cooking myself." Curt's teasing tone brought her around. She'd been so busy worrying, she hadn't even heard him coming.

She could read the compassion in his dark eyes as he crossed the kitchen and took her in his arms. "Don't worry, Yvonne. We're going to get through this, I swear. Hanover's not going to kill anyone else I love."

Anyone else he loved. So he'd been thinking about Genna while he shaved and dressed. It was perfectly natural, so why was she surprised? Did she really think that their making love last night had erased his feelings for the woman he'd almost married? She hated herself for the flash of jealousy that swept through her, but it hurt to even think that someone else had known the wonder of his kisses, the magic of his...

She forced the incendiary images away, concentrating on what he'd said. Could "anyone else I love" mean that he now cared that deeply about her? Afraid that he might be able to read her need for his love in her eyes, she hid her face in his shirtfront for a moment, then tried for a light and teasing tone. "If you don't let me get to the stove, you may die of starvation. We're running too low on food to waste any."

"Maybe you'd better give me a list. I can make a quick run to the grocery store after breakfast. I don't want to take a chance on involving Sybil or Jackson anymore."

Yvonne eased the omelet from the pan, expertly transferring it to their plates, then adding bacon and toast. "Maybe you should just call the police and tell them what I've remembered. They could protect us and if everything was out in the open, Hanover would no longer have any reason to hurt you."

Curt's frown deepened. "Don't you trust me to protect you?"

"Of course I do." The question shocked her. "It's you that I'm worried about. And Sybil and Jackson and everyone else. What if he keeps sending bombs to people? I can't be responsible for his killing someone else."

Curt took the plates and set them on the table, then took her hands in his. "Look at me, Yvonne," he ordered, his tone solemn. "You are not responsible for what Hanover does. You were his victim. I'm going to tell Pete what you've remembered when he gets back tonight, but I'm not about to trust anyone else with your safety. You are the key to linking Hanover with the men on the jet and whatever they represent—that's why you're such a danger to him."

"I know that." She forced herself to meet his gaze, seeing the anger behind his concern. "I just don't want anyone else hurt."

"Then trust me a little longer, please."

She nodded, afraid to speak for fear she couldn't keep her feelings hidden. This was no time to burden him with the fact that she'd happily trust herself to him for the rest of her life. She couldn't tell him that she loved him, not until they were both safe and free of Hanover's threats.

Chapter 14

Yvonne moved restlessly through the house. It seemed so much larger now that Curt had left to get the groceries. Larger and emptier. She shook her head, amazed at her own reaction. She hadn't felt this alone since the first months after her divorce. But there was a difference—this time she craved just one man's company. She'd be fine as soon as Curt got back. Meantime, she'd just have to keep busy.

When the phone rang, she dropped the dirty clothes she'd been carrying to the laundry room all over the kitchen floor. Sure it had to be Curt, she grabbed the receiver and gasped a "hello."

"Yvonne?" Jackson sounded shocked to hear her voice.

Yvonne swallowed hard, suddenly remembering Curt's admonition about not answering the phone while he was gone. "Hi, Jackson."

"Is Curt there?"

"He's out getting some groceries. Could I help?"

There was a moment of silence, as though he might be weighing the wisdom of trusting her, then he sighed. "Just tell him that we finally got the report. It was a fair-sized letter bomb rigged to go off when the envelope was opened.''

"Then Hanover's really serious about forcing me out into the open. And he doesn't care who he hurts to do it."

"His message is pretty plain." Jackson's tone was surprisingly calm. "What you're remembering must be a real danger to him."

"And keeping me safe puts all of you in danger."

"Putting Hanover away just might be worth taking a few risks. Besides, nobody got hurt this morning and now we know what he's up to, it's not going to be so easy for him to try again. You tell Curt not to worry, I'll take care of things here."

"Oh, Jackson, I just—" Her throat closed over the sob that formed there and hot tears burned in her eyes. "I owe my life to all of you."

"We were glad to help, Yvonne. Tell Curt I'll give him a call later, if we get any more information." He was gone before she could tell him how much she appreciated what they'd done for her.

A letter bomb! She shuddered as she leaned against the counter. Though she'd never seen Curt's office and, except for Jackson, didn't know any of the people who worked there, she had no difficulty picturing what the bomb could have done. If it had been her office...

Gwen! The faces of her office staff filled her mind. How could she have been so stupid? If Hanover was willing to send a letter bomb to Curt's office, why not hers? Her hand shook as she reached for the receiver and punched in the familiar numbers. She had to warn Gwen of the danger before it was too late. As the call went through, she closed her eyes, praying that she hadn't waited too long.

"Realty Specialists, may I help you?" The voice was unfamiliar.

"May I speak with Gwen Verona, please." Her heart was pounding so loud she wondered if it was echoing over the lines to California.

"I'm sorry, Miss Verona is not available. May I ask who's calling?"

Yvonne controlled her urge to demand the name of the woman to whom she was speaking. Right now warning Gwen was all that mattered. ''This is Yvonne Worthington and it's essential that I get in touch with Gwen immediately. Do you have a number where I can reach her?''

''Miss Worthington? Oh, I'm sorry, I didn't know it was you. Miss Verona didn't tell me that you might call, but I'm sure she'd want me to get your number so she could call you back.''

''I'm at—'' Yvonne caught herself, swallowing hard. ''I'm sorry, I don't have a number where she can reach me. I'll have to call her. Are you sure she didn't leave a number?''

''She didn't, but if you want to try again later, I'm sure she'll have called in by then.''

''She's all right, isn't she?'' The question came out before she could stop it.

''Yes, ma'am, she's fine, just real busy since you've been on vacation. She'll be happy you called, I'm sure.''

Yvonne muttered the proper words courtesy required, then hung up the receiver, not sure whether she should be relieved or more concerned. Why would Gwen leave the office without giving a number where she could be reached? And who was the woman who'd answered the phone? Where were Janice and Faye?

As she slowly collected the clothes she'd dropped, her head spun. She'd been gone a week today and it seemed as though she'd been out of touch for years. She'd left so many deals in limbo, things that Gwen really wasn't well enough informed to handle. So why hadn't Gwen wondered about her sudden vacation? She groaned, getting her memory back seemed to have generated more questions than it had answered.

The phone rang again as she put the clothes in the washer, but this time she ignored it, having realized that Curt wouldn't be calling, since he'd told her not to answer the phone. Jackson was the only other person who had this number and he already knew Curt wasn't here. So it was probably a random, computer-dialed sales call. Unless it was Hanover. Or whoever had shot her.

Feeling trapped and abandoned, she turned off the security system so she could go outside. Why didn't Curt get back? He'd said he'd be gone about an hour and it was nearly that now. She wandered to the seven-foot block wall, following it around the edge of the property until the heat drove her back inside.

Should she have warned the stranger who'd answered the phone at her office about the danger of a letter bomb? She'd been so worried about reaching Gwen, she hadn't even thought of it at the time. Now she nibbled at her lower lip as she studied the phone. The woman would probably think she was crazy, but still . . .

Yvonne fixed a glass of iced tea and settled down at the kitchen table to wait for the washer to shut off so she could put everything in the dryer. She had to calm down and think logically; panic could lead to serious mistakes—the kind that would put Curt in worse danger.

Feeling more in control of herself and the situation, she considered her fears. Would Hanover bomb her office? If he thought she was in Phoenix, bombing Realty Specialists would be a waste of time. Besides, if he really meant to get rid of her, why destroy her company? Whatever plan he had for them taking over Ocotillo Mall could probably go ahead with Gwen in charge.

If she just disappeared, Hanover got everything he wanted. Gwen wouldn't do as good a job developing the mall, but if he just wanted to use it to launder money, it really wouldn't matter if the legitimate businesses were successful. All he needed was someone who would keep the spaces rented without asking too many questions about how they were used.

Her stomach knotted as she realized just how easily that could be accomplished. Gwen would be delighted to accept her friend Keenan's advice about tenants. As long as the profit margin was good and Keenan suggested other prospective properties, Gwen wouldn't suspect a thing.

Was that why he'd invited her out to his ranch? Had this whole thing been planned in advance? For a moment she honestly wasn't sure, then she remembered that, initially, he'd wanted to put off the meeting for a day; she'd insisted on seeing him immediately. And he had sent her away; it had been her choice to return to look for her watch.

That decided, she felt better, safer, then she realized that Hanover's original intentions made no difference at all. If she was gone, he'd be in charge. The thought chilled her.

Curt pulled into the driveway with a sigh of relief. He'd hated spending extra time making sure that he wasn't followed from the grocery store, yet he couldn't take any chances with Yvonne's life. It disturbed him to realize how precious she'd become to him. He really needed some time away from her to analyze his feelings, make sure that he wasn't getting in over his head, but the idea of her being here alone and vulnerable made every minute they were apart painful.

Once this was over and Hanover was behind bars, things would be different, he told himself as he picked up the sacks of groceries and started up the walk. The door opened before he reached it. His heart lifted at the proof that she'd been waiting for him, wanting to see him. Then he saw her face and nearly dropped the sacks.

"What the hell happened? Are you all right?"

"I'm fine, really. I just . . . You were gone so long and I started thinking . . . Well, all kinds of dumb things." An embarrassed flush rose in her cheeks, making her look far better than she had when she stepped out to take one of the sacks.

"You were worried about me?" He couldn't help grinning like an idiot at the idea that she cared so much.

"After what happened this morning, why wouldn't I be worried? Hanover tried to bomb your office, it's obvious he wants to hurt you." The words came out sharp, angry— mostly in reaction to his pleased grin. Did he enjoy scaring her to death? she wondered as she led the way to the kitchen.

"Now we're not sure..." Curt began, then let the sentence trail off as he realized that her agitation had to be more than just the result of being home alone for a little over an hour. "Did something happen while I was gone, Yvonne?"

Yvonne turned away, busying herself with the contents of the grocery sack. "Jackson called."

"What did he..." He gulped. "You answered the phone?"

"It was a reflex. I was carrying some clothes to the washer when it rang. I just..." She shrugged. "Jackson said to tell you that they had the report. It was a letter bomb and it could have done a lot of damage if he hadn't stopped your receptionist from opening it."

Curt cursed for a moment, then controlled his temper. "Did he say anything else?"

"Just that he'd call back later, if he heard anything more about it." She sighed. "He said he'd take care of things, for you not to worry."

"Right. That bastard Hanover goes after my friends and my company and Jackson says don't worry. Damn, but I wish Pete was here. The sooner he hears your description of the man from the jet, the better. I want to get this thing over before anyone else gets hurt."

Yvonne swallowed hard. He wanted it over so he could get back to his life. So why was she feeling bad? If it was over, she could go on with her life, too. Go on without Curt? The very thought made her heart ache.

"Hey, you can't let this get to you, Yvonne. It's going to be fine, really. Thanks to what you've remembered, we can get Hanover on a number of charges—kidnapping and attempted murder for instance, since he had you held against your will." He slipped his arms around her, pulling her close.

She rested her head against his chest, drawing strength from his nearness and the steady pounding of his heart beneath her cheek. "I'm just glad you're back," she told him as soon as she had her emotions firmly under control once more.

"Me, too." He pressed his lips to her hair for a moment, then forced himself to release her. "So let's put the groceries away, then we can take a swim before lunch."

"Good idea." Taking her cue from him, she banished all thoughts of the future, determined to concentrate on what they were sharing now. Being with him, loving him, feeling his warmth and caring—that had to be enough since the future was anything but secure.

As the day wound slowly toward evening, she rarely even thought about her call to Realty Specialists, which she knew would make Curt furious—if he found out about it. But then, why should she tell him? She hadn't given the woman there her number and she hadn't tried to call again. Like answering the telephone, it had been a moment of insanity, nothing more.

It was almost ten-thirty when the phone rang again. "That's probably Pete." Curt stopped the movie he'd rented at the supermarket and got to his feet. "This shouldn't take long, so leave me some popcorn." He kissed her lightly, then disappeared into the den, leaving the door open.

"'Bout time you got back down from the mountain," he growled when he heard Pete's voice.

"I should have known things would start getting interesting the minute I left town." Pete's tone was sober. "Are you okay? I talked to Jackson and he said the bomb looked like a warning, but I'm getting a different story from the guys assigned to investigate."

"Like what?" Curt sank behind the desk, suddenly wishing that he'd closed the door. He didn't want Yvonne to think he was trying to hide things from her, but he didn't want her scared, either.

"Somebody called in a tip about a disgruntled investor—someone named Newmark. That ring a bell?"

"Newmark?" Curt frowned. The name was familiar, but he felt no tingle of apprehension. "Yeah, I remember him. He was a client of my uncle's and a friend. We handled his investments for him after Bennett died."

"Are you still handling them?"

"No. Like the rest of us, he lost some money in the fall-out from the Savings and Loan mess, but we recouped most of it before he decided to pull out of the company. He didn't leave because he was unhappy with our handling of his funds."

"Do you know where he is now?"

"Not really. He left Arizona, I think. He was talking about going to Mexico and maybe getting into some development there. Said he wanted to live on the water, he was sick of the desert." Curt paused, poking at his memories. "You aren't taking this tip seriously, are you?"

"I'm not saying that I don't think the envelope came from Hanover, but it didn't exactly have his return address on it. And the fact is, Hanover would know that you weren't going to be hurt by it." Pete sounded worried.

"He'd also know that I'd come after him if something happened to Jackson or anyone else in my office."

"You don't think there's any possibility that this New-mark character could have a grudge?"

Curt sighed. "I couldn't guarantee it, but the timing is just a little too perfect, don't you think? It's been over a year since I've seen or heard from the man."

"Well, I'll have the police check out the Mexico connection and see what turns up, meantime . . ."

"Hey, I've got something a lot more important than that to talk to you about." Curt interrupted, quickly outlining for Pete everything Yvonne had remembered.

"She's sure she can identify the man?" Pete's voice was suddenly throbbing with excitement.

"She's positive. Does the description ring a bell for you?"

"It could be any of several people that have become in-volved in money laundering over the past couple of years. Let me get some police photos together and I'll bring them by first thing in the morning. If she can pick somebody out, we can get the ball rolling in a big way."

"You want to come here?"

"Unless you want to risk bringing her somewhere else. I need to be able to ask her questions, Curt, you know that. You can't keep her hidden away forever."

"I had no intention..." Curt let it trail off, realizing that Pete might be right. A part of him didn't want to let anyone else into the private world he and Yvonne were sharing. "Just make sure you aren't followed, okay?"

"I'll give you a call in the morning, let you know when to expect me." Pete paused for a moment, then added, "I'm real eager to meet your lady. Anyone who can hold your interest this long must be special."

Curt swallowed a sharp retort, well aware that any kind of denial would only convince Pete that he was right. "At least it's starting to pay off." He kept his tone amused.

"We'll know how well tomorrow. Keep trying for the other two passengers. Some of these guys are easier to peg by their associates."

"That's my buddy, never satisfied."

Pete's farewell came with a rumble of laughter and Curt replaced the receiver feeling far better for having talked to him. The more people who knew of Yvonne's memories, the better, so long as they could be trusted to protect her. His lazy grin as he rejoined her on the couch was completely genuine. The sooner this was resolved, the better.

And after it was over? He drew her into his arms. Did he really think he could just put her on a plane for Los Angeles and go back to work? The ache inside him made that a bad joke. He wanted Yvonne safe, but he sure didn't like the idea of giving up his role as he protector.

"So what's the latest?" Yvonne asked instead of restarting the VCR. "Have they found out anything more about the bomb?"

"They got a tip that it was a gift from a disappointed client." Curt watched her, curious to see what her response would be.

"Instead of Hanover?" Her frown deepened. "Is that possible?"

"Remotely, but not likely. The man they named was a good friend of my uncle's, so I doubt he'd bomb the company. I think it's just a red herring delivered courtesy of Hanover." He liked the fact that she seemed more angry than worried by the news.

"What about the man I remembered?"

"Pete's going to dig out photographs of some likely candidates and bring them by for you to look at tomorrow morning." He helped himself to a handful of popcorn, then added, "He may want to ask you a few questions."

"I'm sure he will." She sighed, settling her head on his shoulder. "I just hope I can remember a few more details between now and then."

"It'll come when it's ready." He tightened his hold on her, wanting to protect her from those memories and the pain that always seemed to come with them. "Meanwhile, how about we get back to the movie. Knowing Pete, he'll probably arrive at the crack of dawn."

Yvonne caught his hand as he reached for the remote control, sitting up to face him. "If that's the case, why don't we save the rest of the movie for tomorrow afternoon? We're going to need all the rest we can get."

"Rest?" He got his answer when he claimed her lips with a passionate kiss. She was definitely not sleepy. His head was spinning by the time he paused for breath.

"I'll take the tape out of the VCR, while you go set the security system." Yvonne's gaze smoldered. "Then I think I'd like a nice hot shower."

"A nice hot shower? I'm sure that can be arranged." Curt chuckled as he headed for the kitchen. He did love a woman who had her priorities straight. Or could he be falling in love with Yvonne? He didn't know the answer yet, but he had a suspicion that he was going to enjoy researching the feelings she ignited within him.

Yvonne watched him go, then sank back against the couch, uncomfortable with what she'd just done. Though she desperately wanted to spend this night in his arms making love, she knew that a part of her need was based in her fear that tonight might be the last time she'd be here alone with Curt. Once the police came into this, they would be the ones protecting her and Curt could return to his world.

She shuddered, wondering if she'd be able to bear it and sure that she must—no matter how much it hurt. He'd come into her life because she was a victim and needed him desperately; there was no way she'd ever use her need or weakness to keep him close. He had to love her freely and for herself or it would never be enough.

Keeping that in mind, she extracted the movie tape, turned out the living room lights and carried the remaining popcorn to Curt's bedroom. At least she had tonight with him; she meant to make the most of it.

Yvonne stirred and moved closer to the source of warmth. A heavy arm slid over her, pulling her firmly against a distinctly hairy body. She smiled, reveling in the rightness of being here, of waking in Curt's arms. Memories of their night of lovemaking tingled through her; never had she known such sweet passion or felt so complete. Curt's lovemaking satisfied far more than her body's aching need. He'd taught her to trust her heart and given her the will to love again—something David's betrayal had stolen from her.

"I'd like to spend the day just this way." Curt's warm breath tickled her neck.

"You might get hungry."

"I'd find something to nibble on." His love bites found the sensitive skin below her ear.

She couldn't help squirming as her own desire awoke. "I think there's still some popcorn left," she teased.

He groaned when the phone rang. "What do you bet that's Pete?" He licked the spot he'd nipped, then rolled over to pick up the receiver.

Yvonne started to get up, but he pulled her close again. She relaxed, content to rest against his chest while she listened to his side of the conversation.

"Really, that long.... Well, I guess we can find something to do until then.... Of course, I can see why you should wait.... We'll see you then."

"Has something happened?" Yvonne asked as his hands began a stimulating exploration of her body.

"He's waiting for a specific picture to be sent from the Miami area. He won't be out until noon at the earliest. He sends his apologies to you."

"I'll try to bear my disappointment," Yvonne murmured before the magic of his touch banished everything but the miracle of the fiery chariot of their love. For now she was totally his and he belonged to her. As one they made their ride through the glowing stars, then settled back to earth, lost in wonder and joy, content just to hold each other close.

They'd scarcely finished cleaning up after brunch, when the doorbell shrilled. Yvonne started toward the front of the house, but Curt waved her back. "I'll get it. If you hear anything odd, lock yourself in the security room and hit the alarm. And stay there until the cops come."

She wanted to protest, but his hard glare froze the words in her throat. In that moment, he banished the last vestiges of the tender magic they'd shared, reminding her forcefully of all the danger they still had to face. How could she have allowed herself to fall in love now? The answer was simple, she'd had no choice; it had been too late the moment Curt came into her life.

"It's okay, Yvonne. It's just Pete." His voice released her from the feeling of being suspended in time.

"Just Pete, huh! I resent that."

Yvonne looked up into sparkling eyes so dark they were nearly black. She controlled a gasp. Nothing Curt had said about his ex-partner had prepared her for his smoldering movie star handsomeness. When he grinned at her, his teeth flashed against his golden bronze skin and she felt herself smiling in response.

"So you're Yvonne." His eyes missed nothing as she smoothed the skirt of her sundress. "Or should I say, Miss Worthington? Curt's told me so much about you, I feel as though I know you."

She found his friendliness irresistible. "Yvonne, please, if I can call you Pete. I feel the same way."

"You want something to drink, Pete?" Curt interrupted, his expression strictly business.

"You got any coffee? I'm a quart low."

"I just put on a fresh pot and we have some muffins left from brunch, if you're hungry." Yvonne busied herself getting a mug from the cupboard, trying to ignore the blaze of heat that rose in her cheeks when she saw the knowing look that passed between Pete and Curt.

Men! Exactly what had Curt told his buddy? Or were their feelings obvious? As a modern woman, she should be able to shrug off her embarrassment—after all they'd done nothing wrong—but having an outsider know that they were lovers made her feel terribly vulnerable.

"Did you get the picture you were waiting for?" Curt filled all their cups while she set out the butter and the muffins.

"I have a half-dozen photographs, Yvonne," Pete said, producing a large brown envelope. "I'll lay them all out, then I'd like you to look at each one carefully. Give yourself all the time you need to be sure and don't worry if none of them are right. Unfortunately there are an awful lot of people involved in laundering money these days. We might not hit the right group the first time."

"I'm ready to look at them." Yvonne swallowed hard as her head wound began to throb. Not now, she wailed inwardly. She couldn't let the blackness stop her memories while Pete was here, not when she might finally be able to end the nightmare. She took a couple of slow, deep breaths as she waited for Pete to put all the photos on the table.

Curt caught her hand, wrapping his warm fingers around her cold ones. She could feel his strength surrounding her, helping her fight the encroaching blackness inside her head. As long as he held her hand, she was safe. She was glad when he moved to the table with her.

"Just focus on one at a time." Pete's voice was soft as he sat down across the table from the line of photos. "Take a good long look."

The photographs weren't great. The first looked like a blowup of a newspaper picture. The second seemed to have been snapped on a busy street and the third was poorly lit. Still, the faces were clear enough that she knew she hadn't seen them before. The fourth seemed slightly familiar, though not in any context she could place. She studied it for an extra moment, then moved on to the fifth.

It was him! Even though the picture showed him smiling, she still felt the impact of his cold eyes. "That's the one." She couldn't quite bring herself to touch the photo, but she managed to point it out. "He's the man on the stairs, the one from the jet that landed."

"What about the last picture?" Pete asked.

It was a pleasure to shift her gaze from the frightening image, especially when the last picture was that of a stranger. She shook her head. "Number four looks sort of familiar, but not from that night. Number five is the only one I saw there."

"Who is Number five, Pete?" Curt's arm slipped around her shoulders.

Pete picked up the photo and turned it over. "Mr. Paxton is a Bahamian banker who has prospered from operating a tiny money exchange stand in Nassau to owning one of the richest banks in the islands. All in less than ten years. A man of amazing talents, not the least of which seems to be his ability to avoid being seen anywhere he shouldn't be."

"Until now." Curt's tone was stern, but she could hear the excitement, could feel it in his accelerating heart rate.

Pete grinned as he picked up the rest of the photos. "By the way, Number four is a Vegas gambling kingpin. He gets into trouble often enough that you might have seen his picture in the L.A. papers."

"Of course." Yvonne winced as she made the connection. "I met him once. I think my ex-husband owed him money." She sank onto one of the wrought-iron chairs and Curt did the same.

"So what happens now?" Curt asked. "Can we get this guy?"

"That depends on a lot of things and a lot of people."
Pete sipped his coffee and looked directly at Curt.

"How so?"

Yvonne looked from one to the other, aware that they
were communicating in a way she didn't quite understand.
She found the sense of being shut out both frightening and
irritating. This was her life they were discussing. "What
things?" she demanded. "And what people?"

Pete's eyes stayed on Curt until he nodded slightly, then
Pete turned his gaze her way. "That particular photo was
hand-delivered this morning by a gentleman from Miami.
He's in a very special task force dealing with money laundering. He'd like your testimony as a part of a larger case
that he's working on."

"No." Curt's sharp refusal startled her. "We need to get
Hanover now, not some shadow banker in five years. I
know how these federal cases work."

Pete shrugged. "We're going to need cooperation from
them if you want to do more than just embarrass Hanover. He's not going to rollover and admit to anything and,
besides you, Yvonne's got no witnesses to anything that
happened to her."

Yvonne waited for Curt to protest, but he just sat there,
looking frustrated and angry. A chill slipped down her
spine. "But it's all true. I wouldn't make up something so
crazy. He had someone shoot me. They meant to kill me."

"Can you identify the shooter?" Pete's gaze probed her.

Her head throbbed viciously. "Not yet. I can't seem to
remember anything that happened after I fell on the stairs."

Pete swore softly, then looked at Curt. "You want to talk
to this guy?"

"You haven't given him Yvonne's name, have you?"
Curt had a lean, hungry look that made him a stranger to
her.

"No way. He doesn't even know for sure who you are,
though he may have been able to make the connection if he
took a look at the local papers." Pete's grin was bitter as he
set a newspaper on the table. "In one of the stories an

'unnamed source' accuses Hanover of being behind the bomb." Curt's picture smiled up at her.

"Jackson?" Curt didn't seem that disturbed.

"According to the bomb squad, he was a tad upset when they arrived." Pete seemed amused. "You want to talk to my man?"

Curt sighed. "Do I have a choice?"

"Not if you want this nightmare to end."

Yvonne shifted in her chair. Even though Curt still held her hand, she felt invisible. "What about me?"

"You stay here." Pete and Curt both spoke at the same time.

Yvonne looked from one to the other, her temper flaring. "It's my life you're talking about."

"Precisely why we want you safe." Curt reached out to touch her cheek, his fingers gentle. "Just trust me a little longer, Yvonne. Let me find out what he has to offer, then we'll decide what to do. Okay?"

When he looked at her that way, she couldn't argue. Besides, she suspected he was right. "When do you have to go?"

"I'll make a phone call and set it up." Pete headed for the phone.

Yvonne clung to Curt's hand, looking deep into his eyes, suddenly very much afraid of what might lie ahead. She'd wanted the nightmare to end, but what if emptiness was all that waited on the other side.

Chapter 15

She was alone again, but this time it was worse. This time it wasn't just the empty house that echoed around her, it was the fear that yawned inside her. Could Pete be right? Was it possible that Hanover would escape prosecution for what had been done to her? Just because she couldn't remember the person who'd fired the shot.

Ripples of terror shook her so hard she had to hang on to the edge of the table to keep from collapsing. What would happen to her if Hanover wasn't prosecuted? Would she have to run and hide the rest of her life or would they give up after a while?

Her panic was rising to the choking level. Knowing she had to get a grip on herself or end up lying on the floor screaming, Yvonne forced herself to her feet, got a glass of iced tea and picked up the newspaper that Pete had left behind. She carried them both into the living room.

Reading about the attempted letter bombing wasn't exactly soothing, but there was a photograph of the office building where BCM Investments was located and a sidebar story about Curt gave her some insights into just how

ugly things had gotten for him after Genna's suicide. She
understood now why he'd preferred to keep a low profile
where she was concerned.

Feeling better, she turned to the business section, curious to see if there were any related items there. A small
headline caught her eyes immediately.

Ocotillo Mall To Open Soon
New owner-developer Realty Specialists, Inc. of
Los Angeles, California, vows that the mall will be in
operation by the beginning of the tourist season.

There was more, but the words scarcely registered as she
scanned them. Gwen had gone ahead with the mall acqui-
sition! If she didn't stop her soon, Hanover would have a
line to her company and... Her head throbbed viciously at
the picture of all he could do. She headed into the den. She
had to stop Gwen!

The same woman answered her call, but this time she
recognized Yvonne's voice. "Miss Worthington, I'm so
glad you called. Miss Verona was frantic when you didn't
call back yesterday. She needs to talk to you most ur-
gently."

"So put me through."

"Oh, I can't. She's not in the office. She's in Arizona on
business. She's at the Scottsdale Desert Resort, Bungalow
Eight. Let me give you the number there."

Her fingers moved automatically, noting the number on
the pad beside the phone. Gwen was here, staying at the
same resort she'd been in. Gwen might even now be meeting with Diane Collins or with her friend Keenan Hanover.
As a full partner, Gwen had every right to sign the papers
to take over the mall. Especially since she no doubt thought
Yvonne had lost her mind. Nothing else would explain her
sudden vacation in the middle of a negotiation.

She closed her eyes, wishing mightily that Curt was here.
This was something he needed to know. But could she afford to wait? The article hadn't been specific about when

the papers were to be signed, but if Gwen was here... She punched in the numbers and held her breath, wondering what she was going to say to Gwen when she reached her.

The busy signal registered after several minutes. She replaced the receiver, then leaned back in the padded chair, closing her eyes against the headache—a genuine one this time—that had begun the moment she saw the article. She needed to decide what to tell Gwen—how much.

She tried the number every five minutes for the next half hour, her frustration growing with every try. Finally, unable to bear it any longer, she went to the window, looking out, hoping that she'd see Curt turning in. It was then that she realized the rental sedan was still sitting in the driveway. Curt had gone with Pete in his car.

Not sure exactly what she was going to do, Yvonne headed for the bedroom. The car keys were on the dresser, right where Curt had put them when he changed clothes after he got home yesterday. She picked them up, then tried the bungalow number one last time. It was still busy.

Since the rental came with a city map, getting to the resort wasn't difficult, but as she drove her fears began to grow. What if Hanover was at the resort? What if it was too late? What would Curt do when he got back to the house and found her note telling him to wait for her call?

She turned into the resort, noticing that the parking area near the main building was quite full. Her fears ebbed a little. This wasn't like the ranch, where she'd been totally at his mercy. There were plenty of people here. One scream and... She banished that train of thought. She definitely hoped there wouldn't be any reason to scream.

The area of the bungalows was much more deserted. Obviously with the end of the busy winter tourist season, most of the resort business was kept in the main building. Her stomach knotted as she headed for number eight. She'd just drive by. If there was more than one car parked there, she'd go back to the resort office and call again.

A small sedan, identical to the one she'd rented, sat in the parking space. She slowed, still not sure what to do. Why hadn't she stopped at the resort's main building and requested an employee to accompany her? As she watched, the drapes over the window stirred and she glimpsed a hand. Gwen was there, possibly waiting for someone!

She parked and jumped out of the car, hurrying across the desert landscaping. The door opened just as she reached it. A hard hand grabbed her arm and jerked her inside, slamming the door behind her.

"Gwen?" After the bright sunlight, the room was so dim, it took her eyes a moment to adjust so she could see.

"Guess again, Yvonne." The voice was male and familiar, even after five years.

"David!" It came out a squeak as the pounding in her head rose to a crescendo of pain, then shattered like black glass under the assault of memories. "It was you. At the ranch and then in the desert. You! You tried to kill me!"

The pictures filled her mind as she stared at the bearded stranger watching her with David's pale blue eyes. This was the face behind the gun in her nightmare. Her ex-husband, David Rogers, who'd arrived in the second car just as the two thugs were hitting her. She'd cried out to him, thinking he meant to save her from the beating, but instead he'd produced a gun, yelling at her tormentors to get out of his way.

"You look surprised, Yvonne. Why is that? You recognized me out there in the desert." He sighed, suddenly looking old and tired. "Good old, Yvonne. Always in the wrong place at the wrong time. Who would have thought that you'd get mixed up with a high roller like Hanover? I always thought you were such a straight arrow. Now I find out you like the good life every bit as much as I do. Too bad it's too late."

His smile sent a chill down her spine as she gasped, "I thought you were dead."

"That was the plan. You're looking at Roger Davidson, new identity, new man and no old debts to be paid back. I don't even gamble that much now. It's more fun playing for the high stakes as legal rep for a very profitable banking consortium in the Caribbean.''

"Paxton.'' The moment she said the word, she knew she'd made a mistake.

David's eyes narrowed and his fingers tightened on her arm. "Exactly how much do you and your nosy boyfriend know?''

The pain in her head was ebbing now, leaving her mind clear at last, but she winced at the reference to Curt. How much did they know about where she'd been the past week? "About what?''

"My boss.''

Maybe she could throw him off. "I just identified a photo for the police.''

"No, you didn't. The cops don't know zip about what happened. You've never been reported missing. Hanover's kept a good check on that. They don't even suspect that he's implicated. They're too busy chasing some phantom bomber.''

"Maybe your buddy Hanover doesn't know as much as he thinks he does.'' She tried to pull free of his hand, but his grip only tightened.

"He's no buddy of mine. Just a nice handy tool.'' David's chuckle chilled her. "A funnel, for money.'' His evil grin vanished to be replaced by a frown even more intimidating. "Now suppose you tell me exactly how much you've told that bastard who's been hiding you.''

Yvonne forced back her fear. What should she do? Would it be better if he thought Curt knew everything or nothing? Playing for time, she looked around the bungalow. "Where's Gwen?''

"Your greedy partner?'' The grin returned. "You do know how to pick them, don't you, Yvonne? She's back in L.A. making arrangements to accommodate the financial pipeline Hanover is about to insert into your precious Realty Specialists. That company is going to be worth millions in six months, too bad you won't be around to enjoy it.''

"She's in on this?" Her knees weakened at the thought of such a betrayal. She felt too sick to resist as he guided her to the couch and sat down beside her.

"She'd have to be pretty dumb not to figure out that the deal Hanover offered her is too good to be legitimate and, as I recall, Gwen's one bright lady."

"She didn't come here to meet with Hanover?" She had to ask, had to know the depths of her friend's betrayal.

"No need, he's sent a rep to work with her. The lady who gave you this number." His frown returned. "What took you so long, Yvonne? We've been expecting your call for a week."

She lifted her hand to the side of her head, touching the healing furrow the bullet had left. "Let me go, David. Too many people already know about what's happened, who's involved. If you kill me, they'll never give up."

"Don't you mean Macklin will never give up?" His gaze was mocking. "Don't worry, babe, I have plans for him, too. Unlike Hanover, when I'm asked to clean up a mess, I don't leave loose ends."

"What's that supposed to mean?" She stiffened. His smirk irritated her as much now as it had five years ago. He'd always thought he was so clever.

"The boss wanted a suicide pact last year. It would have been so much more practical that way. No Macklin left alive to make noises about his precious Genna. But Hanover was too squeamish." David sighed. "Clean disposal, all the loose ends gone, it's the only way to go—even Hanover understands that now. He'll have to be a cooperative funnel once he owes us for you and Macklin as well as tidying up the mess he made with the cop."

Yvonne stared at David, suddenly finding it hard to breathe. She didn't want to believe her ears. This couldn't be the man she'd married. Her David had been weak, but not evil. Surely not this evil. "You killed Genna?"

"Of course not." David glared at her. "I wouldn't have screwed it up that way. I just made the arrangements for Keenan, as a favor from my boss."

"Murder is a favor?" His lack of emotion was more frightening than rage would have been.

"It was a suicide according to the police. Poor woman was caught with drugs and couldn't handle the disgrace, so she killed herself. Sad case, but it happens. There's just so much money in drugs these days." For a moment she thought she saw a flash of something in his eyes, but it was gone before she could be sure. He glanced at his watch. "Time for you to call your boyfriend."

Fear knotted her stomach as she remembered the note she'd left. She had no doubt that Curt would be waiting by the telephone. Never had she wanted him more. "No way."

David's lip curled slightly. "Love, Yvonne?"

"I won't lead anyone into your trap, David, and nothing you can say or do will make me give you his phone number."

"Brave words." David's smile was cruel. "When you called back today, the stupid broad in L.A. finally remembered to activate the device we installed, so we have your phone number."

Her stomach twisted and nausea burned in her throat as David dragged her across the room to the telephone, which was off the hook. He replaced it, then dug a piece of paper out of his pocket. Her heart dropped as she recognized the phone number.

"He won't be there," she stated, praying that she was right. "He was busy meeting with the police to set them on your trail."

David chuckled as he held the receiver to his ear for a moment, then extended it to her. Tears burned in her eyes as she recognized the desperation in Curt's voice as he called her name. It took all her self-control to keep from answering him.

David swore, then reached out and grabbed her hair, yanking it viciously. She couldn't keep back a scream. His smile chilled her.

"Did you hear that, Macklin? That was Yvonne. She didn't want to talk to you, but I thought you'd like to hear her voice."

"What have you done to her?" Curt's voice was thick with rage and fear.

"Nothing too painful as yet. That could change, however, if you aren't at the Hanover Ranch within the next hour and a half. And you'd better come alone and unarmed. You know how easy it is to watch the road in. You come, you get to see her one more time. You bring company or a gun or get there late and you can pick up the pieces." David gave her arm a twist, making her cry out again. "Do I make myself clear?" He hung up on Curt's threats.

David dragged her off the bed. "Time to go, Yvonne. Give me your car keys. We wouldn't want to be late to our meeting with your lover, now would we?"

She stiffened her body, fighting his pull on her arm. She had to stop him. If she screamed maybe...

The knife appeared in his hand as if by magic. He brought it up to her cheek, touching the tip against her skin. "Don't make me cut you, Yvonne. I really don't want to hurt you, but I will if I have to. Just come quietly and I'll make sure you don't suffer. Give me trouble and your lover will be the one to pay. He'll be there, you know. And if you're already dead, he's going to be a long time joining you."

She wanted to doubt him, but when she looked into his eyes, she knew that he was perfectly capable of such evil. In a very real sense, the man she'd married had died in a boating accident; this man was a stranger to her. She offered no resistance as he escorted her to the sedan, handcuffing her hands behind her back before he drove away from the resort. She felt as though a part of her had already died.

Curt felt the sweat trickling down his spine as he drove Pete's unmarked car along the highway. Even with the air conditioner going full blast, he was sweating. Fear did that, along with the images that filled his mind every time he remembered the cries he'd heard. And that mocking voice.

Who the hell had her and what were they planning? And most important, how could he stop them? Pete would do what he could, but there was no way he could get close to the ranch without being spotted. His belly knotted. He was driving into a trap with his eyes wide open, but he couldn't turn away—not while Yvonne's life was at stake.

The tires screamed in protest as he spun off the highway and bounced along Indian Cliffs Road. The car shimmied wildly, but he fought the wheel, keeping his speed up. No way was he going to be too late this time.

Yvonne leaned back in the seat of the small plane. This was the last thing she'd expected. David had driven directly to the small airport where the plane and pilot were waiting, now they were flying toward the Superstition Mountains. The scene below was beautiful and the pain of all she was going to lose made her eyes burn with tears. She blinked them back, refusing to cry in front of David.

To distract herself from the deep pain of having dragged Curt into a trap, she asked, "What are you going to do to us, David?"

"Why nothing, my dear." His smile was malicious. "The truth is, you two lovebirds are going to have a fatal car accident up in the mountains. One that probably won't be discovered for several weeks since no one will have any idea that you were out there exploring." He shook his head. "Sad, two lovers out in the mountains for an afternoon drive and they just never come back."

Protests rose in her throat, reasons why he shouldn't do this, pleas for decency, promises... But she kept her lips closed. One look into his eyes told her that there were no words that would change his mind. He was just doing his job—a job that he apparently enjoyed. Shuddering, she looked out the window. Not far below she could see the ranch house and off in the distance the blackened face of the cliff that had once sheltered Curt's cabin. She felt the irony of returning to the place where it had all begun.

Yvonne looked around as they entered the rear door of the ranch house. First David had sent the plane away, now the house seemed empty of life. Not that she'd expected a brass band, but somehow she'd thought that a whole group of men with guns would be waiting for them. "Where is everyone?"

"You want me to call those two creeps that were slapping you around last week?" David seemed amused. "Or were you hoping for a bunch of cops in ambush?"

She swallowed hard, aware that she had been hoping for something like that. "Actually, I thought Hanover might be here to take notes on your cleanup methods."

David chuckled. "I'm glad you haven't lost your sense of humor, but don't worry about Hanover. He's arranged to be out of state on very visible business today."

"Naturally."

"We won't be lonesome for long. And I do have people watching the place, so forget reinforcements for your boyfriend. They tell me he's on his way and he appears to be alone. If he is, I may even give the two of you a few moments to say your goodbyes before we get you ready for your accident." He was obviously enjoying his power over her.

"Then what?"

"You really don't want to know, Yvonne." His gaze grew cold. "Let's just say you won't be staying here long enough to get attached to the place and once we're safely away from here, well, your destination won't matter."

She shivered. He was too sure of himself, of his plan; it frightened her. Still, she had to try to do something. She wasn't going to die whimpering. "Please take off the handcuffs, David, my wrists hurt."

He reached out a hand and lightly stroked her cheek. "Poor baby, you never were very good at lying. I could always read your intentions in your eyes. I never did understand how you could be good at real estate."

"That's because you never understood that I didn't have to lie to my clients. I didn't cheat people." Her skin crawled where he'd touched her.

"Still the moral indignation." He shook his head. "And to think I actually thought you might grow up. You never did live in the real world, Yvonne, so you're probably lucky to be escaping it."

"Now you're doing me a favor by killing me?" Her temper flared hot, banishing her fears.

"Would you rather spend your life running from Hanover's goons, while he and Gwen turn your company into a money machine?"

"I'd like to live knowing that you and all your friends were going to jail because of what you'd done to me and to Genna." She glared at him, wishing that her hands were free so she could attack him. For the first time in her life, she felt the urge to actually kill someone.

David laughed as he moved to the window. "I see a cloud of dust on the horizon, so I expect that's your lover. He must drive like a maniac. I figured we'd have at least another five or ten minutes to chat."

Yvonne gasped as she saw that David now held a gun in his hand. For a moment sheer terror made her whole body shake. Was that the gun he'd used to shoot her? She closed her eyes, fighting the blackness that threatened to engulf her. She couldn't give in to her fear now; she had to be strong and help Curt. Curt would have a plan—he had to!

"What's the matter, Yvonne? You remember my gun, don't you? Did you really think I'd just bring a knife to this meeting? I know your lover used to be a cop—there's no way I'm going to give him a chance." His face was as totally devoid of expression as a mask.

She stayed where she was, huddled near the dining-room door. Where would Curt come in—the front door or the back? He couldn't know that David was alone here, so he'd probably be expecting gunmen everywhere. Would he be armed? She couldn't believe that he'd come unarmed; he had to know that they were both marked for death.

"Damn it, Yvonne, do I have to shoot you now?" David's tone had an edge of irritation.

"Won't that mess up your car accident scenario?" Knowing that Curt was near made her reckless. If David shot her now, Curt would hear the sounds and know that he was too late. Maybe he'd be able to escape.

"Stupid bitch!" David came striding toward her, but she scarcely saw him. Her gaze was on the window, the car skidding to a stop outside. A desperate plan began to form in her mind.

"Sure, you're a big man with a gun, aren't you, David? Is that what attracted you to your new line of work? Just being a lawyer wasn't exciting enough, was it? You always needed more. Is this your new form of gambling—playing for big stakes with other people's lives? Does it make you feel like a man?"

He was swearing now, oblivious to what was happening outside. Yvonne concentrated on his bulging eyes, moving away from him, continuing her taunts as she tried to keep his back to the door. If only Curt would hurry; if only he heard her words and realized what was happening; if only...

She was still alive! That was Curt's first thought as he heard Yvonne's taunting voice. He'd made it in time. They hadn't killed her. He inched up to the living-room window and cautiously peeked inside.

Where was everybody? The place seemed almost deserted. Of course, there was room to hide an army in the house, but— His heart stopped as he saw Yvonne across the room, backing away from a man with a gun. She was shouting, her eyes flashing fire as she tanted him.

"Curt doesn't need a gun to feel like a man or to make me feel like a woman. He's a great lover. He made me realize just what a lousy lover you were. Isn't that ironic, David, you try to kill me and the man who rescues me turns out to be the man of my dreams. I guess maybe I should thank you."

What the hell was she doing, trying to get herself killed? For a moment, his fear turned to anger, then he realized what she was up to. She was distracting the man! Which must mean there was no one else in the room.

She'd pushed him too far, Yvonne realized as David lunged at her, his face red with fury. Trying to twist away, she caught her foot in the leg of an end table and staggered wildly as his fist crashed against her jaw, cutting off her scream and sending her hurtling into darkness.

Praying that he'd read Yvonne right, Curt raced back to the car, started it and gunned the engine as he headed for the window he'd just looked in. Curt rolled out of the car just before it plowed into the house with an explosion that shattered the desert quiet. Curt leaped through the broken glass and splintered wood, looking around frantically for Yvonne.

The bearded man straightened up, shooting. Curt felt the sharp burning in his side, but he was already rolling behind the overturned sofa. Where the hell was Yvonne? The terror that raged through him didn't slow his hand as he reached into his boot for the small gun Pete had loaned him.

"You're going to die for this, Macklin." The man shouted.

"You didn't invite me out here to talk." Curt edged along, ignoring the pain and the hot seeping blood. Where was Yvonne? What if he was too late!

He picked up a piece of broken wood and sent it rolling back toward the car, then eased forward trying to see through the opening between the couch and an ornate chest. The man had moved, but where? The hair on the back of his neck prickled and he lunged forward, sliding awkwardly into the space between couch and chest. Shots thudded into the spot where he'd been.

Guessing at where the shots had come from, Curt kept moving. The pain from his side was getting worse and so was the volume of blood flowing from it, which meant he didn't have a whole lot of time before he blacked out. A sound alerted him and he gripped the gun with both hands, rolling over just in time to see the man aiming in his direction. He squeezed off two quick shots, then rolled back the way he'd come.

Another shot echoed through the room, then silence. Curt waited, every sense quivering. Where was he? Was it a trick? Slowly, painfully, he eased back around the end of the couch and peered into the shadows. A dark shape lay huddled between couch and wall. Dead, injured or playing possum? Checking the man was the only way to find out and he'd have to chance it now, while he could still shoot.

Curt edged along the floor carefully, trying hard to spot the gun. The man didn't move, not even when he reached out to touch him. Curt felt along the side of his neck, seeking a pulse, then rested his fingers over his mouth. Nothing!

Still not trusting his luck, he edged the body over and saw the two bullet holes in the man's chest. Feeling sick and weary, he pulled himself to his feet, wavering as the pain increased and dizziness made the room spin. "It's okay, Yvonne, he's dead. You can come out now."

The silence seemed to eddy around him like a chill wind. Nothing moved and the only sound was the creaking and groaning of the wounded house and battered car. He called again, a fresh surge of adrenaline giving him the strength to leave the couch and make his way across the room to where he'd last seen Yvonne.

She was lying on the floor, half under an overturned table. Fear gnawed at him, but he clenched his teeth and knelt awkwardly beside her. If that bastard had . . . His fingers pressed the delicate skin beneath her jaw and the relief was almost too much. Her pulse was strong and normal.

Shaking, he pushed the table out of the way, seeking for visible wounds, but he couldn't find any. He shook her, trying to rouse her, but she remained limp and unconscious. Muttering curses, Curt limped back to the car and eased into it, reaching for the radio, praying that it was still in working order.

When Pete answered his call, he had just enough strength to ask for paramedics before the darkness overwhelmed him.

The pain woke him. He was being attacked. The bearded man was trying to kill Yvonne and he had to...

"Damn it, Curt, if you don't lie still, I'm going to handcuff you." Pete's voice penetrated the nightmare and he stilled instantly.

"First you turn my car into junk, then you screw up the bandage." Pete's tone was as gentle as his hands.

Curt opened his eyes, memories flooding back. "Yvonne?"

"She's on her way to the hospital already. They couldn't find any sign of injury, but since she was unconscious and had a recent head injury, they didn't want to take any chances. I told them you were tough enough to ride in with us." Pete's grin was so wide, Curt knew just how worried he'd been.

"What about the shooter?"

"Dead. You're still a damned good shot."

"What about the rest of Hanover's boys?"

"We picked a couple off that cliff you used to be so fond of and there were a couple more in a gully near the road. We spotted them from the chopper and called in the locals to pick them up. I don't know what we can charge them with, but maybe Yvonne will be able to identify them."

"If he hurt her..." Curt tried to sit up, then gasped as the pain in his side expanded.

"You ready for a chopper ride?" Pete's strong arm helped him to his feet, then kept him there as the room tilted. "The paramedics said the bullet went through clean and nothing vital was hit, but you've lost quite a bit of blood, so you can make your statement at the hospital."

"I just want to see Yvonne."

"If she saw you now, you'd probably set back her recovery. You look like hell." Pete helped him out of the battered living room to where a helicopter waited.

"That's pretty much how I feel, too." Curt leaned against his friend, grateful for the help.

"At least you made it in time."

Curt nodded, then closed his eyes. For the moment, that was enough.

Chapter 16

Yvonne leaned back and closed her eyes, fighting frustration and weariness. Two hours they'd been at it! Two hours of going over every minute of yesterday, repeating every statement David had made, describing over and over exactly what had happened from the time she arrived at the bungalow until David's fist had sent her into darkness.

"Are you all right, Yvonne?" Curt's worried tone forced her to open her eyes.

"Just tired." She looked at him, then away, afraid of what he might read in her eyes—or of all that she wouldn't see in his.

When had it all changed? He'd been at her hospital bedside when she awoke last night. He'd held her and kissed her and told her over and over how glad he was that she'd survived. Then the doctor had ordered him out and she hadn't seen him again until this morning, when he'd come in with the two men who'd been questioning them both.

Was it because he'd found out that she'd betrayed his trust with her first call to Gwen? Was he angry because she hadn't told him about it? She'd seen the shock in his face when she'd told the two men about her calls and about Gwen's involvement in Hanover's schemes.

"We just have a few more questions," the taller of the two men told her. He'd introduced himself as Smith and his partner as Jones, a pair of fake names, if she'd ever heard them.

Yvonne forced herself to sit up straighter, adjusting the pillows on the hospital bed. This had gone on long enough. "I've told you everything that happened."

"Do you have a note or anything from Mr. Hanover that would indicate that you were invited to his ranch the night you claim the attempted murder took place?" This was the third time Mr. Jones had asked that question.

Yvonne gave him a cold stare. They'd probed her memories of her first day in Phoenix as completely as her description of yesterday's events. She was thoroughly sick of all of it. She just wanted to finish the whole sorry episode, so she could begin to live like a normal person again. Could start exploring the new feelings that had developed between her and Curt and...

Aware that Jones was expecting a reply, she forced herself to focus on his question. "I would have told you if I did. Perhaps if you checked with Diane Collins, she could give you more information. As I said, she escorted me around that day, introduced me to prospective tenants, that sort of thing. Perhaps Mr. Hanover told her..." She let it trail off, sick to death of repeating herself. "I don't know what you want me to say, gentlemen. I can only tell you what happened, what I did, what Hanover did. I don't invent things."

The two men exchanged meaningful glances, something else they had been doing with disturbing frequency. Yvonne frowned. When they'd come to her hospital room with Curt, she'd assumed that they were policemen, but now she was beginning to wonder. "You know," she began, "I never did ask exactly who you work for. Are you with the Phoenix Police Department?"

Silence was her only answer. To her surprise, both men turned to look at Curt. Her stomach knotted. What was going on here? "Curt?" Her voice sounded a little high and frightened, but she couldn't help that. She definitely didn't need weird now, not after everything that had happened.

"These gentlemen are part of a special task force that has been looking into money laundering. They were hoping that you would be able to help them make their case against Paxton, by giving them Hanover." Curt's tone was flat, his mouth hard as though he was holding in some kind of anger.

Sensing there was more going on here than she was being told, Yvonne continued to press for answers. "I've told you that Paxton came to meet with Hanover, what more do you want?"

Mr. Smith sighed. "You've told us a large number of things, but unfortunately, we have only your word for most of them."

"You don't believe me?" She was stunned.

"Frankly, we believe every word you've told us," Mr. Jones assured her. "The problem is, you have no proof."

"Proof?" Anger boiled up. "How do you think I ended up here? I was almost killed—twice. You've heard Curt describe what happened to me at the ranch yesterday, and I'm sure the doctor would be happy to supply you with medical descriptions of the bullet wound on the side of my head, so..."

Mr. Jones consulted his notes for a moment, then flipped the notebook closed. "We're not disputing your injuries, Miss Worthington. It's simply that you admit they were inflicted by your ex-husband. You tell us that he was employed by Paxton, but we have no proof of that. Mr. Hanover claims that Davidson, or Rogers, broke into his house illegally yesterday. That everything that happened was merely a ploy by unscrupulous men who wished to use it to blackmail him into laundering drug money. Something he claims he's never done."

"And you believe him?" Yvonne felt as though the ground had been cut from under her.

"No, but he has a half-dozen people who were at his house that Tuesday night and they all say that you weren't there." Mr. Smith's gaze was faintly mocking.

"But I met..." She let the protest die. "They're part of it." It wasn't a question.

"Most likely potential investors in companies that Hanover plans to finance with the drug money." Mr. Jones seemed pleased that she'd grasped the obvious.

Her anger began to change into something close to fear. "What about the men who tied me up and kept me in the guest bedroom? The ones who were beating me out in the desert when David came after me."

"No one has been able to find them," Curt answered for them. "I gave Pete the descriptions, but my guess is that Hanover sent them out of town the next morning. Word is, he's not real tolerant of failure."

"And the men David said were watching the ranch?"

Mr. Jones's short bark of laughter held no humor. "You mean the cowhands who were out looking for strays? They were very disturbed to learn that someone had broken into the ranch while they were busy."

Yvonne sank back against the pillows. This couldn't be happening. She'd nearly lost her life because she'd wanted to remember what had happened and now that she knew it all, it seemed Hanover was trying to change the facts.

"What about Gwen?"

Jones shook his head. "We'll be scrutinizing every deal she's made, but my guess is that this one was to be the beginning of her relationship with Hanover."

Yvonne groaned in frustration.

"I'm sorry, Miss Worthington. Believe me, we'd be very happy if you could give us even one shred of proof of what you've told us, but as it stands, Hanover comes out looking like a victim of the man Macklin shot. We'll definitely follow up on the leads you've given us, but until we are able to prove a link between Hanover and Paxton, our advice would be for you to try to get into the witness protection program." Mr. Smith stood up. "Perhaps at some later date, if we can find a corroborative witness, you could be called to testify."

Mr. Jones rose as well, putting his notebook into his briefcase. "I'm sorry, Miss Worthington, Macklin. We really thought this might be the link we needed, but with nothing to refute the testimony of the other guests..." He didn't even look her way before he followed Smith out the door. "We'll be in touch."

Curt clenched his fists as he watched Yvonne's face grow pale. Why the hell hadn't he been able to protect her from this? He'd spent a couple of hours with the Feds after the doctor threw him out of Yvonne's room last night and they'd assured him that Yvonne could be protected until time for her to testify. They hadn't said anything about a permanent new identity.

"Curt?" The terror in her voice broke through his anger and he hurried to her bedside, ignoring the steady throb from his bandaged side.

"Don't be scared." He edged onto the bed beside her, pulling her into his arms, stroking her hair. "It's going to work out. We'll find some way to nail Hanover. He's not going to get away with hurting you, too."

She pressed her face against his chest, drawing in the soothing scent of his body, concentrating on the steady pounding of his heart. She would be safe as long as he held her. And how long would that be? The chill of Smith's words moved into her heart.

"Why did he say I should enter the witness protection program? What did he mean?"

Curt ground his teeth for a moment, hating the two Feds for leaving him to deliver the bad news, yet knowing that he wouldn't have allowed them to tell her without him. She needed his strength, his love to cling to. Almost as much as he now realized he needed her.

"Curt?" Yvonne pulled away, frightened by his silence and the desperation she sensed in his embrace.

"You are the only person who can link Paxton and Hanover, Yvonne. Whether you have proof or not, you saw them together and they know it. There's no way they can let you go on telling people about it." Curt's dark eyes were bleak. "Paxton might not care, but a lot of Hanover's power comes from his reputation as a businessman. If the truth comes out..." He didn't have to finish.

Yvonne stared at him, the sickness closing her throat. The nightmare wasn't over at all—it was just beginning! She swallowed hard, fighting the waves of horror that set her to trembling. Though the main question in her mind had to do with abandoning the magic they'd just discovered, she couldn't bring herself to put that into words. Instead, she focused on the obvious. "But what about my company, my life? I can't just walk away from everything. I don't want to be anyone else!"

Her wail of protest tore through him with far more impact than yesterday's bullet had. Her pain wrenched at his guts, becoming his. He crushed her to him. He couldn't let her go! They'd just found each other. They'd fought so hard to survive everything that had happened to them and, against all odds, they'd made it. No way was he going to let Hanover win. He'd already had to accept the fact that there wasn't enough evidence to try the man for Genna's murder; he wouldn't let the man destroy what he and Yvonne had discovered.

But how could he stop him? He controlled his emotions, forcing himself to think like a cop. "There has to be something, some way we can prove you were there that night. That's all we really need. Just enough evidence to destroy the credibility of Hanover's witnesses. What about the servants? Do you think any of them would testify?"

Yvonne closed her eyes, forcing back the waves of fear so she could concentrate. She remembered four different women. The youngest a girl who'd taken her stole and purse, then appeared from time to time to clear away the dirty glasses and dishes. Two slightly older women who had tended the buffet table and served the drinks and toward the end of the evening, she'd glimpsed another, older woman in the kitchen.

"Do you remember them?" Curt prompted, not because he really thought that they'd testify against Hanover, but because he wanted to believe there was hope.

"They were all Hispanic, very quiet, polite. I'm sure I'd recognize them again." Yvonne paused, considering her memories. "But I don't think they'd help me. They seemed very timid, like they were afraid of Hanover or of losing their jobs. I know, when I came back to look for my watch, I—" She stopped, gasping as she realized that she hadn't told Smith and Jones everything, probably because their questions had been focused on what happened to her later, not how she'd gotten into the mess. "I forgot all about not finding my watch!"

"Do you think it's possible it's still there?" Curt met her gaze, reading the brilliant light of hope in her eyes. Though his experience told him to be cautious, he couldn't help responding to it.

"I was searching the guest bedroom when I heard the plane and I sort of forgot about it. If it was still there... Would that be enough proof, Curt? If the police could find my watch upstairs at the ranch, wouldn't that prove that I was there?"

Curt considered for a moment, then nodded. "If Jackson, Sybil and I all testified that we noticed that you didn't have the watch when I brought you to the house, it just might be enough—if it's still out there."

"I know Sybil will remember that I didn't have it. I was always complaining about not knowing what time it was." Hope had set her heart to pounding so hard, she was sure Curt could see it through her thin hospital gown.

"And Jackson will remember that I stated you had no jewelry when I found you." Curt took a deep breath, trying hard to keep his objectivity. "Is the watch distinct enough for you to be able to identify it?"

"It's engraved to me with love from my parents on my twenty-fifth birthday." Tears burned in her eyes. "Oh,

Curt, it has to be there, either in the bedroom or the up-stairs bath.''

Curt tightened his arms again, then bent his lips to hers. He'd meant the kiss to be light and reassuring, but his desperate longing drove him to deepen it. When he finally forced himself to free her lips, he was shaking inside. "If it's there, we'll find it. I'll call Pete and see about getting a search warrant right away. You just hang on. We're going to get that bastard yet!"

"Be careful." He was gone before the words left her mouth.

Yvonne settled back against the pillows, torn between hope and despair. The witness protection program! The words chilled her, though all she knew about it came from watching television. Would she be forced to leave everything and everyone behind, to become someone else and live forever in hiding? How could she even consider leaving Curt? The prospect was too horrible to contemplate when her lips still tingled from his kiss.

Remembering his kiss eased some of her fears. At least he still wanted her, cared about what happened to her. But was that enough? She'd seen his face when she repeated David's words about Hanover ordering Genna's murder. How much of his excitement about finding her watch came from his desire to keep her around and how much was motivated by his need to make Hanover pay for his crimes? It scared her to realize that though she knew she loved him, she still wasn't sure how he felt about her.

"I did everything but tear up the tile, Curt. There is no watch in that bathroom." Pete stood in the doorway of Hanover's guest bedroom, looking every bit as frustrated as Curt felt. "How are you doing?"

"I've looked everywhere it could have fallen." Curt sank onto the bed, too sick and weary to even curse. "What the hell could have happened to it?"

"Hanover found it and got rid of it." Pete's tone held more sympathy than his words.

"According to what the Feds dug up, he left before dawn Wednesday morning and hasn't been back to the ranch since. Do you think he turned it up while he was entertaining Paxton?" Even though his head told him the watch wasn't in the house, Curt couldn't give up. It was Yvonne's only hope.

"Someone must have found it." Pete met his gaze squarely. "Hey, man, you know I want Hanover as bad as you do, but if it isn't here..."

"Someone." Curt leaped to his feet. "Like a maid?"

Pete frowned. "You think his help picked it up and took it home?"

"Maybe." Curt hesitated, then headed for the night table, opening the drawer that he'd ignored earlier. It was empty. So was the first drawer of the dresser, but the second wasn't. A neatly folded, brown and gold lace stole was in the drawer and, on top of it, someone had placed a woman's watch. "Bingo!"

"Don't touch it!" Pete's warning was unnecessary.

"Come on, I'm no civilian. Call in your photographers and the print boys. I want this all neatly tied up with a blue ribbon when we present it to the Feds."

Pete peered at the watch. "You think she can prove that's hers? It looks like a lot of other watches."

"If there's an inscription on the back, it is. She said it was a gift from her parents. My guess is, the stole is Yvonne's, too. The maid probably came in to clean Wednesday and found the stole lying in the room somewhere, so she put it away. When the watch turned up, she just added it to the pile. Like you said, it's not that distinctive. She probably forgot to even mention it to Hanover."

"So give your lady a call and ask her to describe the watch." Pete's indulgent grin told him that he probably looked like a kid on Christmas morning, but he really didn't much care. He'd lived too long with fear and misery. He headed across the hall to what had to be Hanover's bedroom and dialed the number of the hospital. He could hardly wait to make Yvonne feel as good as he did.

* * *

Yvonne closed the paperback novel with a sigh and got up to pace. Her hospital room was rapidly becoming a prison. Where was Curt? She hadn't heard from him since his excited call yesterday afternoon. He'd promised to come by as soon as he could, but it was now nearing evening and she was still alone.

A tap on her door made her heartbeat quicken. It had to be Curt. She turned with a smile as the door opened. Her joy died as Mr. Smith entered carrying a suitcase. Yvonne took a step back, suddenly deeply afraid.

"What's going on?" she asked, hating the way her voice shook.

"A friend of yours packed up your belongings and brought them to the police. I thought you might like to have them." Smith put the case on the bed and opened it.

Yvonne relaxed slightly when she recognized the clothes that Sybil had bought for her. "Where's Curt?" she asked.

"Safe." Smith's gaze was unreadable.

Anger flooded through her. She'd had more than enough of being kept in the dark. It was time for some answers. "You have your proof that I was at Hanover Ranch. When can I go home?"

"A month, maybe six weeks." Smith's small, tight smile chilled her. "We're building our case now."

"What do you mean? I can't stay here that long. I thought if you had proof you could arrest Hanover and I'd be safe." She had to sit down, her knees refused to support her.

"I'm afraid you won't be safe until your testimony is on the record, Miss Worthington. I'm here to tell you that we're making arrangements for your protective custody now. Your business will be overseen and you'll be safe. We'll move you out of here shortly. That's why I've brought your things. When everything is set, you'll have to move quickly."

"I'm not going anywhere." Her anger boiled over. "I've been pushed around and nearly killed and the only thing I'm guilty of is being in the wrong place at the wrong time.

I want my life back. I want to see Curt." There was more, but she could feel the sobs filling her throat, so she stopped. No way was she going to cry in front of the stone-faced Smith.

"I'm sorry for you, Miss Worthington, but there is nothing I can do. You have to be protected. If we let you walk out of here on your own, you won't survive twenty-four hours. You know too much." He looked like a man used to delivering bad news.

"What about Curt?"

"He's no longer in Phoenix. It was deemed in his best interest to remove him from the area. You will both be hidden in separate locations until the trial." Smith sighed, then looked around. "Please go through the contents of the suitcase and if there is anything else you'll need, let me know. I'll be in touch." He was gone before she could protest.

The next twenty-four hours were the longest and worst she'd ever lived through. She saw no one but the guard on her door and the nurse who brought her meals, neither Smith nor Jones came by. Her phone had been removed, so she couldn't call anyone. It was as though the outside world had ceased to exist—or she had.

Fear and doubt tormented her. Where had Curt gone? And why hadn't he at least come to tell her "goodbye"? Or had he gone? What if something had happened to him and Smith and Jones had decided not to tell her? Dozens of terrifying scenarios suggested themselves as she prowled the confines of her room.

Was her life going to be like this until the trial? And what if Hanover got off? What if her testimony wasn't enough? She resumed her pacing until time to go to bed.

She hadn't been asleep long, when a soft sound woke her. Though the hospital was never totally quiet, she'd grown accustomed to the normal night noises; but this was different. She tensed, opening her eyes slowly. Someone was in her room! Terror held her paralyzed for a moment, then her anger banished the fear and she drew in a deep breath, ready to scream for her guard.

"It's me, Yvonne. Don't scream." Sybil's whisper stopped the scream in her throat.

"Sybil?" She sat up, staring at the white-clad figure beside her bed.

"I've come for you. Is your suitcase packed?" Sybil looked around the room. "Don't turn on a light."

"The suitcase is in the closet. Everything is in it but the clothes I left out to wear tomorrow and the things in the bathroom." Yvonne didn't move from the bed. "What's going on?"

"I don't have time to explain now. Will you trust me? Jackson's waiting with a car outside the hospital, but we have to go soon and we have to do it without being seen." Sybil's voice quivered with excitement. "I've brought you a nurse's uniform, too. Put it on while I pack the rest of your clothes. The guard will be called away from his post again in about twenty minutes giving us just enough time to get you out of here."

Yvonne took a deep breath. Did she trust Sybil and Jackson? The answer was obvious, she trusted them a whole lot more than she trusted Smith and Jones. She slid out of bed and took the folded uniform Sybil offered her, then got her underclothes from the chair where she'd set them earlier. "I'll hand you the stuff from the bathroom as soon as I'm done."

"Good girl." She could hear the relief in Sybil's voice, but there was no time to speculate about what was going on as she ducked into the bathroom to change. Whatever Sybil and Jackson had to offer must be better than what she'd known the past couple of days.

When she came out, Sybil was at the door, listening, the suitcase at her feet. There was a mound in the bed and what looked like a head on the pillow. Yvonne started over to investigate, but before she could, there were shouts from the corridor outside her room, then the sounds of running feet.

Sybil eased the door open a slit, then grabbed the suitcase. "Follow me."

It was like running a maze. Sybil led her through corridors and down stairways until they reached an area of mysteriously humming machinery. Sybil didn't hesitate there, just opened an unmarked door and led Yvonne through more halls and up a flight of stairs.

Yvonne was panting by the time Sybil paused at still another door. This one opened to the outside world. The moment they stepped through it, a car headed in their direction and both the front and back doors swung open. Sybil shoved her and the suitcase into the back seat, then jumped in the front. "Go!"

Strong arms grabbed Yvonne and pulled her close. "Thank God we were in time." Curt's voice was rough as his lips sought hers. "I was so afraid they'd ship you off somewhere before I could make the arrangements."

"Curt!" That was all she could gasp before his lips claimed hers in a kiss that made her forget everything but the magic that flamed between them. For a moment she knew only that she was home, that she felt safe and loved and happier than she'd been since the last time she'd been in Curt's arms. She held him as tight as he held her.

Reality intruded only when the car bounced out of the hospital parking lot. "I think we're clear," Jackson said from the front seat. "There's still no light in your room, Yvonne."

"Then let's get the hell out of here." Curt's growl came as he trailed kisses along the tender skin beneath her ear.

Yvonne took a deep breath, forcing away the cloying wonder of her emotions. Rescue was great, but sanity demanded a few details. "What's going on? Why did we have to sneak out?"

"Because the Feds have their own plans for you . . . for us." Curt stroked her cheeks with gentle fingers. "They set up separate safe houses for us, one on each coast. When I found out, I decided I preferred to make my own arrangements. I was going to ask you what you wanted to do, but they wouldn't let me anywhere near you."

"Why not?"

"Control. We're their case. They figure they own us." Curt looked slightly guilty in the light reflecting through the windows. "They'd keep you safe, Yvonne, but it could be months before the trial. I couldn't wait that long to be with you."

Jackson chuckled. "What he's trying to say is that he's kidnapped you, but he'll take you back, if you want him to. This was just the only way for the two of you to talk."

Curt muttered something about privacy, then touched her lips with his fingers. "What I'm saying is that I love you, Yvonne, and I want you with me. If we go now, to-night, I think we can elude both the Feds and any of Hanover's people, but there could be danger. The Feds can offer a lot more guards than I can."

Yvonne looked into his eyes and the love she saw there made her heart sing. "I don't want guards, I want you. You took a chance when you rescued me the first time— I'm not afraid to take my chances with the man I love."

"Love? As in forever?" His lips were inches from hers.

"As in forever." She raised her mouth enough to seal the promise with a kiss that bared her soul to him. As long as he loved her, it didn't matter where they were going or what lay ahead. They'd already proved they could face anything together.

"To the plane?" Jackson asked, breaking the spell.

"Definitely." Curt's arms tightened. "And I will be in touch, Jackson, just not right away."

"As long as Pete gives me an alibi, this never happened, so there should be no problem." Jackson sounded more amused than worried. "You two be careful—we're counting on hearing your testimony at Hanover's trial."

Sybil's relieved chuckle made Yvonne smiled. "If you're really leaving, I guess it's just as well I'm going back east to visit my parents next week. Things are going to be awfully dull with you two gone."

"I resent that." Jackson's tone was teasing.

"I just hope it's dull where we're going," Curt whispered. "I've got some plans that require long stretches of time with nothing to do."

Shivers chased down her spine as his fingers caressed her back through the crisp uniform. "I'm sure that can be arranged," she purred, slipping her fingers beneath his shirt to touch the bandage there. "We can play nurse and patient."

"I can hardly wait." His lips claimed hers in a kiss that promised the fulfillment of all her dreams.

*   *   *   *   *

SILHOUETTE·INTIMATE·MOMENTS®

COMING
NEXT MONTH

#437 SOMEBODY'S LADY—Marilyn Pappano

Zachary Adams and Beth Gibson were as different as chalk and cheese. Zach knew the beautiful attorney could never be interested in a country lawyer like himself. But when an important case forced him to seek Beth's help, he took advantage of the opportunity and pleaded *his* case. After all, what better place for a courtship than a courtroom?

#438 ECHOES OF ROSES—Mary Anne Wilson

Music was everything to Sam Boone Patton—until he met Leigh Buchanan. Sam thought Leigh was the perfect woman. She was beautiful, sensitive and creative. But then he learned that she was also deaf. Sam cared for Leigh, but he couldn't imagine life without sound. Until he realized that life without love was even worse....

#439 WHOSE CHILD IS THIS?—Sally Tyler Hayes

Kate Randolph was a woman with a secret—J. D. Satterly knew that much. What he *didn't* know was whether her foster child was the baby he was searching for—his baby. He'd already had his share of dishonest women, and he didn't want another. Unfortunately, his body kept telling him otherwise....

#440 PAROLED!—Paula Detmer Riggs

Dr. Tyler McClane had lost so much—his medical license, his daughter, his freedom. And the one person he'd thought would help him had been instrumental in convicting him. Now Caitlin Fielding was back, asking for forgiveness. True, they had once shared something special. But as much as he wanted Cait, could he ever learn to trust her again?

AVAILABLE THIS MONTH:

#433 UNFINISHED BUSINESS
Nora Roberts

#435 TRUE TO THE FIRE
Suzanne Carey

#434 WAKE TO DARKNESS
Blythe Stephens

#436 WITHOUT WARNING
Ann Williams

Take 4 bestselling love stories FREE

Plus get a FREE surprise gift!

NORA ROBERTS

Love has a language all its own, and for centuries, flowers have symbolized love's finest expression. Discover the language of flowers—and love—in this romantic collection of 48 favorite books by bestselling author Nora Roberts.

Two titles are available each month at your favorite retail outlet.

In June, look for:

Opposites Attract, **Volume #9**
Island of Flowers, **Volume #10**

In July, look for:

Search for Love, **Volume #11**
Playing the Odds, **Volume #12**

Collect all 48 titles
and become fluent in

THE LANGUAGE of LOVE

Silhouette®

FREE GIFT OFFER

To receive your free gift, send us the specified number of proofs-of-purchase from any specially marked Free Gift Offer Harlequin or Silhouette book with the Free Gift Certificate properly completed, plus a check or money order (do not send cash) to cover postage and handling payable to Harlequin/Silhouette Free Gift Promotion Offer. We will send you the specified gift.

FREE GIFT CERTIFICATE

ITEM	A. GOLD TONE EARRINGS	B. GOLD TONE BRACELET	C. GOLD TONE NECKLACE
# of proofs-of-purchase required	3	6	9
Postage and Handling	$1.75	$2.25	$2.75
Check one	☐	☐	☐

Name: _____

Address: _____

City: _____ State: _____ Zip Code: _____

Mail this certificate, specified number of proofs-of-purchase and a check or money order for postage and handling to: HARLEQUIN/SILHOUETTE FREE GIFT OFFER 1992, P.O. Box 9057, Buffalo, NY 14269-9057. Requests must be received by July 31, 1992.

PLUS—Every time you submit a completed certificate with the correct number of proofs-of-purchase, you are automatically entered in our MILLION DOLLAR SWEEPSTAKES! No purchase or obligation necessary to enter. See below for alternate means of entry and how to obtain complete sweepstakes rules.

SI3U

ONE PROOF-OF-PURCHASE

To collect your fabulous **FREE GIFT** you must include the necessary **FREE GIFT** proofs-of-purchase with a properly completed offer certificate.

(See inside back cover for offer details)